Force and Fraud
A TALE OF THE BUSH

ELLEN DAVITT

with an introduction by KEN GELDER *and* RACHAEL WEAVER

 Grattan Street Press

ALSO IN THIS SERIES

The Forger's Wife by John Lang

Published by Grattan Street Press 2017
Introduction copyright © Ken Gelder and Rachael Weaver 2017
Series introduction, note on the text, modernisations and all other material
copyright © Grattan Street Press 2017.

Grattan Street Press is the imprint of the
teaching press based in the School of Culture and
Communication at the University of Melbourne,
Parkville, Australia.

THE UNIVERSITY OF
MELBOURNE

Cover illustration, *Site of Luna Park about 1885* (1885)
by Elizabeth Parsons, sourced from the State Library of Victoria.
Force and Fraud originally published in serial form in the
Australian Journal 1865.
Force and Fraud was first published in book form in 1993.

Grattan Street Press
School of Culture and Communication
John Medley Building,
Parkville, VIC 3010
www.grattanstreetpress.com

Printed in Australia

National Library of Australia Cataloguing-in-Publication entry

Title: Force and Fraud/ Ellen Davitt; Ken Gelder; Rachael Weaver.
ISBN: 9780987625328 (paperback)
Series: Colonial Australian popular fiction; Vol. 2.
Notes: Includes bibliographical references.
Subjects: Crime and mystery stories.
Sydney (N.S.W.)--Fiction.
Other Creators/Contributors:
Gelder, Ken, editor, writer of introduction.
Weaver, Rachael, editor, writer of introduction.

CONTENTS

SERIES INTRODUCTION

The Colonial Australian Popular Fiction series brings the excitement and diversity of colonial Australian fiction to the attention of contemporary readers – and there is certainly some remarkable fiction to read here.

Encompassing both novels and short-story collections, the series will include a range of popular genres that flourished during the colonial period: the bush sketch, the Lemurian novel, crime and detective fiction, the colonial romance, the Gothic tale, the convict novel, the goldfields adventure and the bushranger novel. Some of the authors were bestsellers in their day, and their work can still take us by surprise. We aim to make colonial Australian fiction accessible to contemporary readers – and we hope the design and layout of these works will be helpful here. But we also want to honour the original forms of these works. So we have reprinted from first editions or from the original serialisation of a work in newspapers or journals. Each publication includes a short introduction written by academic specialists, which provides a brief biography of the author (or authors) and offers critical insight into the work and its contexts. We would be particularly pleased if some of our publications become set texts in university or senior secondary courses. We believe that all readers have much to gain from these vibrant works from our turbulent colonial past.

The Colonial Australian Popular Fiction series is an ongoing collaboration between Grattan Street Press and the Australian Centre, both based within the School of Culture and Communication at the University of Melbourne.

INTRODUCTION

Ken Gelder and Rachael Weaver

Force and Fraud: A Tale of the Bush was Australia's first murder mystery. Its author, Ellen Davitt, was born in Hull, Yorkshire, in 1812, the eldest daughter of Edward and Martha Heseltine. She married Arthur Davitt, an accomplished French scholar and well-qualified educationalist, in Jersey (one of the Channel Islands) in 1845, and spent several years teaching drawing at the Irish National Board's Model School for Girls in Dublin. In July 1854, the couple came to Australia, having been appointed to act as principal and superintendent of the newly established Model and Normal School in East Melbourne. But their philosophical differences and bureaucratic struggles with members of the National Board of Education, together with financial problems, resulted in the school's closure after only a few years, in 1859. The Davitts were offered £500 compensation and dismissed. Arthur Davitt died of tuberculosis in Geelong just one year later.

Following an unsuccessful attempt to establish an independent school for girls in Carlton, Ellen Davitt turned to public speaking as a source of income in the early 1860s, presenting a series of lectures at mechanics' institutes and lyceums in Melbourne and in regional centres such as Ballarat and Portland. Her topics included 'The Influence of Art', 'The Vixens of Shakespeare', and 'Wit and Humour'. The lectures were well attended and regarded in local newspapers as entertaining, 'elegant and charming' and intellectually sophisticated.[1] By the mid-1860s, Davitt had also begun writing fiction. An early work, *Edith Travers*, has now been lost, but *Force and Fraud* was serialised in the popular,

---

[1] 'News of the 'Day', *Age*, 23 April 1861, p.5.

long-running literary periodical, the *Australian Journal*. In fact, its serialisation began with the *Australian Journal's* first issue, in September 1865.

After a prolific beginning, with two novel-length serials and two novellas published within two years, Davitt's writing career seemed to have lost momentum. She produced her final serialised novel, *The Wreck of the Atlanta*, for the *Australian Journal* in 1867, along with a few minor works: a travel piece called 'A Souvenir of Havana' in 1866, and a couple of short stories, 'The Highlander's Revenge' in 1867, and 'A House to Let' in 1868. A short time later, Davitt returned to teaching, this time at Kangaroo Flat near Bendigo – where Anthony Trollope, the celebrated English novelist who had married her younger sister Rose, came to visit. But this distinguished family connection did not appear to improve her material circumstances, and, worn down by institutional sexism and petty politics, she retired.[2] Davitt's persistent efforts to gain financial compensation from the Department of Education were unsuccessful and she died of cancer in poverty in the Melbourne suburb of Fitzroy on 6 January 1879.[3]

One of the few accounts of Ellen Davitt's early experiences in Melbourne comes from the historian J. Alex Allan. His book

---

[2] Victoria Glendinning notes Trollope's failure to mention his visit to Ellen Davitt in 1875, erasing any account of his sister-in-law: 'it seems hard that she has no place at all in the family letters and annals. It is as if her existence were suppressed.' See Victoria Glendinning, *Trollope* (London: Random House, 2002), p.3.

[3] For more biographical details, see Lucy Sussex, 'Introduction' to Ellen Davitt, *Force and Fraud: A Tale of the Bush* (Canberra: The Mulini Press, 1993); Warwick Eunson, 'Arthur Davitt', *Australian Dictionary of Biography*, National Centre of Biography, Australian National University, http://adb.anu.edu.au/biography/davitt-arthur-3380/text5115; and Brenda Stevens-Chambers, *Friend and Foe: Caroline Chisholm and the Women of Kyneton, 1840-2004* (Kyneton: Springfield & Hart, 2004) Eunson seems to be mistaken about Davitt's place and date of birth, listing these as Dublin 1820.

about the training college the Davitts had helped establish, *The Old Model School: Its History and Romance 1852-1904*, characterises her as a formidable personality – easily offended, imperious and difficult. 'While one has a certain deep sympathy and admiration for her husband,' he wrote, 'the idea one gathers of Mrs Davitt … is that of a certain hardness, priggishness, and overbearing self-esteem.'[4] More recently, Lucy Sussex has championed Davitt's legacy – highlighting her literary and artistic accomplishments, and combing back through primary documents for biographical details and evidence to counter Allan's view of her as rather severe and dour. Davitt's literary work also reveals a different side to her character. Amongst other things, *Force and Fraud* displays a keen sense of humour, a connection to popular culture, gossip and frivolity, a willingness to laugh at propriety, and an engagement with the salacious fascinations and complex social drives of modern metropolitan and rural culture in colonial Australia of the mid-nineteenth century.

Force and Fraud's light-hearted literary tone was very much in keeping with the stated objectives of the *Australian Journal*, which printed its first editorial, 'To Our Readers', alongside the first instalment of Davitt's novel.

We do not appeal to a sect, a clique, or a class; for we design to interest, to amuse, and, if possible, to instruct everybody who will read us.

Yet do we hope to embrace a wide and genial audience: to record the phases of Colonial literature; to direct attention to the triumphs of art; and to explain the most recent efforts of mechanical genius; until these pages reflect the

---

[4] J. Alex Allan, *The Old Model School: Its History and Romance 1852 – 1904* (Melbourne: Melbourne University Press, 1934), p.21.

Literature, Art, and Science of Australia. Neither shall we
neglect to satisfy our readers with abundance of matter
for mirth and entertainment. . .

The ablest Colonial pens of the day will be engaged on
our staff. Historical Romances and Legendary Narratives
of the old country, will be mingled with Tales of Venture
and Daring in the new . . .[5]

A distinctively Australian flavour combined with familiar English literary elements is precisely what Davitt's novel offers. From *Force and Fraud*'s opening pages we are struck by its population of colonial Australian character types: Harry Saunders, the honest bush worker; Herbert Lindsey, the young artist/dandy (although the novel quibbles over the latter term); Pierce Silverton, the smooth-talking land agent; Angus McAlpin, the bad-tempered squatter; and his attractive, spirited daughter, Flora McAlpin. These Australian bush types rub shoulders with colourful Dickensian characters with allegorical names – the pungent boarding-house keeper Mrs Garlick, with her improvident daughters and loafing sons; Argueville the barrister; the respectable Mr Lovelaw; and Dick Thrasham, the violent thug and ne'er-do-well. We also meet with 'that most uncomfortable of all bipeds', the 'new chum', along with the 'old colonist' and the resident 'man of progress', and hear their lively impressions of the rapidly developing colonies along the way.

But the novel also gives a completely new twist to its material by marrying the squatter romance to a crime narrative in an unprecedented way. The squatter novel had emerged as a recognisable form relatively early on in colonial literature, beginning with Thomas McCombie's *Adventures of A Colonist; or Godfrey Arabin, the Settler* (1845), a picaresque tale of a young

---

[5] 'To Our Readers,' *Australian Journal*, 2 September 1865, p.1.

emigrant settler who buys a station and sets about making his fortune. Other novels with squatter protagonists soon followed, notably Samuel Sidney's *Gallops and Gossips in the Bush of Australia; or, Passages in the Life of Alfred Barnard* (1854), William Howitt's *Tallangetta, the Squatter's Home: A Story of Australian Life* (1856), and Henry Kingsley's *The Recollections of Geoffry Hamlyn* (1859). Many of these early squatter novels included criminal elements – with the security of station life imperilled by threats from escaped convicts, bushrangers and so on. As Stephen Knight notes in his discussion of colonial squatter novels, 'a wandering bushman will at times turn out to be a dangerous ex-convict or, later on, just a wild menace.'[6]

What sets *Force and Fraud* apart from these other squatter romances is that it begins with a major crime – all in the fresh surroundings of the Australian bush – and the story of how it came to happen (and the eventual identification of the culprit) is what drives the rest of the narrative. Kate Watson notes the innovation of this plot structure, which anticipates 'the now familiar generic crime and mystery pattern.'[7] '*Force and Fraud* is pioneering', she writes, 'in its status as the first murder mystery in Australia, and the first "whodunnit."'[8] The contemporary feel of *Force and Fraud's* structure is also intensified by its budding interest in forensics – which sees characters rushing to investigate the crime scene, strategically disturbing chains of evidence, considering autopsy details, and so on.

In contrast to many contemporary murder mysteries, however, *Force and Fraud* has no expert detective working to get to the bottom of the crime. Instead, the mystery is solved partly

---

[6] Stephen Knight, *Continent of Mystery: A Thematic History of Australian Crime Fiction* (Melbourne: Melbourne University Press, 1997), p.41.

[7] Kate Watson, *Women Writing Crime Fiction, 1860-1880: Fourteen American, British and Australian Writers* (Jefferson: MacFarland, 2012), p.163.

[8] Watson, *Women Writing Crime Fiction*, p.161.

through the efforts of the interested parties: the accused, Herbert Lindsey, his sweetheart, Flora McAlpin, and those they turn to for assistance and advice. Their friends and supporters, together with members of the local township, also have an important part to play: community gossip acts as a catalyst to the revelation of evidence – as well as registering the excitement of the scandal – and even the police recognise social networks as the best resource for useful intelligence about the suspects. When the drunken habitués of the local dive, the 'Wild Boar', go on a gruesome field trip to the crime scene, a wily 'member of the Melbourne police' takes the opportunity to go after them 'for well he knew that the character of every individual in the neighbourhood would be freely canvassed'. Popular opinion counts for a great deal in this novel. Alongside this, there is a hearty disrespect for legal authority: the magistrate O'Twig is the object of sustained ridicule, for example. Generally, the local population is presented as close-knit and genial but also insubordinate and unruly.

When the patrons of the 'Wild Boar' flock to the crime scene, Davitt titles the chapter 'The Lovers of Sensation' in a good-humoured nod to the popularity of the sensation novel that peaked in Britain, Europe and America in the 1860s. Wilkie Collins's *The Woman in White* was published in 1860; Mary Elizabeth Braddon's *Lady Audley's Secret* was published in 1862. Braddon was especially popular in colonial Australia, her novels immediately advertised by the local booksellers and impatiently waited for by local readerships. Sensation novels were also routinely serialised in the colonial Australian periodicals and newspapers.[9]

---

[9] On Braddon's popularity in colonial Australia, see Toni Johnson-Woods, 'Mary Elizabeth Braddon in Australia', in Marlene Tromp et al, eds. *Beyond Sensation: Mary Elizabeth Braddon in Context* (New York: State University of New York Press, 2000); and Susan K. Martin and Kylie Mirmohamadi, *Sensational Melbourne: Reading, Sensation Fiction and* Lady Audley's Secret *in the Victorian Metropolis* (Melbourne: Australian Scholarly Publishing, 2011).

Force and Fraud is interesting for the way it energetically localises the tropes of sensation literature: the fascination with crime, convoluted marriage arrangements, intrigues and mysteries, contested fortunes, and double-dealing. It takes all this out of its more familiar metropolitan English contexts and then unleashes it into the Australian bush. Everyone seems to know about sensation literature: early in the novel, for example, a hutkeeper's wife and a squatter's wife are 'both afflicted with a morbid love of the sensational' and 'entertained each other with stories of accidents and adventures in the bush' – all of which send the novel's heroine, Flora McAlpin, into a state of delirium.

The sensation novel, as Pamela K. Gilbert puts it, appealed 'directly to the "nerves", eliciting a physical sensation with its surprises, plot twists, and startling revelations.'[10] In *Force and Fraud*, the courthouse is the place where startling revelations occur, which is why the locals flock to it: 'On they came through the burning streets – along the ill-made road – over vast plains; in carriages, coaches, buggies, dog-carts, gigs, drays … on thoroughbred horses, on horses half broken, and on horses of every description.' The city, too, is a place that draws curious colonials, and *Force and Fraud* depicts its characters travelling down to Melbourne to enjoy the bazaars, the amusements, the zoo, the museum, Royal Park, and so on. Here, Melbourne celebrates its modernity as a place for pleasure-seeking and the ready purchase of consumer goods. It also has a kind of metropolitan erotics, a libidinal economy of buying and selling for its own sake. One of the protagonists, Pierce Silverton, finds himself 'assailed *en voyage* by a shoal of saucy little girls, who are in the habit of going up and down, thrusting their shoulders

---

[10] Pamela K. Gilbert, 'Introduction', in Pamela K. Gilbert, ed. *A Companion to Sensation Fiction* (London: Wiley-Blackwell, 2011), pp.1-2.

out of their frocks, and hawking flowers or tawdry cushions, or something equally useless'.

Davitt's novel is also a romance that plays around with gender roles. Silverton is a beautiful, effeminate young man, pale and fragile, and prone to nervous excitement. 'Violently lively young ladies', the novel tells us, 'are sometimes too fatiguing for the nerves of delicately organised young gentlemen.' In *Force and Fraud*, the women are often cast as powerful and driven. Mrs Garlick and Mrs Roberts (for all their faults) are two robust, opinionated matriarchs, and Flora McAlpin gains in strength as the novel develops. As she comes to 'stand apart from tamer and less vigorous women', Pierce in particular finds her increasingly attractive: 'If he had *loved* her when surrounded by the graceful attributes of domestic life, he *adored* her in her present strange and almost isolated position.' Flora is not a murderous anti-heroine like Braddon's Lucy Graham in *Lady Audley's Secret*, but she is capable of great jealously and impulsive decisions. She tells Pierce at one point, 'I defy the law!' *Force and Fraud* gives this defiant voice some license, mobilising popular support for a sceptical view of legal justice and a sense that a strong, determined character can produce a better outcome when crimes have been committed.

KEN GELDER is Professor of English and Co-director of the Australian Centre at the University of Melbourne.

RACHAEL WEAVER is an ARC Senior Research Fellow in English at the Australian Centre at the University of Melbourne.

WORKS CITED

Allan, J. Alex, *The Old Model School: Its History and Romance 1852 – 1904*. Melbourne: Melbourne University Press, 1934.

Eunson, Warwick, 'Arthur Davitt', *Australian Dictionary of Biography*, National Centre of Biography, Australian National University: http://adb.anu.edu.au/biography/davitt-arthur-3380/text5115

Gilbert, Pamela K. 'Introduction', in Pamela K. Gilbert, Ed. *A Companion to Sensation Fiction*. London: Wiley-Blackwell, 2011.

Glendinning, Victoria. *Trollope*. London: Random House, 2002.

Johnson-Woods, Toni. 'Mary Elizabeth Braddon in Australia', in Marlene Tromp et al, eds. *Beyond Sensation: Mary Elizabeth Braddon in Context*. New York: State University of New York Press, 2000.

Knight, Stephen, *Continent of Mystery: A Thematic History of Australian Crime Fiction*. Melbourne: Melbourne University Press, 1997.

Martin, Susan K. and Mirmohamadi, Kylie. *Sensational Melbourne: Reading, Sensation Fiction and* Lady Audley's Secret *in the Victorian Metropolis*. Melbourne: Australian Scholarly Publishing, 2011.

Stevens-Chambers, Brenda. *Friend and Foe: Caroline Chisholm and the Women of Kyneton, 1840-2004*. Kyneton: Springfield & Hart, 2004.

Sussex, Lucy, 'Introduction' to Ellen Davitt, *Force and Fraud: A Tale of the Bush*. Canberra: The Mulini Press, 1993.

Watson, Kate, *Women Writing Crime Fiction, 1860-1880: Fourteen American, British and Australian Writers*. Jefferson: MacFarland, 2012.

A NOTE ON THE TEXT

This edition of Ellen Davitt's *Force and Fraud* brings together the serialisation of the novel in the *Australian Journal* in 1865. The novel was serialised across twelve weekly issues: 2 September (chapters 1–3), 9 September (chapters 3–7), 16 September (chapter 8–11), 23 September (chapters 12–13), 30 September (chapters 14–15), 7 October (chapters 16–18), 14 October (chapters 19–20), 21 October (chapters 21–22), 28 October (chapter 23), 4 November (chapters 24–28), 11 November (chapters 29–31), 18 November (chapters 32–35).

Force and Fraud was reprinted by The Mulini Press in 1993, with a detailed introduction and bibliographical notes by Lucy Sussex.

The editors of the present text have sought to balance scholarly accuracy with readability. Some punctuation, capitalisation and hyphenation have been changed for the sake of consistency (e.g 'had'nt' to 'hadn't'). Scholars seeking an unamended text of this edition should contact us at info@grattanstreetpress.com for details.

Force and Fraud
A TALE OF THE BUSH

CHAPTER I

The Artist

'TAKE CARE, MASTER, or you'll fall into the creek; those old boughs are not always to be trusted,' said a labourer to a young man who, to aid himself in climbing a steep bank, caught at the branches of a tree; and the speaker to illustrate his remark, uprooted another at a little distance.

'Thank you, my friend, for your advice, but I shall go no farther at present,' replied the traveller, seating himself among the brushwood.

'These old sticks are of no good but to make fires,' continued the first speaker, disdainfully kicking away the uprooted tree.

'Leave it where it is, if you please; it is just what I want,' said Herbert Lindsey (for such was the name of the traveller).

The labourer obeyed, but he looked inquisitively into the face of the stranger, who, as he thought, must have a peculiar taste if he cared anything about a decayed tree.

It was a pleasant face to look at, as the features, if not strictly classical were remarkably good; a cheerful smile rested on the handsome mouth, and an expression of high intellect lighted up the dark grey eyes. This latter characteristic might have escaped the observation of Harry Saunders, for his pursuits had never led him to the study of physiognomy, but when the stranger threw aside the large felt hat which had hitherto covered his noble forehead, the labourer was instantly attracted by an expression of goodness and candour: qualities which are equally appreciated by the unlettered and the refined.

Whether from some sudden feeling of sympathy, or from a desire to gratify his own curiosity, Saunders lingered about the spot, although he was evidently neglecting his duty – that of driving home a herd of cattle – and, when asked if he would be so good as to remain a few minutes longer, he cheerfully replied, 'Glad to serve you any way, master!'

'Thank you; then just stand as you are. Aye, that's right. Look me full in the face.'

'Why, it's taking my picture you are!' exclaimed Saunders in surprise, as the stranger rapidly sketched the well-formed figure of his companion.

'Exactly; but don't stand so stiffly – you were better before.'

'Ah! But I don't know how to look; I never had my picture made.'

'Well, then, try to root up another tree, that old red gum by your side.'

'That fellow's too strong. He won't be pulled up this many a year.'

'Never mind, suppose you try.'

Harry Saunders laughed and pulled away with all his force; but the tree resisted his efforts, and then Herbert

Lindsey laughed too, he had obtained what he wanted – a fine spirited sketch – as the exertion required threw the figure of his companion into an attitude expressive of great vigour.

'Now come and drink a glass of wine,' said the artist as, his sketch being completed, he drew a bottle out of a small knapsack. Saunders drank off the wine, and then looking at his own portrait, exclaimed, 'Dashed if I don't think it's like me! And you made it without putting my head into a frame, as the photograph-man does! I never could put up with that sort of thing – hang it!'

'Yes; you see I did not want the frame.'

'But it's so natural like; just as a man *does* pull up a tree.'

'There's nothing like nature. Now, I'm going to draw that cow, and I don't suppose she would relish the frame more than you do.'

Saunders laughed again, but he seemed rather solicitous respecting the manner in which the cow should be permitted to gaze, as he twisted her about in a way neither to her satisfaction nor that of the artist. Nevertheless, the new friends soon understood each other very well; and Saunders admitted he had often thought that the bit of country just there would make a first-rate picture, particularly when the hills looked purple and the sun shone on the water as it did then. Saunders was an artist at heart, though his occupation was that of a day labourer. At length, after another glance at the sketch, he remarked, 'That he liked coloured pictures best.'

'You shall see this coloured, if you can wait long enough,' replied the artist.

Saunders expressed his desire to witness the process, and Mr Lindsey, opening his case of watercolours, laid his camelhair pencils in order, and prepared to moisten the paper with a sponge. Saunders, who was watching these preliminaries with eager curiosity, perceived that the stranger suddenly turned very pale, exclaiming, as if to himself, 'How careless!'

Lindsay plunged the sponge into the creek, but on wringing it great heavy drops of blood trickled into the stream; it was rinsed again and again, and Mr Lindsey, at length satisfied that it was fit for use, applied it to the drawing paper.

His natural colour had now returned, and his hand did not appear to tremble when set to work on his sketch. But Saunders, who was an acute observer, noticed that he had previously drank off another glass of wine.

Perhaps the colouring of the drawing absorbed the attention of the artist more than the outline had done, for he remained silent, and Saunders, from some cause or other, ceased to ask questions.

The labourer, if he did not speak, watched the rapid movements of the skilful hand that transferred to paper the representation of the familiar scene. He admired those delicately shaped fingers, he thought the diamond ring that sparkled on one of them very handsome, but he felt an involuntary distrust of the artist, as he saw on the wristband, which had been turned over the coat sleeve, dark red stains like those which had lately dripped from the sponge.

Herbert Lindsey appeared strong in health and sound in limb, and Saunders thought those stains had no business there; he did not like to ask any questions, but he began to fear that he had taken too sudden a liking to his new acquaintance. When Lindsey resumed his conversation, the idea was for a while dispersed, but again it returned as on an inspection of the portfolio, *one* likeness was repeated in numerous sketches – this being a portrait of the greatest ruffian that had ever been known in the district.

At length Saunders' curiosity got the better of his discretion, and he asked, 'How did you come across this fellow, master?'

'By chance – just as I came across you, my friend,' replied the artist.

'There's not much likeness between him and me, I hope,' answered Saunders proudly.

'I dare say not; but I don't know anything about him. I said I met him by chance, and I met you by *chance*, you know.'

'A queer thing that *he* should let you draw his face! Jailbirds don't often like to have their pictures taken.'

'O, that's it! Is it? But you know my friend, that an artist sometimes takes a likeness of a man who is not conscious of the fact. This fellow was breaking in a vicious horse, and I thought his attitude would serve me for a particular purpose.'

'It must be a very ugly picture that he's to be put into!' remarked Saunders, rather gruffly; but his good humour returned when Mr Lindsey said, 'A fine handsome fellow like you would not serve for the part *he* is to represent.'

The sketch was now terminated, and the artist, collecting his materials, rose, and holding out his hand to his companion thanked him for his civility and hoped that they should meet again some day. The bright smile, which illumined his face as he spoke, seemed to restore the impression it had first created, and Saunders replied, 'Shall always be glad to oblige you, sir.'

They parted – Saunders went on his way thinking over the little incident that had broken in on the monotony of his usual occupations; he felt somewhat flattered at the recollection that he had been asked for *his* portrait, although his vanity was sorely diminished by knowing that the likeness of Dick Thrasham was in the same collection.

'There's always something to spoil a man's pleasure,' he exclaimed to himself, 'It's just like seeing that fine young fellow turn pale at the sight of a few drops of blood, and what the dickens they had to do on that sponge, I'm blest if I know.'

The young artist, on his part, gave a passing thought to his late companion, whom, physically speaking, he regarded as a fine model, and morally, as a good-hearted fellow. But it will presently be seen that Herbert Lindsey had, at that moment, a subject for consideration more nearly affecting his welfare.

The scene where this incident had taken place was on the outskirts of an Australian forest, which formed a picturesque object, notwithstanding the monotony of its colour and outline. It formed the 'middle distance' of the picture, and contrasted advantageously with the purple tints of the more remote mountains. Between mountain and forest a lagoon was perceptible, the mist arising from which lent the hazy line to the extreme distance, that impressed even the untutored eye of Harry Saunders with a sense of 'the beautiful'.

On one side of his picture, Mr Lindsey had skilfully managed to introduce a sharp outline of the steep bank; and, on the other, a little cascade that fell into the creek and sparkled beneath the sunbeams. Above all was the deep blue of the glorious Australian sky, but the sun, though shining brightly, was a little on the decline, and thus imparted to the scene that strange effect of *chiaroscuro*, which forms one of the beauties of warm and brilliant climates. No dwelling was in sight, neither was there any trace of a *made* road or fence, nor anything that indicated the work of man; but, though all around was wild, the scene was attractive; the glowing hue of the cattle, as well as the vigorous figure of Saunders, gave life and animation to the picture, without diminishing the effect of majestic grandeur conveyed by the dark forest and the trackless plain.

Herbert Lindsey, like all true artists, was an enthusiastic admirer of nature, and during that day he had greatly increased his collection of Colonial scenery. There was a sketch taken by sunrise; and the sparkling lights on the topmost trees might have been touched in by Claude de Lorraine[1] himself. There was a scene in the depths of a gloomy forest where giant trees had either been blighted by lightning or scorched by a bushfire, and rocks upheaved by an earthquake, invited to form a design that would have delighted Salvator.[2]

The portfolio contained several other drawings, slight and sketchy perhaps, but truthful nevertheless. Herbert Lindsey was satisfied that he had done a good day's work, and yet these drawings had rather occupied his time than his thoughts.

After parting with Saunders, he walked rapidly on; so rapidly indeed that he soon became heated, as he well might under the summer sun of Australia. He opened his vest which (for the season) he had worn rather closely

[1] A 17th century French landscape painter.

[2] Salvator Rosa, a 17th century Italian Baroque painter.

9

buttoned to his throat, but, on glancing at a stain of blood on his otherwise unsullied linen, he once more closed his vest, and notwithstanding the heat, again quickened his pace.

Another hour brought him to a small township, and he immediately took his way to the principal hotel. Mr Lindsey was well known to the landlord who came out to welcome him, as did the landlady, the ostler, barmaid, and half-a-dozen other people.

'Glad to see you again Mr Lindsey, you've been quite a stranger of late,' said the landlord.

'Yes, I've been on a tour in New South Wales, I suppose I can have a bed as usual.'

'To be sure, but supper will be ready in half an hour.'

'Oh! I shall have time for a wash before then. Mary, get me a jug of water, there's a good girl.' And so saying, Mr Lindsey stepped upstairs as if he had *not* walked twenty-five miles under a blazing sun.

He had brought a change of linen and a vest of Chinese silk, and substituting a coat of a light coloured woollen material, (which he had carried across his arm) for one of grass-cloth, which he had previously worn, he cut as good a figure as any traveller in the bush could possibly do.

Herbert Lindsey, though no 'dandy', was scrupulously particular in the cleanliness of his attire, so, before descending to the supper room, he summoned the chambermaid and requested her to send his linen to the laundress.

The hotel of the Southern Cross being admirably conducted, especially in the important matter of the table, naturally mustered a great number of guests, and when Herbert Lindsey entered the room, from twenty to thirty persons were seated at supper as the repast was called, although it bore a nondescript character: various joints and pastry, as well as tea and coffee, being served at the same time. Ale and porter, as well as wine and spirits, were, however, in many cases demanded. Mr Lindsey was known to the greater number of the company, and by them welcomed as warmly as he had previously been by his host. It was quite natural that he should be so, as his character was eminently social, for he had always plenty of anecdotes and was ever ready to sing a capital song.

Supper passed gaily over, the viands were excellent, and the appetites of the company not amiss. 'May good digestion wait on such.' However, there is little to be apprehended in this respect amongst such vigorous constitutions. Herbert Lindsey gave proof positive how well *he* relished his landlord's good cheer, he drank cup after cup of tea like a thirsty bushman, and then submitted to be toasted and pledged in a most genial fashion.

CHAPTER II

THE ARTIST'S FRIEND

SUPPER WAS SCARCELY concluded, when a gentleman, who was also well known in the neighbourhood, entered the room, and advanced towards the traveller with apparent pleasure.

'Pierce Silverton! My dear fellow, how are you?' exclaimed Lindsey, taking the offered hand.

'Quite well. And you? It must be nearly a year since you were in this district,' returned the newcomer.

'Nearly an age!' replied Lindsey impetuously; then suddenly changing his tone, he asked, almost in a nervous manner – 'And Flora, how is she?'

'Very well; do you intend to see her?'

'Do I *not*? What else should bring me here?' cried Lindsey, more impetuously than before.

'Take care what you are about – McAlpin is more irritated against you than ever.'

'Pshaw! The obstinate old fellow! What crotchet has he taken into his head *now*?'

'Nothing fresh that I hear of; but as his daughter will soon be of age, he is, perhaps, afraid that she may follow her own inclination.'

'She loves me still! Her father's threats have had no effect on her? Tell me at once, Silverton.'

'At all events she has refused half a dozen offers, a circumstance that seems greatly to annoy McAlpin, for he swears she shall not have a farthing till his death, and you may be very certain he would not let her have any then if he could help it – but he cannot interfere with her mother's property.'

'He can't interfere with that, and he can't live for ever,' said Lindsey quickly, but again changing his tone, he added, 'not that I wish *his* death or *her* money – Flora would be a fortune in herself.'

'A fortune in a wife is better than a fortune with a wife. Eh?'

'Come, Pierce, don't give us any wise saws,' said Lindsey, interrupting his friend.

'Very well; then I suppose you find the arts a paying speculation?'

'No, faith; the time has not come for that. I'll be bound to say that you make ten times more money as McAlpin's agent than I do as an artist, aye; or than Titian himself would do could he be resuscitated and start on a fresh career in this part of the world. But I envy you your privilege of seeing Flora, far more than all your percentages on wool, your mining shares, or any other species of good luck.'

'You know I shall always be rejoiced to serve you, Lindsey; but come, these gentlemen will think that I am monopolising your company.'

The above conversation had taken place on the verandah: the two friends now re-entered the supper room, and the remainder of the evening was passed amidst songs and jokes and general hilarity.

Certain individuals who pretended to be great physiognomists had occasionally remarked that Herbert Lindsey and his friend, Pierce Silverton, formed an admirable contrast to each other. As the former has been already described, we will briefly notice the general appearance of the latter, considered by some to be the handsomer man. So he was with regard to regularity of features, each of which bore a just proportion to the other; with some trifling exceptions they might have been cast in the Greek mould; but a few *trifling* exceptions sometimes combine in making a great difference. The Greek forehead is certainly not high, but that of Pierce Silverton was just a very little *lower;* his blue eyes were well shaped, but he had a habit of looking under his brows, more frequent in women than in men – not proud women – but those who affect to excite sympathy. His lips, the colour of pink coral, were rather contracted; his teeth of a bluish white, like those substituted by dentists, who sometimes outdo nature. Altogether, there was a consumptive look about the mouth, and this expression was imparted to the other features by a delicate complexion, as well as by the habitual drooping attitude of the head; very different to that of Herbert Lindsey, who, in this respect at least, had more of the Ancient Greek, as (especially when he walked) his head was thrown proudly back. Silverton's hair was particularly beautiful – of a light brown, gently waving, and worn rather long. His nose was perfect, and his profile nearly so. What, then, prevented him from being a handsome man? There was a deficiency somewhere, and what it was we shall, perhaps, discover by and by. His voice was 'gentle and low' – *not* an excellent thing in *man*, whatever it may be in *woman*; and with women, in general, Pierce Silverton was *not* a great favourite. It is true that women are apt to take likes and dislikes; a habit that cannot be justified, as nobody ought to be liked or disliked till well known. So it may be inferred that women act without judgement, as animals do. A strange thing that women and animals should sometimes be *right* in their *impulses*, whilst men are *wrong* in their *judgement!* Let it not be supposed, however, that Pierce Silverton was entirely discarded by the fair sex, as, on the contrary, several young ladies thought him a 'very interesting man'; though upon the whole he was more appreciated by matrons who had daughters to marry; and here he had decidedly the advantage of his friend, for Pierce Silverton, who in a few years had amassed a competency – who never got himself into a scrape – was generally patronised by the mammas, whilst Herbert Lindsey, who had squandered a fortune in eighteen months, entangled himself in more than one political outbreak, and thrown away the chance of advancing his interests in a lucrative profession, was not likely to be regarded with views matrimonial.

But as there is no rule without an exception, Herbert Lindsey had, in one instance, been accepted by a very charming matron, as her daughter's future husband, merely because that matron considered him to be an honourable, talented, energetic young man, who could make her child happy. Nearly four years had passed since that consent was given, and the gentle matron was now in her cold grave, but the compact, formed by her deathbed, was still unbroken, notwithstanding the reproaches and menaces of the surviving parent.

It was in reference to this engagement that Herbert Lindsey was now conversing with his friend, Pierce

Silverton, the privileged companion of Flora McAlpin, and the trusted agent of her father. They sat on the verandah of the Southern Cross a full hour after the other guests had dispersed; at length Silverton, in his turn, prepared to go, saying, 'Well, Lindsey, as you will have another long walk tomorrow morning, I ought not to detain you; it would not be proper for Flora to go far into the forest to meet you.'

'I will take care of that; I shall be at the boundary of her father's station by eight o'clock in the morning.'

'Can you manage that? You will have a walk of a dozen miles.'

'I shall rise at daybreak, take a cup of coffee, which will be ready for the coach passengers, and that same coach will give me a lift, thus saving me three or four miles.'

'It will set you down at the entrance of the forest; but take care you don't get entangled amongst the branches.'

'Not I, indeed. The forest that I passed through this morning is more dense; but I chopped away the branches like a thorough bushman, I can tell you. I have a first-rate bowie knife: look here.'

Lindsey felt in his pockets for the article, and suddenly exclaimed, 'Why, where the deuce has it got to? O, upstairs in my other coat I suppose. But I was going to ask, if there is any likelihood of McAlpin returning tonight? Not that I care for the old fellow; but I don't want to give him a pretext for tyrannising over my darling Flora.'

'No; he only started yesterday. I almost wonder you did not meet him.'

'There is no horse track through the part of the forest I travelled. I purposely kept out of his way. The obstinate old fellow, to turn against the son of his best friend for such a trifle!'

'Men of McAlpin's stamp do not regard the squandering of three thousand pounds in less than two years as a trifle.'

'Especially as I spent it. Men of his sort are more ready to find an excuse for swindling and speculation than for the follies of a youth who is led astray by the fascinations of the Continent. I do not mean to vindicate myself; I did spend my fortune, and now—'

'True – spent your money like an ass, and now you have to earn it like a horse.'

'I wish you wouldn't talk proverbs, Pierce. I hate that sort of humbug; besides, they are generally nonsensical. Asses don't spend money though they earn it sometimes for their masters – and I never had a master – and, by Jove, I never will.'

Lindsey spoke with more temper than he had hitherto done, and Silverton added, 'It is not only having *spent* your money that irritates McAlpin, but he thinks you will never settle to anything.'

'Tell him to give me a station and his daughter, and I will be the steadiest fellow in the colony. I should like to know how a man is to settle when he is obliged to tramp about the country looking out for chances as I do.'

'He thinks you might have followed the profession of medicine. You walked the hospitals for a year, did you not?'

'Yes, and got sickened with horrors – I can't bear the sight of blood, Pierce.'

Herbert Lindsey turned pale, and entering the room through the window of the verandah, drew from the filter a glass of water, which he drank eagerly.

'I have often wondered to hear you say so – a brave fellow like you, Lindsey!' repeated his friend.

'Pshaw! A mere physical defect that I inherit from my mother; she was frightened a short time before my birth. But I do not permit this disgust to take a morbid possession of my faculties. I would not turn away from a sight of pain if I could do any good, and thus nerving – but no matter. I did *not* choose to become a surgeon, and, perhaps if I had never got amongst those students, I might have been a rich man today.'

'Another of McAlpin's objections: he says you suffer yourself to be led away by any wild fellow.'

'Six years since probably I *did*, but I am another man now. Can't he allow a poor devil a chance to reform? But I never was vicious, I never did anything to leave a stain on my name, and that's more than some people can say. I tell you, Pierce, that McAlpin is an obstinate pig-headed old Highlander, and I'll marry his daughter in spite of him.'

CHAPTER III

THE ARTIST'S LOVE

S OME PORTION OF the young artist's past career may be gathered by the dialogue recorded in our last chapter. It will easily be seen that Herbert Lindsey had been a spendthrift, in fact, like many other young men who become possessed of wealth in early life, he once thought that money would never come to an end. At the age of twenty-one he became entitled to £3000, and, two years later, not a shilling remained. To his credit, however, be it recorded that a great part of it had been absorbed in the purchase of valuable books: scientific, artistic, and historical, and (when disgusted with the profession of medicine, which he had once prepared to follow) in the expenses necessary to qualify himself as an artist. He had travelled in France, Italy, Spain, and Germany, studying in the best galleries, and under the best masters: thus, after all, Herbert Lindsey had spent as little money in foolish extravagance as the generality of young men would do under similar circumstances.

Like many others, he had paid a high price for 'experience', having been robbed and defrauded by those on whose good faith he relied. But never having been addicted to 'vice', when he found himself nearly penniless, he could at least commence a fresh career, unembittered by the pangs of remorse.

About two years after having devoted himself to the Arts, being on a sketching tour in Germany, he met Mrs McAlpin and her daughter, the former having been recommended by her physicians to try the waters of Baden. Mrs McAlpin was an English lady of good family, refined and highly educated. In her youth, she had been very romantic, and after reading *The Lady of the Lake*, amidst the scenes described in that beautiful poem, she married a great strapping Highlander, because she fancied he resembled Rhoderick Dhu.

As that renowned chieftain died a bachelor, it would not be fair to surmise what sort of husband he 'might have made'; nevertheless, the poet has not indued him with the sweetest of tempers, and so it is probable that poor Lucy discovered, when too late, that her husband resembled the hero of her romance in one very undesirable point of view.

Poor Lucy McAlpin! Her illusions were dispelled one by one, and she at last became aware that her lord and master cared more for making money, than for either his gentle wife or his pretty daughter; as, having heard that, in Australia, he could easily become possessed of vast and valuable lands, he resolved to go thither at *once*.

A considerable delay would have been caused by waiting till his elegant and somewhat fastidious wife had made, what she thought, the indispensable preparations, till a suitable governess could be procured for Flora, and till various other preliminaries could be arranged. Her husband told her that she was making a fuss about things that were not of the least consequence, and the result was that Angus McAlpin set off alone, having readily assented to his wife's proposal that she should remain behind till Flora had finished her education.

On arriving in the land of his adoption, McAlpin congratulated himself on the steps he had taken, the wild life of the wildest part of the bush being just the thing for the hardy Highlander, but not quite adapted to the tastes of a fanciful lady. Thus Mrs McAlpin continued to dwell amongst her own relations, occupying herself, for a period of five years after her husband's departure, with the education of her child. At the end of this time, a complaint, with which she had long been afflicted, assumed a threatening appearance, and (as we have stated) she was recommended to try the waters of Baden.

Unable to enter into the pleasure of that gay scene, she gladly welcomed the society of Herbert Lindsey. The more so, that she had known him since his childhood; *his* father and *her* husband having been early friends.

The young man fearlessly related the history of his past career. He spoke with enthusiasm of his present occupations, and anticipated, with all the ardour of a sanguine temperament, success for the future. Mrs McAlpin was naturally disposed to regard errors like his with indulgence. Herbert Lindsey had been 'more sinned against than sinning' and would, probably, have obtained forgiveness from a sterner judge than the amiable Lucy. Flora, at that time seventeen years of age, was always present during the visits of the young artist, and he was occasionally permitted to accompany her on her rambles if the distance happened to too great for the declining health of the delicate mother.

At first, their conversation was of art, of poetry; then, as will readily be imagined, of love. Herbert Lindsey, with all the frankness and loyalty of his nature, immediately informed Mrs McAlpin of his passion for her daughter, and, after some persuasion, obtained her consent to their future union. It is true that the lover had not a shilling beyond what his pencil procured, but what did that signify? Could they not live on love? So at least thought Flora.

'And on my exertions – my untiring exertions,' said Herbert.

'Such genius as yours must surely meet its reward,' added the mother, whose fading eyes rekindled with enthusiasm as she spoke. Alas, and aday! It may chance that the young girl's dreams were not more idle than those of the travelled artist, or of the mature and accomplished woman! Mrs McAlpin, however, was not altogether imprudent in sanctioning this attachment, as in the first place, she relied on the good principles, as well as the genius of her future son-in-law; in the second, on a competency that it was in her own power to bestow, and on which the young couple could exist till the death of Herbert's uncle, when the artist would become possessed of considerable property.

In this manner, Herbert and Flora were betrothed, and passed several months very happily in each other's society. Suddenly, however, Mrs McAlpin's complaint developed itself in an alarming manner, and in a few days she was no more.

Poor Flora, who had never yet witnessed death, was frantic with grief and fear; but a kind matronly lady took charge of her, and accompanied by her lover, she returned to England immediately after her mother's funeral. Scarcely had she landed ere a letter was received from her father, ordering the presence of his wife and child. His wife!

Perhaps he repented his imperious command on finding that she was forever beyond his control; but the recollection of past severity did not render him more gentle towards his daughter when she, in compliance with his request, joined him in Australia.

The irritable temper of McAlpin was excited by the knowledge of the engagement Flora had contracted, and still more increased by a visit, a few months later, from Herbert Lindsey.

'An artist, indeed!' exclaimed the enraged Highlander. 'What a fool the fellow must be to think he can make a living by painting pictures in a colony like this!'

Herbert Lindsey had certainly given proof of his folly in fancying anything to be improbable, but he had also proved his honourable love, having resisted his inclination to accompany his betrothed on that long voyage; as when she refused to marry him without her father's knowledge, he let her depart in the care of a respectable family, and the next week, followed on her track.

McAlpin forbade Lindsey access to his house, but Flora, though unwilling to disobey her father, resolved that if Herbert was not to be her husband, nobody else should. In this manner were these three years passed away, during which time the lovers continued occasionally to meet; and it was to see Flora that Lindsey had now traversed many a weary mile of plain and forest, his ostensible object being an artist's tour.

Pierce Silverton, their mutual friend, as the agent of McAlpin, was a frequent visitor of his house, and he had therefore been enabled to convey to the lover the intelligence that the father of his betrothed was about to absent himself for a few days, and, with a joyful heart, Herbert Lindsey now found himself close to the extremity of the forest that skirted one boundary of McAlpin's station.

It was early morning, and fresh, and pure as dawn, was the fair girl, who came tripping over the light brushwood. A fit subject for an artist's love was Flora McAlpin, with her soft eyes that spake a world of sweet tranquil thought. Her dark brown hair, which, as it waved back in the breeze, reflected a golden tint, that peculiar hue, so rare, but so appreciated by a painter; the colour of her cheek, the carnation of which Titian himself might have worshipped; and her graceful figure arrayed in that pretty flowered muslin. On she comes, and Herbert Lindsey, springing over fence and scrub, catches her in his arms.

'Herbert! Dear Herbert!'

'Flora! My darling girl!'

They mutually exclaim, and feel a long absence forgotten in that happy meeting.

They sat under the shade of a spreading tree, talking for a little while of the 'past', but their conversation, like that of all true lovers, soon turned to the 'future'. They spake of happy years yet in store, when no barrier should exist to mar their bliss – when the father's opposition should be surmounted, the fortune gained – and life become one scene of hope and joy.

'Six weeks,' said the happy girl, 'and I shall be of age, Herbert! and then—'

'You will be my wife – my own wife – *my* Flora,' interrupted the lover.

'I do not mean that – at least, not quite so soon. I should not like Papa to think that the first use I made of my liberty was to run away from him. No, I intend to be very submissive for a little while, and if *that* does not soften his heart, perhaps I may show him what I *can* do.'

Flora drew herself up, and the artist, who had studied all sorts of attitudes and expressions, thought she looked very queenly, and said in a jesting tone, 'You inherit your father's love of power, but I hope you do not mean to be tyrannical, Flory.'

'No, not if you behave yourself; but Herbert, it is very pleasant to know we *can* do what we like.'

'Dear Flora, your money is your own – I would not touch a farthing of it for the world – no, not even to enable me to marry you!'

'O, Herbert! Can you suppose that I was thinking of such a vile thing as money?' asked Flora, in an accent of reproach.

'Ah, Flora! I once thought money a vile thing, but I have learned that we cannot live without it.'

'At all events, we will not *talk* of it. Papa's friends have scarcely another idea in their heads. But I mean to give you my money – that is, if *I do* marry you.'

'*If* you do, Flora?'

'Very well, *when* I do. But Herbert, which is worth the most – my hand or my fortune?'

'Your hand, a thousand times, Flora, and you know it.'

'Well then, if I give you my hand, surely I may give you what is so *very* inferior. But not another word of my fortune, or I'll go back this minute, and talk to one of Papa's old money-grubbers.'

'I little thought that the quiet retiring girl I once met at Baden would ever exhibit such an independent spirit.'

'Baden is a very different sort of place to Australia, and when poor dear mamma was alive, I submitted everything to her; besides people grow very independent in this colony.'

Herbert Lindsey told his betrothed that he would take her back to Baden, and tame her, and then he uttered a few more threats, demonstrating how well bachelors can rule *their* wives.

Gaily and happily the hours passed away, but, at length, the lovers knew that they must part, or they would be observed by the labourers returning to their dinner, and Herbert, unwilling as he had ever been that the conduct of Flora should be open to censure, tenderly bid her farewell, entreating her to meet him on the same spot, on the following day.

To this she cheerfully assented and, with light step and still lighter heart, returned to her father's house.

Either it must be that presentiments do not foreshadow every calamity or there are some individuals not subject to their influence, for on entering the house, the first intelligence that greeted Flora McAlpin was . . . that her father had been discovered *dead* – murdered on the plain!

CHAPTER IV

The Inquest

VERY LITTLE EXCITEMENT was, at anytime, required to collect a crowd about the bar of the Wild Boar, the frequenters of which place were generally sufficiently attracted by the various beverages it afforded, as *drinking* seemed to be the vocation of the whole neighbourhood, and, although there was an 'ordinary' at a stated hour, at which substantial fare was set forth, the consumption of viands was by no means equal to that of liquids – the proportion which Falstaff's 'pennyworth of bread' bore to the inordinate 'quantity of sack', may give some idea of the manners and customs of the *habitués*. Either from courtesy or custom, the Wild Boar was called an 'hotel', but such a place in England would have been merely designated a 'public house', in Scotland it would have received the still more appropriate appellation of a 'tippling house', and at the Wild Boar everybody did *tipple*, not excepting some grave magistrates and a few other dignitaries, who should have known better; in fact, the only exceptions were 'a lot of slow fellows who had taken the pledge' (for such they were generally termed), but as the pledge was generally broken, the exceptions to the prevailing rule of intoxication were few indeed.

The bar of the Wild Boar had originally occupied a very small space, but as the population increased, and their propensities became more confirmed, a partition was removed, which, by adding another room, extra accommodation was afforded, and thus a little quarrelling and crowding around the counter were avoided. A couple of pillars, supporting the ceiling, were placed where the partition had stood, and against one of these a large stove had been fixed, by the side of which numerous guests would congregate in wet weather to dry their feet, and at all seasons to help themselves to hot water, when such might be required to dilute their potations. By this stove, winter and summer, early and late, was seated a modern Bardolph;[3] perhaps the landlord fancied that he was giving proof of his own hospitality in suffering the perpetual presence of this individual, although the very *few* rational beings who saw him shuddered at the sad state to which a man may reduce himself when he 'puts an enemy into his mouth to steal away his brains'.

But, at the moment to which this portion of our story refers, there was other excitement than that afforded by 'nobblers', for a murdered man lay in the house, on whose body an inquest was about to be held! No drinking was going on in *that* chamber, perhaps for the first time in *his* presence; he had been a good customer during his life time – and was so even now – for what so natural as that his acquaintance should require a stimulant after 'such a sight'?

---

[3] Thief and companion to Falstaff, who appears in a number of Shakespeare's plays.

'Here comes Harry Saunders! He looks quite flabbergasted; and well he may, for he has lost a good master,' exclaimed 'Mine Host'.

'Shut up, Drainwell. McAlpin was never good but to fellows like you,' replied the most abstemious of the group.

The entrance of Saunders probably prevented an angry argument, for even the humblest labourer who had once served the murdered man was now invested with a kind of interest.

'Have a nobbler, Harry?'

'Come, Saunders, I'll shout,' cried a couple of the bystanders in a breath.

'Get out of the way. Is it drinking I'm thinking of whilst the poor master lies dead in the house?' said Harry, as he pushed through the crowd, and hastened to the chamber where lay the body of his late employer.

When McAlpin was about to start on his last earthly journey, Harry Saunders had brought out his horse, as well as that of Mr Silverton, for they had ridden forth together; the labourer was therefore considered as an important witness, as he might be likely to give some account of his master's apparent health on that morning, as well as of the several details connected with the saddle bags and other accoutrements. Everybody felt convinced that Saunders would speak the truth, no matter who might be implicated; and so, doubtless, would Pierce Silverton, who had likewise been summoned to attend the inquest. There was no reason to suspect either of these individuals as guilty of the deed.

Mr Silverton was the last of the two to be in the company of the deceased, but another person voluntarily came forward, and stated that he had met McAlpin after Mr Silverton had parted with him.

'He was then riding at a brisk pace,' said Mr Dixon, 'and as I thought he seemed in haste, I only bade him "Good morning". He answered me in rather a surly tone, but that was his way. Afterwards, I overtook Mr Silverton, and recollect saying to him that Mr McAlpin did not seem in the best of tempers. He replied, "No, he has lost a great deal of money lately by some mining shares." Mr Silverton asked me where I met him, and when I named the spot, he said, "I did not think he could have got so far." This was on the open plain, about three miles from the place where his body was found.'

Mr Silverton and Mr Dixon corroborated each other's statements, but no light was thrown on the mystery, either by their evidence, or by that of Saunders.

It was supposed that McAlpin, after meeting Mr Dixon, had crossed a portion of the plain, which was covered with 'scrub', amongst which some person lay in ambush awaiting his approach, as, from a wound on the back of the head, the murdered man had apparently been stunned. Being a crack shot he had probably seized his revolver, which he always carried when travelling, but it might have been knocked out of his hand, as the right wrist bore the mark of a heavy blow.

The 'death-wound', however, was in the centre of the throat, and had evidently been inflicted by a large knife.

A surgeon, who was present at the inquest, said it was his opinion that at the time the stab was given, McAlpin's head had fallen back – probably he was faint from the effects of the previous blow – the surgeon said that death must immediately have followed the wound caused by the knife, although there might previously have been a struggle. He also thought the assassin must have been shorter in stature than his victim, the knife having penetrated in an upward direction.

Whether the murder had been committed for the purpose of robbery or not remained a matter of doubt. Mr Silverton and Harry Saunders, who were both acquainted with the habits of the deceased, said he seldom travelled with much money on his person; but of this circumstance his murderer would probably have been unaware. A cheque book was found in his pocket – watch, there was none; but, when someone suggested it had been stolen, Harry Saunders said his master had broken the glass as he was mounting his horse, and given *him* the watch to take back into the house, which he immediately did; therefore, if the murderer had been led to the commission of the crime from a love of gain, he could not have been greatly enriched. The motive of *revenge* seemed not improbable, McAlpin having been an exacting landlord and a tyrannical master, and consequently, an unpopular character.

Nevertheless, a feeling of deep indignation at the savage deed, if not one of regret for the victim, was expressed; and a verdict of 'Wilful murder by some person or persons unknown', unhesitatingly returned, after which resolution, the jurors adjourned to the dining room of the Wild Boar, to restore their nerves by such stimulants as their various tastes might suggest.

CHAPTER V

THE LAST HOME

THE INTELLIGENCE OF her father's death was conveyed to Flora in the most abrupt manner, as on her return from meeting Herbert Lindsey, a smart girl came running towards her, exclaiming, 'Oh! Miss Flora dear, the master's killed!'

The moral shock, succeeding to physical exertion, overcame poor Flora, and she fell senseless on the ground, whilst her incautious informant screamed with all her might, 'Och! Murder! Sure she's kilt too! Och? What will I do?'

Flora was carried into the house, and, after some delay, a doctor arrived, who prescribed a composing draught and *quiet*; but the latter remedy was not very easily obtained in that agitated household. The hut-keeper's wife, a woman of some experience in sickness, volunteered her services, and a few hours later the wife of a neighbouring squatter came to offer her sympathy and assistance.

Poor Flora's state was not likely to be much amended by the presence of either of her nurses, for although extremely kind, and not devoid of skill, they were both afflicted with a morbid love for the 'sensational', and whilst in attendance on their patient, entertained each other with stories of accidents and adventures in the bush. The squatter's lady had a tale of a murdered man, who some years previously had been tied to a tree, having died apparently in the greatest agony; and the hut-keeper's dame related the capture and death of a bushranger, under circumstances equally appalling. Most graphically did these good wives detail the account of ghastly wounds and every horrible circumstance, talking *sotto voce* all the time, but in that tone so painfully audible to the delirious invalid, and Flora, who lay in a state of half consciousness, both from the effects of her attack and its remedy, raved about her father and also frequently uttered the name of Herbert Lindsey.

'I hope they will not see you, Herbert! Oh! I would not have you meet my father for the world! Yes, very soon there will be nothing to prevent our marriage!' were the disjointed exclamations of the feverish girl, which, as will readily be imagined, created great wonder and dismay. These expressions, together with the symptoms of the patient, were told to the doctor, but he made no comment, desiring, as before, that Miss Flora should be kept perfectly quiet.

A few hours after the news of McAlpin's death had reached the station, Pierce Silverton, who had previously heard of the calamity, arrived there; he had come with the intention of breaking the intelligence gently to the orphan girl, and therefore seemed very much shocked when told of her condition. He then resolved to seek Herbert Lindsey, and inform *him* of what had taken place; but the lover had also heard of the occurrence, as on his return to his hotel he found all its inmates in a state of the greatest excitement relative to the murder of McAlpin.

'Great God! You don't say so, Mrs Roberts?' exclaimed Mr Lindsey to his landlady, who came forward to relate her version of the disaster.

'Yes, it is too true! But – bless me! Mr Lindsey, how pale you *do* look! Here, take a little brandy.'

Herbert accepted that universal panacea for all evils, whether moral or physical, and (although by no means addicted to strong liquors) drank off the fiery draught as if it had been water.

'Poor Flora! I must go to her at once, Mrs Roberts!' cried Lindsey as soon as he had himself recovered from the shock of the terrible intelligence.

'Ah! Poor dear! They say she takes on greatly,' replied the sympathising hostess, who, for some time, had been in the lovers' secret.

At that instant, Pierce Silverton entered, and, with some difficulty, convinced his friend that all attempts to see Miss McAlpin would be useless; a notification that greatly increased Lindsey's anxiety. Mr Silverton, however, could delay no longer, having been summoned to attend the inquest, the particulars of which have been already related.

The funeral was fixed for the following day, and Mr Silverton, though he entrusted the immediate arrangements to an undertaker, busied himself a good deal in mustering the principal gentry who resided in that locality; but it was against his advice that Herbert Lindsey insisted on attending. Carriages of various kinds followed the hearse; after them came a long train of horsemen, chiefly squatters and farmers, who had been intimately acquainted with the deceased; although the procession was lengthened by a number of people belonging to the Freemasons' lodge, that of Odd Fellows, and several other societies. And thus, the Son of the North was laid in his southern grave.

CHAPTER VI

THE LOVERS OF SENSATION

TWO DAYS OF unusual excitement had passed away, and on the third, the population in general began to 'suffer a recovery'. The public mind being in this state, all business was out of the question, and when someone proposed a visit to the spot where the body had been discovered, the idea was adopted without a dissenting voice; therefore, after fortifying themselves with the usual stimulants, away some dozen enterprising individuals started from the hotel of the Wild Boar.

On their way they met Harry Saunders, who was saluted by one of the party with the remark, 'Well, Harry, lad, thee'll have to look out for another maister, and I hope thee'll get a better – Mac was a gruff un.'

'Whate'er he was, he's dead and gone, and I won't hear a word agin the dead.'

'But what's thee going to do for a billet, lad?'

'Stay wi' the young mistress, to be sure, and may be I shall have a young master one o' these days. There's a gentleman I know of who – but … Hang it! 'Tis'nt fair to blab…'

Harry was not much prepared to reveal his secret: the softer emotions that a love tale might call forth being stifled by the more exacting interest attached to murder. The merits and the demerits of the deceased, the inquest, and the funeral were all discussed – the *male* gossips almost rivalling the good wives whose taste for the sensational had been exhibited by the sick-bed of the orphan girl.

Amongst the party was a member of the Melbourne police, who, perhaps, was not averse to gather any scattered hints afforded by local associations; for he well knew that the character of every individual in the neighbourhood would be freely canvassed.

Very little reticence in this respect was observed, a great many remarks being made which might have implicated several individuals, but, fortunately for them, they were, at the time of the murder, hundreds of miles from the scene.

The experienced eye of the official at once detected that there had been a struggle, the grass adjacent to the spot where the body was found being rooted up, as if by the scuffling of feet, several twigs were also broken from the hardy scrub, some of which were clotted with blood, to which adhered particles of human hair; some of these were raven black, slightly mixed with grey. These were easily identified as having belonged to the victim; a few others were also scattered about, of a lighter colour. The dying man had probably grasped at the locks of his assailant, as several brown hairs had been found between the cold and stiffened fingers.

McAlpin's revolver was discovered amongst the branches of the scrub, but the unerring aim and strong hand of the Highlander had been equally unavailing, as the weapon was still loaded. It was thought that McAlpin could not have been on horseback at the time of the attack, for the animal was found quietly grazing at a little distance. Perhaps, on that last journey his master had led him down to the creek, the heat of the day having no doubt rendered the horse, as well as his rider, extremely thirsty. This circumstance was remarked, as McAlpin, though harsh to his fellow man, was merciful to his beast. 'Weel, weel! His last act was of mercy, and the Lord grant it to him now,' exclaimed an old shepherd, who had accompanied 'the Laird' from his native land, and followed his fortunes ever since.

The policeman then examined the saddlebags, which had evidently been ransacked. They contained a change of linen, but nothing else of any value whatever; the murderer might have been a thief, although he had not proved himself on this occasion a horse stealer.

Souvenirs of the occurrence were sought by many of the party, the blood-stained twigs and scattered hairs forming matter of dispute; but the latter were claimed by the official as *his* right.

'Hallo! What's this?' exclaimed one of the bystanders, as he stooped to pick up a large bowie knife.

'That has taken *his* life, and the Lord grant I may live to see the murderer swing one o' these days,' cried the faithful shepherd.

The knife was stained with blood, and on the handle was a small silver plate engraved with the letters 'U. L.' With eager curiosity, the crowd pressed forward to obtain a sight of the fatal weapon, which a few continued to touch, and then they went through pantomimic gestures, indicative of those the murderer might have assumed. The official sternly bade them 'stand off'. Anyone might have taken him for a naturalist, who had caught a delicate butterfly and was apprehensive lest the down, which rendered it so *fair*, should be brushed from its wings, so careful was he that the knife should not lose the stain that made it so *foul*.

'Stop a bit. Here's something else,' exclaimed a keen sighted individual, as he drew forth a strip of linen from under the branch of the scrub. That also was polluted by a dark red stain; but it bore other distinguishing peculiarities – it was of fine lawn, something less than three-quarters of a yard in length, and a half-quarter in breadth, a selvage running down one of the long sides, the other being frayed and ragged; the two ends were hemmed, and had a ribbed sort of border, the letters 'U. L.' being marked in one corner; it was thus easy to perceive that this fragment of linen had once formed part of a pocket handkerchief. It was also appropriated by the official, and there were certain individuals in the crowd who envied him the possession of his treasures.

CHAPTER VII

HARRY'S MISGIVINGS

'THEE DOES LOOK downhearted, Harry, lad. Come in an' ha' a nobbler; it'll rouse thee,' said the man, who, on a former occasion, invited Saunders to partake of a remedy to which he himself had recourse on all occasions of excitement. Harry accepted the offer, though he did not drain his glass with his accustomed cheerfulness. His entertainer then proposed a second, but this Harry refused.

'Did thee look as glum as that when the painter made thee picture, lad?' asked his inquisitive acquaintance.

'Drat the painter! I wish I'd never seen him. I never was so dashed in all my life,' replied Harry abruptly, then, muttering some hasty excuse about being wanted at home, he rode off from the Wild Boar.

When he had proceeded a little way, he was overtaken by Mr Silverton, who asked him if he had accompanied the other men to the spot where the body was found.

'Yes, and I wish I'd been a thousand miles off,' was the reply.

'Why? Surely nothing fresh has occurred?' asked Pierce Silverton.

'Fresh? No – but you see, Mr Silverton, a man who loves truth had better keep a close mouth these times.'

'An honest man should never be afraid to speak the truth.'

'Not about his own doings; but there's a deal of deceit in the world.'

'Ah! I see. You are thinking of the murder – a shocking transaction, though not one usually termed *deceit*. It was a deed of violence and—'

'I wasn't thinking of *that* altogether, but, you know, Mr Silverton, a man takes fancies sometimes, and likes people without knowing why.'

'True – that species of charity we should entertain for our fellow creatures; it is a virtue we are all commanded to practice.'

'Virtue or no virtue, it's a thing that's apt to get a man into a fix. Did you look into the Wild Boar, and see the things that the policeman has got, Mr Silverton?'

'I understand you now, Harry. Ah! I'm afraid we've a great trial before us.'

'There *will* be a trial, then? It's a sad world, Mr Silverton.'

'It is indeed, but let us hope that no friend of ours will be implicated in this affair. Come, cheer up. You did not put on that dismal face when Mr Lindsey took your likeness. I saw the sketch in his portfolio. Mr Lindsey and I are old acquaintances, you know.'

'And you never knew anything agin him?'

'No, not exactly – at least with the exception of his determined pursuit of Miss Flora; but love drives a man mad sometimes.'

'I don't see that, Mr Silverton. It's two year sin' I fell in love with Mary, the chambermaid of the Southern Cross; and though her father's turned me out of his house, I wouldn't do anything agin him. I don't mean to say that Mr Lindsey has done anything either; but I'm right down bothered, and no mistake.'

'I do not wonder that you are confused, and I respect your feelings too much to press this painful subject farther upon you, being convinced that no consideration would ever induce you to deviate from the path of truth, and, called upon, as I am to stand prominently forward in this matter, it is a great satisfaction to know that poor McAlpin had at least one honest and honourable friend, ever ready to cherish his memory and defend his child.'

Harry Saunders did not exactly understand why Mr Silverton should think it necessary to make such a speech, but the soft low tones fell pleasantly on his ear; and though the language was vague – a critic would have called it nonsensical – it conveyed a reliance on his sense of honour and manliness, and Harry at once yielded up his judgement to the gentle flattery, and, with the ready frankness of a bushman, he said, 'Give us your hand, Mr Silverton. It's pleasant to know for a right-down certain truth that one is not talking to a murderer.'

'It is, indeed, Saunders, and we ought to thank Providence that she has not implanted such violent passions in *our* breasts,' answered Pierce Silverton, as he placed his soft white hand in the broad palm of his companion.

They proceeded for some time in silence, till, on approaching the hotel of the Southern Cross, Mr Silverton said in a whisper, 'If we should either of us have formed a suspicion respecting any individual, let us maintain the greatest reserve, and leave judgement to the Lord.'

'Aye, aye. We'll bring it home to the right person – no fear of that,' returned Harry impetuously.

They alighted, and entered the hotel together, Silverton, with the intention of seeking his *friend*, Saunders, his *sweetheart*; but the object of both was frustrated, as, in the first place, Lindsey, who could no longer control his impatience, had gone to make inquiries respecting Flora's heath; therefore, on ascertaining this fact, Mr Silverton hastened to overtake him.

Saunders, on his part, hearing that Mary was engaged in arranging the sleeping apartments of some newly-arrived travellers, walked up and down the courtyard, now listening to various remarks on the all-absorbing topic, now pondering on the events of the last few days; on his hastily conceived liking for Herbert Lindsey, and his former dislike of Pierce Silverton (for such feeling he had once conceived); and the recollection of it causing him a pang of remorse, his generous disposition made him resolve to do all in his power to repair 'the evil he had thought'.

'And it's waiting to see Mary you are, Mr Saunders?' asked a pretty girl, who at the moment came up with a basket of linen.

'May be so; but I'm glad to wait in your company, my dear,' replied Harry, chucking the girl under the chin – for the sight of her laughing face roused him out of his sombre mood.

'Arrah! And d'ye think I'd be bothering myself with another girl, sweetheart?' said the rustic coquette, as she turned away.

'Stop a bit, Biddy; I've got a word to say to you about Dan,' returned Harry, endeavouring to detain his pretty companion.

'Bother Dan! Mother's waiting for me outside, and she would go *on* if she knew I was talking about *him*. La! I wish Mary'd come, I've got a message for her.'

'What is it, Biddy? Can't I tell her?'

'Oh, yes, I dare say you can. It's only that mother couldn't get them stains out of the bosom of the gentleman's shirt; but she says it'll be all right after another washing. Here's the parcel, you may give it to Mary – I've ever so many more places to go to.'

Biddy tripped away; but she had no sooner gone than Harry's curiosity led him to unpin the wrapper in which the linen was folded. He shook his head and sighed, muttering to himself, 'I'm not the man to give Biddy's message. I won't help to put his head in a halter, unless I am bound to speak the truth.'

But he was aroused from his reverie by the sight of a man posting a large placard against a wall. Harry read the heading, 'Wilful Murder', he saw the date of the occurrence, the name of the deceased, the official reward for the apprehension of the culprit, the official signature, and felt a conviction that, ere long, the crime would meet its just punishment.

CHAPTER VIII

SAILING OF THE *ROBESPIERRE*

MEANTIME, HERBERT LINDSEY, having reached the place of his late rendezvous with Flora, was about to advance towards the house when, looking round, he saw Pierce Silverton riding up, and heard him call out, 'Where are you going, Lindsey?'

'To see Flora, to be sure. Saunders told me that she was better,' replied the impatient lover.

'She *is* better, I am glad to say, but not yet well enough to receive company.'

'Company! What nonsense! Am I not her affianced husband?'

'You *were*, but I hear she now reproaches herself with disobedience towards her father, as on the evening before his death he repeated his refusal to sanction her marriage with you, in consequence of which a dispute ensued; therefore, I do not think she would like to act in open violation of his command – at least immediately. Wait till tomorrow, I will then let you know when you can see her; believe me, Lindsey, I will act towards you as if you were my own brother.'

'God bless you, Pierce; you are a true friend, but it is hard to be debarred from her presence.'

'I will tell her you say so – that is, if I am admitted – for I have not yet seen her.'

The young men took leave of each other, and the next morning Silverton despatched a note to his friend, in which he stated that having heard of the proposed departure of Mr Manners (one of Miss McAlpin's trustees) for England, he thought it his duty to see him before he sailed. The note concluded with assurances of friendship, and a regret that Miss McAlpin was not yet able to leave her room.

On arriving in Melbourne, Mr Silverton found plenty to do. In the first place, he had to call on certain detective officers respecting the necessary steps to be taken for the discovery of the murderer; in the second, to seek out Miss McAlpin's trustees. One of these was a mere cypher, who, whenever it was possible, permitted any person to transact *his* concerns; therefore, it was not likely that he would be very energetic about those of other people; but his associate being a very active man would be of the greatest assistance under the present circumstances and, as Mr Silverton thought, might probably be induced to delay his departure. What then was his disappointment on learning that Mr Manners had sailed the very day that the murder had been discovered!

Pierce Silverton censured himself severely for having omitted to note the departure of the vessel – an oversight very excusable at such a time – but it was not till he reached the wharf that he became aware of the mischance.

'Is there any possibility of the *Royal Oak* being detained at the Heads? This wind is against her getting out,' he said to a sailor whom he met on the pier.

'Bless your soul, sir! She has made five hundred miles by this time; this wind will not alter her scourse to signify,' replied the sailor.

Mr Silverton walked up and down in evident trouble; doubtless he was overwhelmed by the weight of his own responsibility. He was not a strong man, and had lately been compelled to witness a sight that strikes terror into the strongest heart; so, after a little while he sat down on the pier, thinking that the sea breeze might restore his nerves, and perhaps envying the robust constitution of a countryman who came up at that moment, for he said, 'Well, Dick, how goes it? You look as well as ever!'

'And why shouldn't I? Trifles don't affect me, you know, Mr Silverton.'

'Trifles don't give me much trouble either, but what I've gone through during the last two or three days is no trifle at all.'

'Come across a dead man, as I hear. Pooh!' exclaimed the countryman, whistling between his teeth, and snapping his fingers.

'It is not everyone who can boast such nerves as yours, Dick,' returned Mr Silverton in a melancholy voice.

'Nerves be blowed! What's a fellow who has to live alone in the bush to do with nerves, I should like to know?'

'Ah, but you have got rid of the bush for some time. You are quite ready for your voyage, I hope.'

'No, I ain't.'

'No? And the *Robespierre* sails tomorrow!'

'She may sail when she likes. If I go in her, I'll be—.'

'Why not? I thought it was all settled.'

'No, 'tisn't. I don't like her name; they say it belonged to a French fellow who sent lots of poor devils out of the world in double quick time.'

'And do *you* care about such nonsense as the name of a ship? I thought you had more sense, Dick.'

'Any how, I havn't got the money.'

'Got no money! And the three hundred pounds I gave you – where's *that* gone?'

'Blowed if I know! That's all I've left of it. You'll have to fork out again, Mr Silverton.'

The stranger drew three or four sovereigns and a little silver out of his pocket, and Mr Silverton, after a pause, said in a whisper, 'I will not desert you, Dick; there is a great prejudice just now against persons who are supposed to be bushrangers, therefore you *might* get into trouble if recognised. Meet me here this evening, I will bring what you require.'

'Knowed you would; but I shall want another three hundred pounds.'

'It will be very difficult for me to procure so much. I will see what is to be done, however.'

'It is a good thing to have a friend who will help a poor devil with a little tin.'

'Hum! But I mean to see you off this time. Don't fail to meet me; and now, goodbye for the present.'

Mr Silverton went to his bankers; and the stranger, apparently relying on his exertions, gave himself no trouble respecting the future, nor, to judge from the look of insouciance his countenance conveyed, respecting the past.

The generous disposition of Pierce Silverton had frequently been extolled by certain ladies, who go up and down begging contributions to bazaars, etc., but they would probably have been surprised at the *excess* of charity which led him so effectually to aid a fellow creature in distress, especially if they beheld the present object, whose powerful frame was sufficient to indicate that he could very well help himself.

'Dick', as he had been styled by Mr Silverton, was a man of middle height, of a square build, with features that might have been cast in an iron mould; the expression of his countenance, if not of absolute cruelty, was by no means engaging; in repose, it wore a look of utter indifference to all external circumstances; but in action, it was strangely energetic; the clenched teeth, the thin compressed lips, conveying an idea of great determination; but the eye added an elevating character that might give an idea of either moral or intellectual worth; all was physical, such as befitted his pursuits, the most creditable of which had been that of a horse breaker; and, when compelling the wild animals to obedience, he would mutter between his teeth, 'If you don't do what I choose, I know how to make you!' And this habitual expression was on his countenance, this phrase on his tongue, as the kind and benevolent Silverton went to procure him assistance!

'I should have thought you would have been more anxious to get away, Dick,' said that gentleman, when, at the stated hour, he returned to the pier, and found his *protégé* carelessly seated, enjoying his pipe.

'When a man has no power to do a thing, there is no use in being anxious about it. I'm as helpless as a babe, Mr Silverton.'

Pierce could scarcely help laughing at this speech, coming as it did from one whose strength appeared to be almost herculean, but he simply replied, 'I have got the money, and arranged about your passage; you will be safer and happier in England.'

'No objection to have a look at the old country, but I fancy it's a slow sort of a place for a fellow who has lived ten years in the bush.'

'Suppose you go to America, *that* is not a slow place.'

'Just what I was thinking of! Any commands there Mr Silverton? One good turn deserves another, you know.'

Pierce coloured a little at this remark, and, after a short pause, replied, 'No, thank you, not at present.'

Upon a post, near the place where they were standing, was a placard similar to that which Harry Saunders had read on the gate of the Southern Cross. During the day it had attracted several observers, and now, although the twilight rendered its characters somewhat indistinct, a host of idlers still lingered in its vicinity, one of whom, being an acquaintance of Mr Silverton, advanced towards him, and striking the placard with his cane, said, 'Sad affair that, Pierce.'

'Sad indeed! It has caused the greatest consternation and regret throughout the district.'

'Consternation, no doubt, but McAlpin was not a man to be much regretted I should think.'

'Well, he's dead, so let us forget his faults, I speak of him as a friend, for such he was to me.'

'That's all right, but a man's memory is the shadow of his life, and I for one, confess to being more shocked than afflicted by this event. But who is that fellow who was talking to you just now?'

'An old servant of McAlpin's; he had placed his little savings in his care, and as McAlpin died without a will, and left no memorandum of the transaction, the poor fellow is hard up at present. We shall take care that he does not ultimately lose his money; but as it is advisable to send someone after Mr Manners, (one of Miss McAlpin's trustees), I am shipping off my friend there.'

'*Apropos* of Miss McAlpin, she'll be a great catch, won't she?' asked Mr Silverton's companion, whose thoughts naturally reverted to the heiress.

'I should think so; suppose you try your luck? But I must wish you good evening for the present; I shall be seeing you again before I leave town.'

The gentleman retired, and Mr Silverton again joined his humbler friend, accompanying him on board the vessel in which he was to embark, and making every arrangement for his comfort on the voyage. On the following morning, 'Dick' sailed for England in the *Robespierre*; and his kind patron, whose nerves had not recovered their wonted tone, resolved to take a trip in the same vessel as far as the Heads.

CHAPTER IX

BOARD AND LODGING IN A CHRISTIAN FAMILY

WAS THE ADVERTISEMENT of Mrs Garlick, a lady who endeavoured to unite two callings rather incompatible with each other, viz. the education of young ladies, and the boarding and lodging of persons of the other sex. She did not find either speculation very paying; although the rent of her house was not high, nor the expenditure of her *housekeeping* very great, everything being done in the cheap and 'not extremely nice' style. It is true that she was highly recommended, but what is the use of *recommending* people, as they generally like to judge for themselves? A great many young men certainly did give Mrs Garlick's establishment a trial but very few remained long with her. One, a mere youth who had been placed there by his guardian, said, 'It was a humbugging sort of a shop, and he'd bolt,' whereupon a little impetus was given to the usual routine, and something more appetising than 'bread and butter' allowed for the evening meal. Sometimes, to vary her advertisements, Mrs Garlick began them with a preamble about 'a lady possessing Christian principles'; on reading which, a wag once said, 'Methinks the lady doth possess too much!' The remark was not inappropriate, as Mrs Garlick *did* possess a great deal, although her *practice* was much more limited. Theoretically speaking, her Christianity comprehended all the severer virtues, and ignored pardon for injuries or indulgence for any weakness whatever. She was bitter against her own husband, although he was dead, because he had left her in difficulties; and more bitter still against her sons, because they, as soon as possible, had shaken off her control; and she was most bitter of all against people of any creed but her own. Her three daughters had been trained to follow in her footsteps, and the eldest had already made considerable progress in the school of acrimonious philosophy, having, at the age of twenty-eight, discovered that the world was bad; that women were nearly all idle, vain, or depraved; and, that men— 'Thank goodness, *she* was not married! Unless indeed to one of those perfect beings who abjure earthly vanities for the sake of a wife!' For the sake of Miss Garlick, few men could forego their inclinations; and she had not hitherto met with such a self-sacrificing individual. The second sister was rather less ambitious in her ideas of a husband, and it was rumoured that she was about to espouse a gentleman who filled the duties of lay preacher and schoolmaster in a country district. The third was 'a gushing young creature,' and though her exuberant spirits sometimes met with the reproving exclamation of 'Oh Bessie!' yet a little wildness was tolerated in consideration of her youth.

Although Mrs Garlick and her three daughters passed for being 'pious', her sons were unquestionably dissipated, as the sons of *such* mothers frequently are. One of these 'black sheep' had obtained a situation in the gay little township where we left Herbert Lindsey, and spent a great portion of his time amongst a rollicking set of young fellows who frequented the Southern Cross. The other held a minor appointment in the Civil Service, was a frequenter of theatres, cafés, and music saloons, and being also an inveterate smoker, and proportionately 'fast' in every other respect, he did not think fit to reside in his mother's quiet home.

Mrs Garlick's *practical* Christianity consisted in giving away small sections of very dry loaves, tainted meat, and useless boots; in having cold dinners on Sundays, and making all the members of her household, over whom she had any control, attend divine service three times a day. Her three daughters obeyed her injunctions, and also possessed a peculiar Christianity of their own, which mainly consisted in promoting bazaars by means of other people's purses. Although these young ladies did not violate all the ten commandments, they had some vague ideas respecting the one that sayeth, 'Thou shalt not steal', for they did not regard the pilfering of little ornaments, of beads, or other trifles, as *theft*, when the objects, thus procured, were to be converted to this fund of charity.

Miss Bessie, in the frolicsome *abandon* for which she was remarkable, had purloined a little article from Mr Silverton's dressing table. Our friend Pierce, when in town, resided in Mrs Garlick's establishment; he had known the family a long time and the choice of such an irreproachable home, in the opinion of some people, added materially to his own respectability. He was the 'pet lodger', and during his stay, *his* comfort was the main object of the mother, as well as of her daughters.

His return from the Heads was now expected, and tea kept waiting on his account; perhaps the tediousness of expectancy had rendered Miss Garlick more cross than usual, as in a tone of reproof, she exclaimed, 'I desire you to put that snuffbox back again, Bessie, before Mr Silverton returns.'

'No, I won't,' answered the younger sister. 'It will just do for our stall; we want something of that sort for the gentlemen to buy.'

'Gentlemen, indeed! I should like to know who'd buy that old-fashioned Scotch snuffbox; it's only fit for a figure at a tobacconist's door.'

'It'll bring more money than that cigar-case of yours.'

'No, it won't.'

'Yes, it will.'

In the midst of this dispute the legitimate owner of the snuffbox entered. Miss Bessie put the relic in her pocket, and the four ladies rose to welcome their favourite boarder.

They 'hoped his trip had done him good'.

'Thought he looked better.'

And were '*so* glad he had come *just* in time for tea'. The meal was hastened, and every delicacy that the house afforded produced. Mr John Speedy (the young gentleman whose guardian had placed him in that immaculate abode) condescended to rise from the sofa and ask a few questions respecting the *Robespierre*; her passengers and crew, her cargo and sailing capabilities; wishing himself at sea, and announcing his intention to '"hook it" one of these days'.

Mr Silverton answered the various queries of the precocious youth, and mildly advised a longer course of study, to which counsel Mr Speedy replied that 'study was *tarnation* slow', and then invited Mr Silverton to go with him to see the new burlesque. Mrs Garlick turned up her eyes at the profane idea and might probably have otherwise expressed her horror, had not Mr Silverton accepted the invitation, and Mr Silverton was too good a boarder to offend.

Miss Bessie wished she was going too, and consequently the reproaches that could not be poured forth on Mr Silverton were heaped on her devoted head – a proceeding which provoked her to exhibit the snuffbox; and on the removal of the tea equipage, whilst her sisters were arranging their bugles, their Berlin wool, their gold thread, and other preparations for the approaching bazaar, she held the stolen article close before Mr Silverton's eyes, calling out, 'There's a fine thing, and a very fine thing, what shall he be done to who owns this fine thing?'

'Give him a swing in the air. There's a new forfeit for you, Miss Bessie,' cried young Speedy.

Pierce Silverton turned pale, and seating himself on the sofa, exclaimed, 'Good heavens!'

The youth laughed heartily as well he might, for the emotion of Mr Silverton seemed greatly to exceed the cause.

'Bessie! You are setting a very bad example,' said Mrs Garlick, glancing at two of the day boarders, who had come to help in working for the bazaar. But Miss Bessie, proud of playing a more conspicuous part than her sisters, maintained possession of the snuffbox – dancing about the room, and holding it up at a distance: then, as Mr Silverton approached, she grasped it tightly, laughing all the while.

'Give it up, Bessie, and be quiet,' said her eldest sister.

'No, I won't, it's sure to fetch a good price at the bazaar.'

'I'll give you one pound for it now; it belonged to that poor fellow who has just started for England, and I promised to keep it for his sake,' said Mr Silverton.

'One pound indeed! It will fetch two and perhaps five, at the Bazaar, besides making fun,' exclaimed Bessie, as she held the snuffbox within Silverton's reach, and when he was about to snatch it, she darted off to the other end of the room; he followed – she leapt over the chairs, mounted on the end of the sofa, and dodged behind her mother and sisters, to their great disgust, pulling off the tablecloth, and scattering bugles and spangles upon the floor. Down stairs she ran, Pierce Silverton after her and young Speedy applauding.

'If you don't give up that snuffbox, I'll kiss you, Bessie, that I will,' said Pierce.

'You'd better not, Mr Impudence,' she replied, holding the box still tighter in her grasp.

Perhaps the threat was not regarded in the light of a punishment, for Bessie, though she allowed herself to be kissed, did not give up the stolen property. She was a great strong girl, more than a match for Pierce Silverton, who at length sat down, exhausted by the unequal strife, and though vexed and half ashamed of the whole affair, yet unable to refrain from laughing.

'You may come to the bazaar and *buy* it, but you shan't have it now,' cried the triumphant Bessie.

'If he can't come, I'll buy it for him,' said Speedy, adding, 'and, now let us be off, Silverton, or we shall be too late for the burlesque.'

Mr Silverton, being obliged to give up the hope of recovering his snuffbox, followed the young man into the hall, whilst Miss Bessie rejoined her mother and sisters in the drawing room, where a very good lecture was awaiting her as the reward of her frolic.

'Never had such a lark in this house before,' said Speedy, as he closed the door.

'What strength that girl has! I am quite done up!' exclaimed Pierce.

'Why didn't you give in sooner? You can't care about that old snuffbox Silverton.'

'No, but, there's no harm in a romp sometimes.'

'I should think not. We don't do much in that line at Mother Garlick's. I mean to skedaddle as soon as you go.'

'Wait a few weeks. I shall be down again very shortly.'

'Do you mean to come to this bazaar?'

'Why, no. I shall not give myself much trouble about that. But the murder has thrown us all into confusion, and will be sure to cause me another journey to town. I don't know how matters will be settled.'

'Faith! If I were you Silverton, I'd marry the heiress. She's a decent looking girl, isn't she?'

'First-rate – but I wish to act as a disinterested friend.'

And such was the character usually attributed to Pierce Silverton.

CHAPTER X

TRANSITION

FLORA McALPIN WAS not long in recovering from her indisposition; its magnitude had been rather exaggerated by her attendants, several of whom possessed that passion for 'the terrible', which induces the imagination to fly off at a tangent on the intelligence of a tragic event, adding one calamity to another as if determined that misfortunes shall not 'come singly'; and thus, Angus McAlpin having been murdered, they prophesied that his daughter would never recover from the shock. But, notwithstanding all these gloomy forebodings, at the end of a fortnight Flora was perfectly restored to health, and quite able to undertake the responsibility of being an heiress.

Since the death of her father, she had remained secluded in her own chamber, but, during the last few days, the motive for so doing had rather been a want of interest in the society of her occasional household. A sentiment of propriety prevented her from summoning Herbert Lindsey to her side, and, as we have stated, he had been recommended by Mr Silverton to absent himself.

At length, his impatience overcame all bounds, and he wrote to his *fiancée*, expressing his devoted affection and sympathy in her grief. Very precious was the reply, though it only said:

> Dear Herbert,
> Come at once to
> Your own Flora.

The welcome permission was immediately complied with, and Herbert, demanding the swiftest horse in the stable of the Southern Cross, gallopped at full speed across plain and forest. The first person he met within the precincts of the station was Harry Saunders, who approached with a hesitating step, his countenance strangely alternating between confidence and dismay, as he exclaimed, 'Is that you, Mr Lindsey? Well, I never!'

'To be sure it is – and why not? Take care of my horse, there's a good fellow,' replied Lindsey, dismounting.

Harry led the horse to the stall, and Herbert walked to the open window, near which he perceived the dark folds of Flora's mourning dress. That sombre attire, added to her previous indisposition, subdued the natural brilliancy of a complexion which had not hitherto yielded to the effects of climate; but if, at this moment, Flora's beauty was of a less dazzling character, it was more touching, and the lover, affected by her unwonted air of languor, exclaimed, as he pressed her to his heart, 'My poor, dear girl! Why was I kept from you?'

'I don't know, Herbert,' she replied, in a mournful tone, 'but I have been ill and *so* unhappy. Oh! Why must I either continue to disobey my father's wish, or—'

'Forget me, Flora! Do you mean that?'

'Oh! Herbert, I can never *forget* you; but since dear Papa's death, I have thought so much of my disobedience.'

'Flora, your mother joined our hands, and, before she died, charged me to console you.'

The memory of her mother increased her recent grief, and, for some moments, Flora wept bitterly. But Herbert, with the sophistry of love, convinced her that having formerly been instituted her consoler, and, for the time, her guardian, he was the fittest person to enact those parts on the present occasion.

Flora smiled, but did not reply, and taking silence for consent, he asked her to become his wife without farther delay.

'No, no. Herbert, I cannot *now*,' she answered, but in such a faltering tone that he probably thought she hesitated, and therefore urged his request with greater ardour. But Flora only replied she could not, she *would* not 'show so little respect' for her father's memory, as '*immediately* to act in opposition to the wish he had so often expressed'.

'You will let someone persuade you that it would be wrong to marry me at even a future period; and so I shall lose you altogether, Flora.'

'Oh, no! Why should you doubt me, Herbert? Have I not always been constant, in spite of opposition?

'My darling girl, you have, but now your *heart* has admitted one argument against me, and it is the suggestions of the *heart*, not the commands of authority, that I fear.'

'Do not fear either, Herbert. I will be thine, but you know it would not look well to marry you just yet.'

Lindsey sighed, and, after a pause, added, 'Perhaps not; but absence is hard to bear.'

'Absence! Why not remain in the neighbourhood? We could meet very often.'

'*That* cannot be. I have made an important engagement in South Australia, one that will be extremely lucrative. Oh! That I should have to consider such motives; but poverty is urgent, Flora.'

'I cannot bear to hear you talk of *poverty* whilst I am rich, Herbert.'

'Not one shilling of your money will I ever touch, Flora. I do not think there is a more contemptible creature in the world than a man who lives on his wife's means. But I am not so *very* poor, and it is to avoid becoming so, that I have made certain engagements. I am commissioned to paint a few portraits at almost fabulous prices, considering the way in which talent is generally rewarded in these colonies. I will only remain absent three or four months; and then, Flora, I mean to claim your promise.'

She put her hand in his, and asked, 'When must you go?'

'Tomorrow, by break of day, Flora. I only waited to see you once more. You will not forget me, dearest?'

The vow of constancy was renewed; and then Flora accompanied her lover to the farther end of the garden, where he mounted his horse and rode slowly away.

Flora returned to the house with a step that had none of the joyous alacrity which once characterised her movements; recent grief more than indisposition had produced a change in attitude, as well as in countenance, although both were rather composed than sad, and as she again seated herself on the verandah, from which she could watch the receding figure of her lover, a faint smile rested on her lips and many fugitive thoughts seemed to flit across her face.

In that mobility of expression, some persons fancied they read indecision of character, but Herbert Lindsay, versed in all the nicer shades of difference, perceived that the wild and wilful girl had become the tender and loving woman.

Events work *their* change, as well as *time*, and it may be that the character of Flora McAlpin is not yet developed.

CHAPTER XI

The Little Cloud

AN OCCASIONAL MELANCHOLY, which is inseparable from all finer natures, tempered the genial disposition of Herbert Lindsey, and as he rode away from his betrothed, he thought of the vicissitudes that chequered his career – of the terrible incident which had overwhelmed Flora with grief, of his own compulsory absence, and of the uncertain future – for he had long since realised the sad truth that talent and genius are seldom rewarded with wealth.

In vain he tried to shake off a feeling of sadness; he sang a gay song, he whistled a lively air, but could not force himself to be cheerful. Then arose the painful reflection that if his earlier years had been irreproachable he might now be happy, and thus self-condemnation aided to depress his spirits.

His imaginative temperament invested outward objects with a deeper gloom, although the scene at that moment was cheerless enough. All at once he remembered on the morning of that day having noticed a 'little cloud' in the western heavens, and (accustomed by frequent outdoor exercise to observe all characteristics of approaching change in the weather) he then thought this little cloud would increase till it spread itself over the entire sky. 'Just as trouble does, sometimes overpowering people altogether,' he said to himself – but at that moment Flora's note was put into his hand, and the cloud and his reflections alike forgotten.

But the cloud *had* increased, and now hung like a great pall over the setting sun – it seemed to have assumed a threatening form, the dark forest appeared to frown, the rising wind to admonish. Lindsey rode on, and presently met a ferocious dog, formerly the favourite of McAlpin, who had, in a fit of irritation, once set the animal on his daughter's suitor; the dog, true to his master's teaching, now assailed Lindsey, endeavouring to bite the legs of his horse until he was beaten off with a heavy riding whip. A little farther on, a great ugly bird flew screaming overhead, and by and by, Harry Saunders, looking as gloomy as the darkening twilight, came in sight; and, pursuing his painful reverie, Lindsey thought that animated nature had leagued with the elements to oppress his spirits. At length he reached the hotel, and having determined to proceed on his journey by daybreak, he paid his bill, took leave of host and hostess, and after putting his little knapsack in order, retired to rest.

For an hour or two he slept soundly, but was then awoke by heavy rain splashing against the shingle roof. The ceiling of the apartment, being of canvas, gave way, and a stream of water came pouring into the room. Lindsey drew his bed away from the wall, and once more tried to sleep. He dreamt first of the 'little cloud', then of the storm. The shower that drenched his pillow might naturally induce him to dream of a torrent; but either from some inexplicable circumstance relating to the vagaries of the imagination during sleep, or from some other cause, that torrent did not appear to be of *water* – but of *blood*! Herbert Lindsey's antipathy – and, oppressed by the vision – he shrieked out, 'Blood, blood! It is everywhere! It will stain my hands and my *soul* forever!' He was awoke by a strong light; his door was open, and *there* stood two men whose dress denoted their calling. These men were accustomed to strange language – to the ravings of fear, the murmurs of guilt – but now they looked with horror into each other's faces as they heard the exclamations of the dreamer.

'What do you want here?' demanded Herbert, as soon as he was sufficiently aroused to speak.

'To arrest you for the murder of Angus McAlpin,' was the reply. And some hours later, Herbert Lindsey was submitted to an examination for the commission of that offence.

CHAPTER XII

REASON AND INSTINCT

ERBERT LINDSEY, UNLIKE Jack Falstaff, did not 'run away upon instinct'; it is very certain that his nocturnal visitors would not have allowed such a step, neither would they have permitted *that* which his instinct *did* take, could they have prevented it, this being nothing less than knocking down the gentleman that acted as leader; a very improper course no doubt, and imprudent, as it did his cause no good. The prejudice conceived against him by certain individuals was also increased by the language he thought fit to employ on being examined, for when asked, 'Why he assaulted an officer in the discharge of his duty?' He replied, 'I awoke and saw a couple of fellows in my room, one of whom was making free with my knapsack, and the first thing that came into my head was to knock one of them down, and most certainly I should have treated his companion in the same manner, if a set of ruffians had not rushed into the room and seized on me in the most cowardly manner. And now, Sir, be good enough to tell me why I have been brought here?'

'Herbert Lindsey, you are here on suspicion of having murdered the late Angus McAlpin,' replied one of the magistrates, in a pompous manner.

'I did *not* murder him, and those that say so tell a confounded lie; as soon as I get out of this den of yours, I'll break the head of the first fellow who dares to insinuate any such thing.'

Herbert Lindsey was reprimanded for contempt of court; in reply to which he used a still stronger expression respecting that institution, not forgetting the magistrates themselves. Cries of 'Oh! Oh!' followed, but these were mixed with cheers; upon which some persons were expelled, and, with great difficulty, order restored.

'I presume it was under a similar impulse of temper that you struck the fatal blow,' said one of the magistrates.

'You have no right to insinuate that I *did* strike the blow, and as soon as I am at liberty I'll make you eat your own words.'

'Your ebullitions of temper will greatly injure your cause; it is my duty to put you on your guard.'

'Is it likely that I am to submit tamely to be dragged out of my bed, and brought here to have my name disgraced? Be good enough, sir, to inform me what *knave* put this idea into the heads of *fools.*'

Although the worthy magistrate's exposition was not remarkable for clearness, Herbert was, at length, brought to understand that a warrant for his apprehension had been issued by the Crown, and, consequently, the inference of knavery was both insolent and inapplicable; unfortunately, however, the gentleman on the bench failed in the attempt to convince *his* listener (or, perhaps, any of his other hearers), that *folly* must necessarily be separated from *his* acts, or those of his colleagues.

A considerable time elapsed ere the suspected culprit appeared to comprehend the gravity of his position; but when the bowie knife was produced he started, and after a few moments' silence, said it belonged to him. He also admitted that the piece of linen formed part of his handkerchief; he was observed to turn very pale at the sight of the blood with which both these articles were stained; nevertheless, he positively asserted his innocence, and denied having met McAlpin at all. When asked if he could account for the blood on the knife and the linen, he raised his head fearlessly, and said, 'Yes, I think I can.' Then on being told to explain, he added, 'As I was going through the forest I met a bushman, who had cut himself with his axe, the wound was just above the knee, and bled profusely; although I have an instinctive aversion to the sight of blood, I immediately offered assistance and bound up the wound.'

'But the knife! How came *that* to be soiled?' asked a magistrate.

'I used one handkerchief to bind up the wound, and tore another in pieces to make the bandage firm. I suppose I must have used the knife to cut through the hem.'

'You *suppose*! Anyone would imagine that you could not forget such a circumstance.'

'I did *not* forget it. I fancied I had used my pen knife, but now see that I must have employed the bowie knife.'

'You seem to have a very imperfect recollection of the occurrence.'

'I recollect it all very well, but other events, for the moment, effaced it from my memory.'

'What events?'

'That is a question I decline answering.'

'What brought you to this neighbourhood?'

'A professional engagement; I was making sketches on the day of the murder.'

The sketchbook was here produced; and some likenesses it contained identified, amongst these were several of one individual, known by the name of Dick Thrasham.

'Was Mr Lindsey acquainted with him?'

Mr Lindsey couldn't say that he was *acquainted* with the man, though he had spoken to him on a former occasion; those likenesses had either been drawn from memory, or without the man's knowledge.

'Why hadn't Mr Lindsey sketched the wounded bushman?' The magistrate thought *he* would have made a nice picture.

Mr Lindsey begged to differ from his worship, as, in the first instance, the subject did not strike his fancy; in the second, there was nothing very striking either in the face or figure of the man.

'Could Mr Lindsey describe him, or state the nature of their conversation?'

Mr Lindsey said that the bushman could scarcely express himself in English, and as his own knowledge of Gaelic was still more limited, any communication that passed between them was chiefly carried on by signs.

'Was there any other circumstance by which the bushman could be identified?'

'Perhaps by a large dog that accompanied him.'

It was remarked as something extraordinary, that, although several persons had been in the vicinity of the forest during the day, no one had seen either the bushman or his dog. This circumstance, combined with others, told greatly against Mr Lindsey, and he was fully committed to take his trial for the murder.

'It is a great pity that young fellow couldn't keep his temper; the expressions he used to the magistrate will tell against him, besides prejudicing that gentleman against him,' said Mr Lovelaw, a great authority in the neighbourhood, to the landlord of the Southern Cross.

'When a man's roused out of his sleep, and finds a fellow fingering his traps, it is a matter of instinct to knock him down. I have known Mr Lindsey these three years, and a more civil and honourable gentleman never came into this house. I'll stick to him through thick and thin,' replied the landlord.

'I am glad to find that he has such a friend; but nothing can excuse the language he made use of.'

'Being charged unjustly is enough to excuse anything.'

'Justice will be done to him at the trial, no doubt.'

'Justice d'ye call it to try a fine honourable gentleman like that?' vociferated Mrs Roberts, a warm-hearted Irish woman, who, since the trial, had been declaiming against the whole transaction.

'Of course, if he is suspected of the murder he must stand his trial,' said Mr Lovelaw.

'Them that says they suspect him had better keep out of this house,' replied the landlady, in an angry tone as she retired to the bar.

The committal of Herbert Lindsey formed ample food for discussion, and such food generally requiring liquids, the bar of the Southern Cross soon became crowded, the bar-parlour invaded, and other rooms in request. The arguments of the speakers varied from sage to silly, although the latter greatly predominated. Mr Lovelaw still remained in conversation with his host, while Mrs Roberts occasionally aided the barman in the discharge of his onerous duties.

'Well, I don't see what O'Twig could do but to commit the young man for trial,' remarked Mr Lovelaw, as he was about to take his departure.

'And more shame for him, the spalpeen!'[4] cried Mrs Roberts, from her sanctuary.

'I think you are rather hard on your countryman, my good lady,' replied Mr Lovelaw.

'It's him that's hard on Mr Lindsey; and he to call himself an Irishman, and bear grudge because a policeman was knocked down! There he comes – the varmint!' and, as the magistrate entered, she added, 'Oh! It's a nice day's work your honour's done! And may be ye'd like to forget it in the drink?'

Mrs Roberts had known Mr O'Twig, as she said, in the 'Ould Country', a circumstance that frequently prompted her to treat him with very little respect. O'Twig was not a general favourite, as he united to the insolence of office, 'the rudeness of the upstart', and having, on many occasions, punished juvenile delinquents with extreme severity, he was not likely to be extremely popular with the matrons.

O'Twig was neither tall nor short, young nor old, dark nor fair, in fact, with one exception, he could best be described by *negatives*; the exception consisted in one eye that seemed to have a great affection for the nose.

'Come don't bother us, there's a good woman, give us a glass of your best English ale; it's thirsty work sitting

---

4 A rascal or a scamp.

in the court all the morning,' exclaimed that dignitary to his hostess.

'Tom, help *Mister* O'Twig,' said Mrs Roberts to her barman.

'And the Lord send it may poison him!' cried a woman present, whose son had lately been sent to gaol for some trivial offence. Mr Lovelaw, who piqued himself on great politeness to women in all grades of society, mildly expostulated with the lady who had uttered this pious wish, saying, 'My dear madam, never let your temper get the better of your discretion. It was temper that—'

But his harangue was suddenly brought to a close by the offended matron, who coming up to him in a belligerent attitude, called aloud, 'Madam! Is it madam, ye call an honest man's wife? Bad cess to ye! Come out. I'll see if ye'll call me madam again!'

'The gentleman did not mean to offend you – madam is a term of respect,' said the landlord, interposing.

'Anyhow, 'tisn't fit for an honest woman, and I'll let him see if I'll stand it!'

The heroine was about to conclude her threats in a summary manner, but Mr Lovelaw had taken shelter in the bar-parlour, where he was followed by O'Twig; upon which Mrs Roberts cried out, 'Your Honour's had *your* say on the *bench*, and I'll have *mine* in the *parlour*. No enemy shall go there!'

'Enemy! My dear Judith! Haven't you and I been friends this many a year?' answered O'Twig, in a coaxing tone.

'Ah! That's true. Sure I remember when your Honour was nothing but plain Tim O'Twig, and never dared take off your jacket, for fear ye couldn't put it on again along o' the rags! And many's the cup o' buttermilk my mother gave ye!'

Mr O'Twig coughed and said the fire smoked, then seizing the tongs, he began to knock the wood about, endeavouring, by the clatter, to drown the voice of his hostess. Perhaps it was to give a turn to the conversation that he addressed the housemaid, who was laying the table for her mistress's dinner, as he said, 'Mary, my dear, get some other sort of wood; that stringy bark is no good.'

'The *gentlemen* never ask me to fetch up wood; there's the bellows, ye may blow up the fire yourself,' said Mary, letting the bellows fall on the feet of the visitor.

'And what is it ye want with a fire in summer, Mr O'Twig?' asked Mrs Roberts, although it had been ordered by herself.

'Don't you see how it rains? You wouldn't like an old friend to be drowned, would you, Judith?' asked the magistrate.

'No fear o' *drowning* for ye, Mister O'Twig,' replied the landlady with marked emphasis.

'Oh! For the matter of *hanging*, that may fall to the lot of the young gentleman who has run away with the hearts of all you women.'

'The hemp to make a cord for *his* neck is not grown yet; but bad luck to ye, Timothy O'Twig, that puts him in danger! Och! Ye needn't be squinting at me with your old cockle eye! I've known ye ever since ye were a bit of a ragged gossoon,[5] and have given ye the shoes off my feet, and *that's* your gratitude!'

'My dear Mrs Roberts,' said Mr Lovelaw, coming to the relief of the magistrate, 'You ought to be reasonable. Does it follow that because you happened to be acquainted with my worthy friend in his earlier days, he should stretch the law so far as to shield a supposed murderer.'

---

[5] From the French *garçon*; a boy or lad.

'I don't care what he stretches, but he shan't stretch them bad legs of his under my table. He may go to the Ordinary, or the Wild Boar, it's more fitting for him than a respectable hotel like the Southern Cross. Mr Lindsey is no murderer; and them that says he is are no friends of mine.'

'Well, well, Judith, my dear!' said O'Twig, in his coaxing tone. 'The young man shall meet with justice; and perhaps this bushman with his dog that talks Gaelic.'

There was a general laugh against Mr O'Twig; and Mrs Roberts taking advantage of it, turned the tables on her countryman, exclaiming, 'Make the likes of him a Jay Pea, indeed!'

'Mr O'Twig is a *P.M.* you know, Mrs Roberts,' said Mr Lovelaw.

'I make no more account of Pea Hens, than Jay Peas,' replied the landlady.

'And I might have been your husband, if you hadn't been in such a hurry to take up with that Yankee chap of yours,' said the magistrate, who, in consequence of sipping at various stimulants, had become rather sentimental.

The anger of Mrs Roberts increased at this insinuation, and she exclaimed, 'And do you think I would have taken up with ye? Though 't wasn't for the rags and bare feet on ye, for honesty can go along with them; but I know ye, Timothy O'Twig; I knew ye when ye kept the shanty in Melbourne, in the old times, and made a power o' money by sly grog selling; and though ye do be a Pea Hen, yez nothing but varmint!'

Mr Lovelaw, alarmed at the idea of what might ensue, took the magistrate by the arm, saying, 'Come along, O'Twig, there is no use in trying to reason with women; they are only creatures of instinct.'

'Bother reason! Women can be good friends, and *that* we all are, in this house, to Mr Lindsey,' exclaimed the landlady, as her guests retired.

'Troth! And we *are*, Ma'am,' sobbed out Mary, who, since the adventure of the morning, had been quite beside herself with grief.

'Does anybody here think *he* did it?' asked Mrs Roberts.

'He! The poor gentleman! We all know he didn't,' replied the girl.

'Don't say you *know*. Say you *hope*, Mary,' said Harry, who was lingering about the bar.

'I'll say what I like, Harry, and I couldn't believe it, unless I'd seen it with my own eyes,' answered Mary.

'I couldn't believe my eyes if I had seen him,' cried Mrs Roberts.

'Come, Harry, you and I will discuss the matter over a glass; these women talk nothing but nonsense,' said the landlord, who now entered.

'There's no good in discussing rationally, Roberts. Mr Lindsey either murdered old McAlpin, or he didn't; and we know he *didn't*,' replied Mr Roberts's better half.

'How do you *know*, Judy, you can't swear an *alibi*.'

'I'm not going to swear at the ale you buy! But I say he didn't do it, because he wouldn't.'

'Well, I don't suspect him myself; the only doubt I have is that he might have met McAlpin, and a quarrel ensued (Mac. was very aggravating) and then no one knows what might have taken place.'

'That's what I'm afraid of. He did turn so terrible white when he saw the blood on the sponge,' said Harry Saunders.

'If you say anything against him at the trial, I'll never marry you, Harry, mind that.'

'I won't do him any harm if I can avoid it, but I must speak the truth on oath,' answered Harry, whose countenance suddenly brightened, and he added, as if struck by a sudden thought, 'Mr Roberts, though they say that knocking down the policeman will go against him, *I* think it looks honest. For you see, when a man's awoke, all of a sudden, he's sure to be flabbergasted; but it wasn't Mr Lindsey's instinct to duck under the bedclothes, or bolt through the window. And, again, I like him because he wouldn't tell them fellows of magistrates, what he came here for; *we* know it was to court Miss McAlpin, but you may depend upon it, a man who doesn't go blabbing a woman's name about, is of the right sort, and—'

Here Harry's logic was cut short by Mrs Roberts crying out 'Oh dear! Oh dear! Poor Miss Flora! How she will take on when she knows.'

'It's just like a story I am reading in *Reynold's Miscellany*,[6] about a man on a black horse—'

But Mary's illustration was interrupted by the entrance of the cook, who came to receive orders respecting the Freemason's dinner, which was to take place at the Southern Cross, on the morrow. At the moment she opened the door, Harry Saunders was dwelling gloomily on the incident of Lindsey's dream, as explained by his waking exclamations, which had been commented on pretty freely during the day.

'Lor bless you!' exclaimed the cook, 'It was all along o' them pork sausages; he did eat a power last night. But, Missis dear, this stir has kept me back with the cooking; there's no end of people who come to the kitchen to ask the new.'

---

[6] Mary means *Reynold's Miscellany of Romance, General Literature, Science, and Art*, a popular mid-19th century British journal.

'And see you tell them all, you know Mr Lindsey didn't do it.'

'Av coorse! I know the poor gentleman is as innocent as that sucking pig, it'll be beautiful tender, but I havn't got enough apples for the sauce, Mrs Roberts; and the butcher's boy, when he fetched the lamb, a bit since, said, he'd bet a new hat that Mr Lindsey *did* murder ould McAlpin.'

'The impudence of him! And what did you do, Bridget?'

'Just walloped him out o' the kitchen with the potstick, to be sure!'

'Served him right! If Mr Steak doesn't want to lose the custom of the Southern Cross, he'll make that boy shut up! Here, take this glass of whiskey, Bridget, whilst I get out the things for the tipsy cake.'

When the cook had received the ingredients required for that delicacy, she retired, and Mrs Roberts once more ensconced herself in the rocking chair; but she was not long allowed to take her ease, as the stagecoach was heard rattling up the street, and she knew it would bring an influx of guests to the Southern Cross; so passing her hand over the braids of her bright black hair, she called up her most winning smile and advanced to meet the passengers.

These, with one exception, were promptly attended to by the various functionaries of the establishment, and *that* exception, by the landlady herself, for *he* happened to be Mr Silverton, and to him she related the disastrous event of the morning.

Pierce Silverton was thunderstruck. Mrs Roberts, thinking he would faint, called to the barman for a restorative; and Harry Saunders exclaimed, 'Why, Mr Silverton! I declare you are more dashed than poor Mr Lindsey was.'

'I *am* shocked! My best friend! Murder the father of the woman he wishes to marry!' exclaimed Pierce.

'Well, I never thought about it in that way – but it seems more unlikely than ever, and I'll swear he no more did it than I did,' cried Mrs Roberts.

'Nobody will suspect you, Judith,' said her husband, 'though you'll very likely be examined at the trial, as you came from your sister's that morning, and the road Tom always takes with the dogcart is just over the spot.'

'Well, I didn't meet McAlpin, nor Mr Lindsey, nor anybody – only, oh dear! Oh dear!'

'What's the matter?'

'Something I picked up when the pin came out of the wheel of the dogcart – but Mr Lindsey didn't commit the murder for all that; I liked him the first time I set eyes on him, and don't mean to turn against him now; no, not if things looked ten times worse than they do.'

As soon as Mr Silverton recovered from his agitation, he asked Saunders if Miss McAlpin had heard of the occurrence.

'Not that I know of, Mr Silverton,' replied Harry, 'but I left the station early this morning, and have not been back since, more shame for me! The poor young lady will want every friend she has got; and I'm her friend, though only a humble one.'

'You are a good fellow, Harry! Get a couple of horses, and we'll ride over together. Poor girl! Her father murdered by her lover! It's a sad world, Saunders!'

'It is, sir; but maybe he didn't do it after all.'

'I wish I could think so, Saunders. But see to the horses whilst I take a cup of tea.'

Pierce Silverton joined the coach passengers at the evening meal, and Saunders followed Mr Roberts into the stable, remarking, as the landlord was selecting a horse for the newcomer, 'How sure some people seem to be about things.'

'Ah, yes! Women often talk in that way: when they take a liking to anyone, they don't give him up in a hurry; and when they *dislike* – by Jingo! It's a terrible down they have on a fellow.'

'It isn't what the women were saying that bothering me just now, Mr Roberts, but I'm thinking that Mr Silverton talks as if he knew for certain that Mr Lindsey did this thing.'

Mr Roberts looked into the face of his companion, and exclaimed, 'Eh?'

'Watch him, that's all, and you'll find he speaks a deal more positive than them that were in court today, and heard all the ins and outs of the business.'

'Hum, that's queer! But what is *your* candid opinion, Saunders?'

'Why, you see, Mr Roberts, I'm *bothered*; one moment I think as the women do, that Mr Lindsey *wouldn't* do it, and another I think as the magistrates did – that nobody else *could*.'

Although everybody had been more than usually idle during the day, the kitchen of the Southern Cross presented a scene of activity. The Freemasons' dinner was always considered an important event, and to prepare for *this*, the 'busy note of preparation' had already been sounded. The kitchen (which was approached by the verandah at the back of the house) was a spacious room, about forty feet in length by twenty in breadth; it was amply furnished with tables, dressers, etc., but its distinguishing features consisted in its facilities for cooking. On entering, the first object that arrested attention was a capacious hearth, of a depth unusual, even in the bush. This hearth was fitted with a colonial oven, of appropriate dimensions, which at that moment, ought to be intensely hot, as beneath it were blazing branches, and above, huge burning logs. From the interior of the chimney was suspended a large crane, to which were attached immense vessels emitting a savoury odour. An American stove stood in a recess connected with the chimney; this article seeming also to be in full operation. A servant girl was at intervals turning the various dishes with which the two ovens were filled; a boy, replenishing the two fires, and a blackfellow, discharging all sorts of promiscuous duties. Over all these presided the queen of that region – Bridget, the cook. She had recently been superintending the cooling of jellies in the pantry, and was now about to prepare some other delicacy, when her eye fell on the son and heir of Mr O'Twig, who was seated under the table indulging himself with apricot jam.

'Bad cess to ye, Mike! Is it there ye are? And what brings ye into *my* kitchen?' demanded Bridget, in a tone of authority.

'Mother thinks Patsey's got the whooping cough, and she'll thank you for a little jelly.'

'There never was a Freemason's dinner, that some o' ye didn't get the whooping cough. But sorrow a taste o' jelly shall ye have.'

'Then, blanc mange will do.'

'No, nor blanc mange neither. I'd rather give it to the blackfellows for a corroboree than to yez. You may tell your mother so with my compliments. I suppose *she's* too much of a fine lady to cook *now*, though I remember the time when— *Will* ye keep your fingers out o' the jam?

With that face o' yours just like your father's; bad luck to him! Sending a real gentleman to gaol for a thing he never did.'

'The governor thinks it was him that settled old Mac.'

'I'll settle ye, Mike, and your governor too, if ye dare say that again. D'ye see this rolling pin?'

'Are you going to make us a cake with it, Bridget?'

'Cake, is it? No, but to whollop the life out o' ye. Off ye go, Mike.'

And, brandishing the insignia of her office, Bridget pursued the boy into the yard, where he was saluted by the magpie screaming forth after the manner of his species, to demand who the young gentleman might be.

'More power to ye, Mag!' cried the cook, as her feathered ally took up her cause by pecking at the feet of the intruder.

'The impudence of them O'Twigs! I'll twig them if they come here, and everybody else who dares say a word against Mr Lindsey,' continued the autocrat of the kitchen.

'I've served out one of the travellers for the like,' said Mary, as she entered.

'And what have you done, Mary?' asked the cook,

'He wanted a large airy bedroom, and I shewed him into the worst in the house, and gave him a cracked looking glass, and a basin with a piece out of it, and the coarsest sheets I could find; and then I put a gentleman that was standing up for Mr Lindsey into the best bedroom. I'll have none of his enemies on the front lobby – that I won't!'

Meantime Mrs Roberts remembered an occurrence which might increase the difficulties of the prisoner's situation, and being determined that, right or wrong, she would not add one link in the chain of evidence, as soon as she could escape from her guests, she retired to her own room, and unlocking a drawer, took out a blue and white necktie (the article which she had picked up at some little distance from the spot where the murder had been committed). Well she knew to whom that little silken tie belonged, for it had been a gift from herself – pretty and fresh-looking when she had proudly presented it to her favourite guest– but now creased and spotted with blood!

The kind-hearted woman sighed and exclaimed to herself, 'For all that, *I* don't believe he did it, but *they* will, so I'll make an end of this.'

A knock was heard at the chamber door, and Mrs Roberts, startled and dismayed, again deposited the necktie in the drawer, which she hastily re-locked, as she said, 'Come in.'

The visitor was only Bridget, desiring other materials for the morrow's feast. But, although Bridget was a friend, her mistress did not think fit to intrust her with the history of the necktie, and she felt a good deal relieved on perceiving that the heroine of the kitchen was too much occupied by the recent ejectment of young O'Twig, to observe *her* agitation. The exploit was related and applauded; and then the two partisans of Herbert Lindsey sat down to regale themselves with brandy cherries.

Mrs Roberts kept her most choice delicacies in a cupboard within her own room, which, the space being somewhat limited, was pretty well crowded with shelves, and as one of these was placed at a considerable height from the ground, it became necessary, in order to reach it, to mount on either a chair or table. Mrs Roberts being by no means tall, required all the elevation possible, to gain which, she placed a box upon a table, and then, with Bridget's assistance, ascended the perilous height, but being earnestly engaged in conversation, she stepped too much on one end of the box and fell *heavily*, for, if not tall, she was by no means slender, and her foot being in an awkward position, received a severe injury; she endeavoured to rise, but the effort caused great pain, and she fainted. Bridget screamed, and half the inmates of the hotel came rushing to the rescue; Mrs Roberts was laid on her bed, and soon restored to consciousness, but she continued to shriek 'Oh! My foot! My foot! Roberts, get along and don't touch it!' as her husband, from an excess of solicitude, pressed upon the swollen ankle.

'Bless my life! I hope there's nothing broke; run off, one of you, for Doctor McDose,' exclaimed Roberts.

Different remedies were recommended by different people, but as the sufferer screamed loudly when the foot was touched, it was agreed that nothing could be done until professional assistance could be procured. Unfortunately, however, the doctor had been summoned to a patient at some distance, and was not expected to return till late. What should they do? Friction might be beneficial, or the reverse, at all events Mrs Roberts would not allow anyone to touch her foot. All at once her husband recollected that the surgeon's assistant was in the house, and as he was considered a skilful young man, he was immediately summoned. The name of this gentleman was Philip Garlick, generally called Phil, and not unfrequently, *Pill* Garlick; he was the eldest son of the austere matron, already introduced, and, like his youngest sister, was apt to indulge in practical jokes. When called to administer his aid, he was surveying the decorations lavished by the various Societies called Friendly, on the hall set apart for their mystic rites, and seeing the letters M.U.I.O.O.F.,[7] newly painted on some device, he seized on the palette of the absent *artiste*, and facetiously struck out the three last vowels, and doubled the final consonant. A very profane act, no doubt, but if *mischief* was the instinct of Miss Bessie, who might be supposed to have benefited from the good example of her mother and sisters, it was not the less likely to invest Mr Philip's character, and to become the more developed as he was frequently applauded by frolicsome young men.

But notwithstanding his love of fun, Philip was good-natured as well as skilful, and on hearing of the accident, he went at once to tender assistance. Mrs Roberts's ankle was found to be dislocated, and it therefore, became necessary, in spite of her shrieks, to press it, and swathe it, and to put her to so much torture that she again fainted.

'I'll run home and prepare a liniment, and you can keep this bandage wet with it,' said Mr Garlick.

'The Missus has got some that the doctor sent when I sprained my wrist,' said the cook.

'So much the better – that will save time. Where is it?' replied the young surgeon.

'The doctor said it was poison, so Mrs Roberts locked it in that drawer, to be out of the way.'

'All right; get the key at once.'

'There's Missus' bunch of keys, and this is the one belonging to the drawer,' said Mary, who was also in attendance.

The drawer was opened, and the liniment produced and applied before Mrs Roberts recovered from her swoon. The young doctor, then saying he would send her something to

---

[7] Manchester Unity Independent Order of Oddfellows, a Friendly Society founded in Manchester in 1810 and established in Melbourne in 1840.

calm her nerves, took his leave; but he had previously taken something else, as, on opening the drawer, his sharp eyes espied a little book of gold leaf, and his imagination still remaining on the gorgeous letters he had recently designed, he appropriated the hidden treasure, and then returned to the Hall to pursue his study of Decorative Art. Unluckily, in abstracting the book of gold leaf, Mr Garlick had caught up the silken handkerchief, which fell upon the floor.

On recovering from her trance, and even before she could speak, Mrs Roberts became painfully conscious of *sound*; she heard the rattling of keys, the turn of a lock, and knew that her drawer had been opened; she kept silent, and, after taking the sedative, turned over, as if to seek repose; this, however, pain would have rendered impossible, but her attendants thinking she slept, and knowing that a thousand things remained to be done, dropped off one by one. No sooner was she alone, than raising herself on her elbow, she perceived the little handkerchief; making a violent effort, she got off the bed and seized it; but she had over calculated her strength, and, a second time, fell helpless on the floor. After the lapse of an hour she was found there, grasping the handkerchief, which was recognised by more than one individual. All wondered, all knew that there was some secret connected with it; all agreed that it would be desirable to preserve silence; and all, from an impulse to gossip, aided in circulating a report prejudicial to the cause of Herbert Lindsey.

CHAPTER XIII

A Storm

ALTHOUGH PIERCE SILVERTON and Harry Saunders had both expressed considerable anxiety respecting Miss McAlpin, neither of them seemed inclined to soften the blow that the sadder tidings of that morning's event must inevitably cause; neither of them offering to become the messenger of ill. It might not be easy to define the motives which, in both cases, were of a mixed nature. Pierce Silverton, by a curious instance of association, suddenly recollected that, whilst in Melbourne, he had attended the representation of *King John* in the principal theatre of that city, and had been forcibly struck with the manner in which the Lady Constance treated the bearer of ill news; so much indeed as to have involuntarily exclaimed (very *mal à propos*), 'Poor Flora!'

A circumstance that caused Mr John Speedy to remark, 'Silverton, my boy, I think it is a case with you.'

'A case! What do you mean?' was the reply of Pierce.

'Why, you called that virago of a princess, *Flora*; and her name's Constance.'

'Did I? Oh! Hem! There's a likeness between the two ladies.' In this instance the immaculate Silverton deviated from the truth, as there was not the slightest resemblance between Miss McAlpin and the fair *impersonatrix* of the injured Princess; but if we take the liberty of looking into our friend Pierce's heart, we shall find that he resolved not to become an object of dislike to the young lady, by revealing a disagreeable fact, lest he should be assailed by reproaches similar to those that greeted the ear of the mediæval messenger. *How* such thoughts *could* have entered his brain *previous* to the committal of Lindsey, is a circumstance we cannot, at present, consider.

The reluctance felt by Harry Saunders to become the bearer of evil news was also of rather a complicated nature. In the first instance, he did not like to give pain; in the second (according to his own reasoning), if anything *could* make him to tell an untruth, it would be the pleading of a pretty woman; for the imagination of Harry had conjured up a picture in which Flora, with clasped hands and streaming eyes, was entreating him not to tell *all* he knew. And thus, poor Flora was left, like many another hapless female, to go through a trial unsupported by her friends, as when the two horsemen arrived at Mount Alpin, she had been fully informed of the whole transaction.

It is certain that human nature must be greatly diversified, for the office of conveying evil tidings, so shunned by Mr Silverton and Harry, had been volunteered by Mr Lovelaw. This gentleman was considered very kind-hearted by some people; by others, as rather officious; and, by a few of the profane sort, as 'an old woman'. Since a great authority has condemned 'good intentions' to such a purpose vile, we will not enquire what might be there of Mr Lovelaw when he offered to tell the tale, but tell it he did; not, however, without taking his wife's smelling bottle, and by way of further preparation, pouring out a glass of water; but, to his surprise, neither of these articles was called into request, for Miss McAlpin, instead of falling senseless on the ground, stamped her foot, clenched her hand, and exclaimed in an angry tone, 'Who dares to attribute such a crime to Mr Lindsey?'

Rather, a thousand times, would Mr Lovelaw have witnessed a fit of hysterics than the passionate aspect of that young tigress (for to such animal he afterwards likened Miss McAlpin), as, with flashing eyes and haughty gesture, she repeated her demand, adding, 'That upstart, O'Twig, shall pay for his insolence.'

'My dear Miss McAlpin,' replied her visitor in his mildest tone, 'Mr, O'Twig is but a medium of the law in this instance, and—'

'Don't talk to me, sir, of mediums or law, or any such nonsense!' interrupted Flora. 'Somebody has thrown a suspicion against an innocent man, and I demand his instant release!'

Mr Lovelaw, who had often hinted that his wife's hysterics were very tiresome, now repented his injustice towards that injured female. What are *hysterics* compared to *such* passion?

At this juncture, Mr Silverton and Harry Saunders entered, both of whom thought almost that McAlpin lived again in his daughter.

The likeness between father and child had been observed by certain individuals, but they were few, as, in order to trace the resemblance, it was necessary to see Flora greatly excited (a most rare occurrence). Her usual appearance was calm as a summer lake, although now wild as a stormy sea; and there she stood, her brow contracted, her nostrils dilated, and her chest heaving with passion; but, on perceiving Silverton, her manner changed, and, approaching him, she asked if he had heard of that infamous transaction.

He took her hands in his, and replied mournfully, 'With the greatest regret; but I still hope he may establish his innocence.'

'You hope! You, his friend! And do you mean to say that you doubt? That you dare to doubt?'

'I do not doubt his innocence, Miss McAlpin, and trust that the *jury* may not at the trial.'

'The jury! The trial! Will it come to this?'

Mr Lovelaw here interposed, saying that he had come to break the intelligence to Miss McAlpin, but she was so excited that he could not explain.

'It is an infamous transaction!' she exclaimed. 'Commit an honourable man to prison! But that insolent O'Twig shall pay dearly for this; and I request that you gentlemen will immediately effect the release of Mr Lindsey.'

'My dear Miss McAlpin,' replied Mr Lovelaw, 'are you so ignorant of the law as to imagine that, in the present state of the case, *we* can do anything. Mr Lindsey must stand his trial; when, as I trust, he will be honourably acquitted by a jury of his countrymen.'

'Yes, yes; of *that* I am sure; and *then* for revenge on his enemies!' The highland spirit of her father flashed forth, and her listeners quailed beneath her fiery glance. Mr Lovelaw said he thought he had better go, and *went*. Mr Silverton *stayed* and trembled; and Harry Saunders whispered, 'Well, I thought those women at the Southern Cross *could* get into a passion, but *she* beats them all to pieces.'

CHAPTER XIV

AFTER THE STORM

'HAS MISS MCALPIN left her room, Margaret?' asked Mr Silverton of a maidservant, the morning after the event recorded in the previous chapter.

'No, sir,' replied the girl. 'But I think she is up, for the window is open.'

'I am very anxious about her; just knock at her door and enquire how she is, there's a good girl.'

Margaret was spared the trouble, as, at that moment, Miss McAlpin's voice was heard calling her. The girl obeyed the summons, and soon returned, saying to Mr Silverton, 'Miss Flora seems very well, sir; she told me to take her a cup of coffee, and to say that she would like to speak to you in the drawing room in a few minutes.'

Pierce Silverton, a good deal relieved from his anxiety, sent word that he would wait the convenience of Miss McAlpin, and turned towards the drawing room, where he was soon followed by the young lady. Holding out her hand kindly, she said she wanted to speak on a matter of importance.

Mr Silverton offered his services; and Flora, motioning him to a chair, seated herself on the sofa, at the same time placing a large desk by her side.

Excepting that she was a little paler than usual, her countenance bore no trace of recent agitation. Pierce Silverton thought he detected a glance of pride in her eye; a tone of authority in her voice, as she said, 'It will be necessary to take steps for the defence of Mr Lindsey without delay.'

'Yes, I intend calling on him to ask what counsel he will like.'

'He would propose Mr Argueville, I *know*. I have often heard Mr Lindsey speak favourably of that gentleman's talents.'

'Poor Lindsey! What message shall I take from you, Miss McAlpin? I will go to him in an hour or two.'

'Say that I am well; but I sent off Saunders with a letter to him at six o'clock this morning, and have since despatched a retaining fee to the barrister.'

'Already?'

'There is no time to lose. I hope you will obtain all the information in your power, Mr Silverton, that may lead to the detection of the real murderer.'

'I will do all I can to shield my friend.'

'His innocence will prove his shield, Mr Silverton.'

'God grant it!'

On Flora's countenance was written 'do not dare to doubt', but she remained silent.

'Will you excuse a remark, Miss McAlpin?' asked Silverton.

'Yes; what is it?' was her careless reply.

'The world is ill-natured, and if you should appear *very* eager in the defence of your father's mur— of the person committed to await his trial for your father's murder, you will be exposed to censure.'

'If the world should suspect him, I can believe any other rumour, and despise those who listen to such.'

'But how will it look to employ the fortune your father left you in this manner? I am as anxious as yourself to establish the innocence of Lindsey, but the conduct we ought to pursue should be—'

'Straight forward; nevertheless, my father's money shall not be spent in the defence of the man who is wrongfully accused. I have other means; the fortune left by my mother, and that cannot be better directed than in saving the life of the man she acknowledged as her friend – as the future husband of her child.'

There was another pause. Then, Mr Silverton, gazing with admiration on Flora, said, 'Although I respect your resolution, I would venture to suggest that this business should be left to your friends; the more so, that being a minor—'

Flora rose from her seat, and looking with determination at her companion, said, 'Mr Silverton, I am legally mistress of my mother's property; I was of age yesterday!'

CHAPTER XV

OF AGE

PIERCE SILVERTON MUST either have fancied Flora to have been younger, or the time had slipped imperceptibly away, so he merely replied, 'Indeed!'

'Yes,' she answered, 'and this desk contains the certificate of my mother's marriage, as well as that of my birth.' 'It was my father's desk,' she added, in a solemn tone, as she raised her eyes to heaven, 'and God knows that, in seeking to defend Herbert, I truly and religiously believe him innocent of the deed with which he is charged; my resolution is fixed.'

The desk was unlocked, and the two certificates discovered. Under the place where they lay was a folded paper, which Flora opened and read. It was headed thus: 'This is the last Will and Testament of me, Angus McAlpin.'

Flora was surprised, as her father had expressed great unwillingness to make a will (but obstinate people are not always firm). She read on, and found that she was to be disinherited if she married Herbert Lindsey, and only to receive half her father's property unless she married Pierce Silverton.

The will, which was duly signed and witnessed, bore the date of some six months back.

Flora looked neither pleased nor angry; neither blushed nor turned pale, as Silverton read the document at the same time with herself.

'Dear Miss McAlpin, I beg you to believe that I was ignorant of this,' said Pierce in a soft low tone.

'I do not suppose that you knew anything of it, but it will make no difference to my proceedings, whatever it may do to my circumstances hereafter. Ah! I see Papa has left you a legacy. I'm glad of that. What's the rest about? Churches or hospitals, or what? Papa didn't care much about building them. Well! I declare! Some old tumble-down place in Scotland! Those who like may administer to the will. I have still my mother's property, which I shall spend as I choose. But won't you go to see Herbert? I shall not visit him at present; so you see I have some regard for appearances; but you may say that I am with him in spirit; that my heart and soul are his, and he shall be acquitted.'

So saying, Flora retired, leaving the will in the possession of Pierce Silverton. He scarcely seemed to heed it, although the legacy left him was something considerable, for he muttered to himself, 'It is valueless without her.'

Then burying his face between his hands, a few tears trickled between his thin white fingers. Half an hour later he left the house, telling the maidservant to inform her mistress that he had gone to visit Mr Lindsey.

And now we must pause to ask what were the sentiments that Flora and Pierce entertained for each other. Some time before the arrival of Miss McAlpin in the colony, Mr Silverton had acted as her father's agent, occasionally residing in Melbourne, but quite as often at

Mount Alpin; and thus when she came he was frequently thrown into her society. She was glad of this, his manners being agreeable, and his conversation greatly superior to that of most persons in the neighbourhood. He was her chief companion, for there was not another station within twenty miles – the township itself being at least half that distance from her father's house – therefore, without the society of Mr Silverton, Flora would have felt almost isolated. It was Pierce who accompanied her on horseback through the tangled forest and over the lonely plain; Pierce who planted her garden with luxuriant flowers, and Pierce who read poetry or played the flute whilst she sat at work.

Always dangerous is this unreserved intimacy between a young man and a beautiful girl, but in this instance he was the only sufferer; for, if he did not actually fall in love at first sight, a very short period had elapsed after the arrival of Flora ere Pierce Silverton felt that he scarcely existed but in her presence. Perhaps, with a woman's clear sightedness, she perceived the impression she had made, and to prevent an avowal on his part, with the consequent refusal on hers, she told him of the engagement existing between herself and Herbert Lindsey.

Notwithstanding her resolution to fulfil this contract, Flora felt most intensely pained, that, in order to do so, she must disobey her father; and Pierce Silverton, conscious of the moral struggle, sometimes thought that filial duty might ultimately vanquish love.

The two young men occasionally met in Melbourne, as well as in the little township to which we have referred; they had also been slightly acquainted in England – a circumstance that generally leads to a close intimacy when the parties again meet so far from their native land.

The position of Pierce Silverton, as confidant, was one of extreme delicacy; he could neither tear himself away from Flora, nor cease to love her; and to love is, with some persons, to hope. It is true that he saw no indication of inconstancy in her character, but he knew that she was friendly, disposed towards himself, and having obtained the goodwill of the father, he fancied that the daughter might hereafter be won. Why McAlpin became induced to select his agent for his son-in-law may appear somewhat strange, as he could easily have found a more ambitious alliance; but McAlpin, although invested with great ideas of his own importance, was not exactly an ambitious man, and perhaps, on account of that very self-importance; as he imagined that nothing could add to the dignity of a McAlpin ; but he liked power – in his youth he had been at the head of his clan, commanding and hectoring all his kin – and he was now resolved never to call that man his son-in-law who would not submit to be commanded and hectored too.

To such treatment the free spirit of Herbert Lindsey would not long submit, although the pliant disposition of Pierce Silverton yielded, or affected to do so, but not always without an attempt at insubordination – just as a vassal in the feudal times might rebel against his tyrannical liege. A relic of the feudal ages indeed was Angus McAlpin, and although merely the owner of a station in one of the youngest lands of the New World, he was as arbitrary as if he had been a Kaiser of old, commanding some half score of petty princes; and to one of these Pierce may rather be likened than to a great vassal, as, instead of defying his lord, he murmured, and – we shall see what else.

Fancy might also trace another resemblance to ancient usages in McAlpin's treatment of his daughter, whom he loved in a peculiar way; and though he could not institute tournaments in her honour, he got up highland sports, and, moreover, bought her everything the colony could produce, or the mother country export – in short, allowing her every indulgence, save that of being happy in her own way. But although he forbade her marriage with Lindsey, he had not thought it necessary to inform her that he had planned her union with someone else.

It is evident that the inmates of Mount Alpin did not at all times live in the most perfect harmony, though the young people sympathised with each other whenever their tyrant was more than usually stern. If a letter from Herbert had been intercepted, Silverton pleaded for Flora's forgiveness; and when the bushfires had been prevalent, or the wool sales not gone off well, and the unreasonable squatter vented his anger on his agent, Flora would say, 'Dear Papa, it is not his fault.'

Sine the death of McAlpin, though Silverton had been prevented from seeing Flora on account of her illness, yet he had surrounded her with numerous attentions, and she was now sure that he would assist her in the present difficulty. Perhaps she thought he might have been more enthusiastic in the cause of Herbert Lindsey, but the character of Silverton was not so much of an enthusiastic as of a reflective turn; and, then, he loved her father's memory – a love that gratitude for the handsome legacy would naturally increase. She was so glad that her father had remembered poor dear Pierce; as for herself, she cared no more for money than she had done four years ago, when she talked of love and a cottage, at Baden.

Such were the reflections of Flora McAlpin respecting her disinterested friend, as she watched him ride off to visit the prisoner; but from these 'maiden meditations' her thoughts reverted to a certain truism, viz., 'If you want a thing well done, do it yourself'; and happening to see Harry, who was engaged tying up the luxuriant branches of a vine, she went towards him, and asked at what hour the stagecoach started for Melbourne.

'At four in the morning, sharp, Miss Flora,' replied Harry.

'It will be very difficult to reach it in time, the carriage road is so far round, and I must take a box of some sort,' added Flora thoughtfully.

Harry looked puzzled, and she continued, 'Tell one of the men to saddle a horse directly, I want him to take a letter to Mr Roberts.'

'I'll go, Miss Flora, in less than no time.'

'Thank you, Harry, but I mean you to drive me to the Southern Cross this evening. I shall sleep there tonight, and go to Melbourne by the coach tomorrow. I intend on seeing the counsel myself. I don't mind telling you, but would rather it was not generally known; and now I must write to Mr Roberts to secure me a place or they will all be taken by the gentlemen returning from the dinner.'

'It's likely that some of them that's fit will be going,' remarked Harry.

Flora retired to write her note; and Harry, as he took his way to the stable, ejaculated, 'The Lord grant he didn't do it, for she is a jewel.'

Flora's messenger was soon despatched, and, a few hours later, she herself followed, having first written to Pierce Silverton stating her resolution to see Mr Argueville herself, and begging him to make every effort that might lead to the discovery of the real murderer.

A little surprise was expressed by some of the bystanders when Miss McAlpin alighted at the door of the Southern Cross. She had often called there before; but to do so whilst a public dinner was at its height was an act not very becoming for a refined young lady. Surely she did not want to hear the songs. A crowd had collected for this purpose, and, the windows of the dining hall being open, these were sufficiently audible; some of them were very good, a great deal better than the speeches, which were partially audible also. It would appear that the gentlemen had passed through the phases of piety and patriotism, and were now waxing convivial. They had toasted royalty and nationality, and all sorts of institutions, home and colonial, and now they were toasting each other.

Miss McAlpin, on entering, encountered Mr Lovelaw, who officiated as master of the ceremonies, being proudly conspicuous by a white satin rosette attached to a buttonhole. He looked rather aghast, perhaps thinking that the young lady had come to denounce Mr O'Twig to his brother Masons; and not wishing to identify himself too decidedly with either party, he vanished into the little parlour communicating with the bar. Visions of sundry other gentlemen were also seen, clad in that very appropriate costume for a semi-tropical climate, viz., a black coat, etceteras black also, a stiff white necktie, and, in honour of the festivity, an apron, that couldn't be useful, and, despite its glossy texture, its blue ribbons, and gold tinsel, was not ornamental.

Those who saw Miss McAlpin seemed rather surprised at her presence, and their surprise was increased when, without stopping to address any of them, she shook hands with Mr Roberts and proceeded with him to his wife's apartment.

The kind-hearted landlady was lying on her bed; she had dressed herself and made an effort to attend to her household duties, but was not equal to the task, and had become almost delirious with pain, with anxiety respecting Herbert Lindsey, and solicitude about the credit of her feast. This was the first time she had not superintended the laying of the cloth, the arrangement of the dessert, and the dishing of the dinner; and though assured that all was perfect, and that the greatest satisfaction had been expressed, she could not help exclaiming, every now and then, 'To think that I should be laid up the day of a Freemason's dinner!'

'My dear Mrs Roberts, I am very sorry for your accident,' said Flora, as she approached the bedside of the sufferer.

'Ah, then, Miss McAlpin, there's another thing that bothers me – that I can't get up and receive you as I ought.'

'Pray do not speak of such a thing; but I hope I am not putting you out of the way.'

'No, not a bit. You are to have Mr Tippleton's room; the waiter says he's fast asleep in the parlour, and he always takes his spell; he won't wake till you are twenty miles from this, and if he should, there's a sofa for him. But I'm glad you've made up your mind to go to Melbourne and tell the judge of the capers of that O'Twig.'

'It's the barrister who is to defend Mr Lindsey I am going to see, Mrs Roberts.'

'Sure, and the judge will defend him too. The impudence of O'Twig to send the likes of Mr Lindsey to the lockup. He no more did it than myself.'

'Thank you for your kind expressions, Mrs Roberts; but can you tell me if public opinion is in his favour?'

'I guess it is with them that comes near me; and it's himself that would go bail for him, wouldn't you, Roberts?'

'I offered any amount; and there isn't a decent man in the district who wouldn't do the same thing,' said the landlord.

'How kind. But why was it not accepted?'

'It is not the custom in cases of this sort. But at the trial we will all speak in his favour; that must have influence. But it is my duty to tell you that circumstantial evidence is against him. It may be that there is something going on we don't know of. I'll have an eye to matters though, and, perhaps, shall find out if poor Lindsey has enemies, as people are apt to speak their minds when they are half-seas-over, and there'll be lots of that sort here.'

The hospitable landlady interrupted her husband, exclaiming, 'Bless my life, Roberts! All this time Miss McAlpin is eating nothing. Ring the bell for Mary.'

Mr Roberts did as directed. Mary entered, received orders, retired, and presently re-entered, bearing a tray containing cold turkey, hot coffee, wine, and a goodly portion of the dessert. Miss McAlpin was compelled to taste some of these delicacies, and others were packed in a basket for the morning's journey. By and by, young Garlick made his appearance, and, after prescribing for his patient, he began to bewail the discovery of his practical joke.

'M. U. F. F. over the head of that slow coach, old Lovelaw! Wouldn't it have been a lark, Miss McAlpin?' he said, in a tone of regret.

'I should not have been at all sorry,' replied Flora, who sometimes was not averse to a little mischief.

'He said you did pitch into him yesterday. And when he got home, Mrs L. treated him to a scene; Mrs O'T., too, flared up in her style. I was called in; and, by Jove! I think the cat had never done so much damage in all her life.'

'What could the cat have to do in the matter?' asked Flora in a tone of surprise.

'Why, don't you know that in all well-regulated households a cat is kept on purpose to run away with cold turkeys and– We'll save her the trouble this time, first-rate bird this, Mrs R., and the sparkling moselle quite stunning! Here's my love to you, and may you soon be on your pins again.'

Mr Garlick helped himself unceremoniously to the good things provided for Miss McAlpin, and the young lady, amused at his gastronomic powers, remarked that he would not leave anything for the cat.

'Well, I see you understand. Now, isn't a cat useful when turkeys are run away with, and glasses come to grief? But Mrs O'T.'s cat breaks the whiskey bottle, and the illustrious matron is overpowered by the fumes.'

'Fumes is it? It'll take more than fumes to overpower Molly O'Twig. She'd a still of her own when Tim kept the shanty,' cried Mrs Roberts from her couch.

The apartment of the good hostess was pretty well thronged with visitors, amongst whom came Mr Silverton, eager alike to condole with the landlady and converse with her fair guest. After performing the former duty, he seated himself by Flora, saying, 'I found your letter on my return from Mount Alpin, and couldn't let you go without bidding you farewell.'

'I am sorry that you took so much trouble, Mr Silverton,' was Flora's reply.

'Trouble! On whom should the care of you devolve, if not on me? But are you resolved to go to Melbourne?'

'Certainly. But tell me about Herbert – how does he look? How does he bear this calamity?'

'The lad's well enough. Though I am sorry to say he does not bear affliction with a very Christian-like spirit. He says that as soon as he is at liberty, he will horsewhip O'Twig.'

'Of course he will,' replied Flora.

'The Lord send it!' exclaimed Mrs Roberts, Bridget, and Mary, in chorus.

'He is not yet at liberty, and you must not take it for granted that he will be. But rest assured that I will do all in my power both for him and for you,' said Pierce, as he took Flora's hand in his.

'I know you will,' she replied, withdrawing her hand. For the first time in her life, Flora felt some embarrassment in his presence.

Mr Silverton was a very temperate man, so it is possible that a couple of glasses of sparkling moselle had got into his head, as his cheeks glowed, his eyes glistened, and he pressed Flora's hand more warmly than he had ever done before. 'Where do you propose staying in Melbourne?' he at length asked.

'I shall go to an hotel at first, and then, I don't know – I hadn't thought about it.'

'An hotel is no place for a young lady, nor is it quite the thing for you to go at all; but as you have made up your mind, perhaps you could not do better than go to Mrs Garlick's. I suppose, Phil, your mother will not object to accommodate Miss McAlpin?'

'No, to be sure not; and I will run down to see you, Miss McAlpin, and keep you alive. I have not been in

Melbourne this twelvemonth. Now don't fret. I'll pay poor Lindsey a visit tomorrow; and we'll manage to get him out of limbo, and no fear.'

Miss McAlpin expressed her thanks to the young man for his sympathy, and turning to Silverton, said he ought not to stay any longer, as it was a long way back to Mount Alpin.

'I shall stay in town tonight, on purpose to see you off in the morning. Mr Garlick will give me a shakedown – won't you, Phil?' said Silverton.

Mr Garlick readily assented; and Miss McAlpin, remarking the feverish appearance of her hostess, suggested that all should retire.

Mr Garlick's conscience began to reproach him with his inconsiderate treatment of his patient, whom he now desired to keep quiet, adding, 'A cooling draught will be more in your line than sparkling moselle, Mrs R., so I will go and brew one and bring it in a jiffy.'

Mrs Roberts was left to obtain all the repose that a swollen ankle and the idea of that kerchief under her pillow could afford, and her guests took leave of her for the night.

The Worshipful Order of the Freemasons was – being uninitiated, we cannot say what they were doing – but as they called themselves brethren, perhaps they were fraternising, nevertheless the popping of corks was heard at intervals, and songs and speeches still succeeded each other, and at length the festivity became a thing of the past.

At half-past three a.m., the coach was heard rattling into the yard – groom and ostler came yawning to their duties, the horses were brought from the stable, the passengers roused from their beds, some of whom (to use the expression of Mr Garlick) looked deuced seedy. The landlord himself had risen to do honour to Miss McAlpin, and, as he assisted her into the vehicle, bade her be of good cheer, for Mr Lindsey's friends would help him out of that fix.

Mr Silverton pressed Flora's hand to his lips, saying he would devote all his energies to her cause; and Mr Philip Garlick told her she was a brick! The driver jumped on his box, the horses plunged and kicked, and the coach dashed into the street in real go ahead Yankee fashion.

Amongst Miss McAlpin's fellow passengers was an elderly gentleman, with whom she had been acquainted some time; he was very attentive to her on the road, pointing out everything worthy of remark, bringing her oranges and coffee, and what was more cheering than all, telling her that he would do all in his power for poor Lindsey. The other passengers slept the greater part of the way – a fact that some of them announced most audibly. The journey was long, the weather hot, and the road dusty; but the coach was at length exchanged for a railway carriage, which in due time deposited its freight at the Melbourne terminus.

Miss McAlpin was received with a considerable amount of impressment by Mrs Garlick and her daughters, who had previously been slightly known to her, and though there was little sympathy between her tastes and theirs, that was a matter of little consequence. What was now of consequence to Flora but the safety and deliverance of Herbert?

The motive of Miss McAlpin's visit was at once explained by herself. It had previously been so, she was informed, by Mr Silverton, in a letter just received. Flora thought his version slightly different from her own, but this might be in the telling – Mrs Garlick being in the habit of employing very long words, fuller of sound than meaning. When the young ladies understood that their visitor was engaged to Mr Lindsey, they seemed to regard her more favourably, not so much from the frankness of her avowal, as from the fact that, if she married Mr Lindsey, she could not conveniently marry Mr Silverton also. It has been said that frankness is a quality never seen in the vulgar, and vulgar the Misses Garlick were, not on account of red faces or extreme coarseness, but as being stamped with that type of the half educated – affectation.

'I think it right to tell you that I am engaged to Mr Lindsey, and that I embrace his cause in the conviction of his innocence,' said Flora to Mrs Garlick. 'Otherwise I should not be warranted in the step I am about to take; and I hope you will not object to accompany me and my solicitor to Mr Argueville's chambers tomorrow morning.' Mrs Garlick assented; and, at the appointed hour, the two ladies waited on the barrister.

Mr Argueville had already received instructions and a fee through Flora's attorney. One of these he pocketed, the other he put aside. The letter containing the instructions was very short, merely stating the wish of the writer to retain the services of the learned counsel, and adding that all particulars would be hereafter supplied. It was signed 'F. McAlpin'; but as F. might stand for either Francis or Frederick, and the writing was rather bold, the lawyer did not suppose his correspondent to be of the fair sex. There was a want of legal etiquette, and a tone of authority about the epistle, that betokened ignorance of, or indifference to, professional formalities, causing Mr Argueville, to whom it had been handed, to say to his clerk, 'Some of these fellows in the bush would be none the worse for a lesson or two.' He was also a little puzzled about another subject – the name of the murdered man and that of the prisoner's friend being the same – but being engaged with a knotty case at the time, he did not give these matters much consideration. His surprise, however, had reached its climax when he saw in his new client a young lady, who, upon being introduced to him, said, 'Mr Argueville, I know Mr Lindsey to be innocent, and desire to prove his innocence to the world. It may appear strange to you that the daughter of the murdered man should step forward to assist the person imprisoned for the commission of the crime; but I know that imprisonment to be unjust. I am his affianced wife – a contract sanctioned by my mother on her deathbed – and I think you will admit that I am justified in this proceeding.' Flora spoke in a low earnest tone; no blush o'erspread her cheek as she told of her engagement; but she raised her eyes to heaven with an expression of fervour and devotedness.

The barrister felt deeply interested, and promised to do his utmost in the case; but when she retired he remarked, 'There are some fools who will ridicule this noble creature, and call her a strong-minded woman.'

CHAPTER XVI

A Bazaar

I F FLORA COMPELLED herself to speak so freely to Mr Argueville, she was doing violence to her own feelings, and, in consequence, suffered from the effects of reaction. Mrs Garlick, who had been rather shocked at so much decision in a girl of twenty-one, said 'She couldn't have spoken out in such a way for all the world.'

Flora carelessly replied, 'No, I don't suppose you could.' Then, as two or three lady friends of Mrs Garlick dropped in, she retired to her room, and thus their curiosity respecting the strong-minded young lady remained ungratified.

The next day Mr Silverton arrived, and, for the first time was received with mixed feelings of joy and sorrow; as, although he stated that the object of his journey was to look after a shipment of wool, he was suspected of being much more enticed by the society of Miss McAlpin.

Miss Bessie, who had been skirmishing about for some time, was resolved on a *coup d'état*, and therefore bluntly told her imagined admirer that she didn't think he'd have much chance in that quarter, as her mamma said Miss McAlpin had frankly avowed her engagement.

'She wished for an excuse in thus openly undertaking the defence of poor Lindsey,' replied Silverton, 'and if it will serve his cause, I have no objection that the engagement should still be regarded as unbroken; but, in consequence of her father's will and another matter to which I cannot becomingly refer at present, I may inform you that Miss McAlpin will never marry Herbert Lindsey.'

The gentleman looked mysterious, the lady angry, and they parted: the former to seek Flora, the latter to resume her preparations for the bazaar.

Pierce had brought a letter from the imprisoned lover; and, either on that account, or from real pleasure in his society, was received by Flora with undisguised satisfaction. Miss McAlpin, who, under ordinary circumstances, acted as girls ordinarily do, volunteered to dress a doll and knit a purse in aid of the bazaar, though she scarcely inquired into the objects of the charity; and as the family was collected around the table after tea, Pierce took his place by her side, fondly watching the nimble movements of her delicate fingers. She seemed very well pleased that he should be there, perhaps because she felt (as she had expressed herself to him) 'Bored with those hypocritical girls', perhaps from some other cause that she had not expressed. Occasionally he addressed her in a low tone; Miss Bessie thought she overheard the name of Lindsey, but was positive about the word marriage; she saw Miss McAlpin blush, and Mr Silverton smile – he really looked handsome. (We have already stated that his appearance was agreeable, and, as a rule, it is becoming to be in love.) The Misses Garlick had all remarked that Pierce seemed to be in stronger health and much gayer than usual, and they naturally attributed the change to Flora's presence.

'I'll spite him for his flirtation, that I will,' said Miss Bessie to her second sister, as they were packing up the articles designed for their stall at the bazaar.

'I wouldn't do anything if I were you, Bessie, people will be sure to say you are jealous,' replied Miss Susannah; who, being engaged herself, was so wrapped up in her own prospects as to be indifferent to those of others.

'People may mind their own business – I'll do as I like,' answered Bessie; and, remembering the eagerness of Mr Silverton to obtain the snuffbox, she determined to cross him in that respect at least.

And now drums and trumpets proclaimed to the good people of Melbourne that a bazaar was about to be opened! Why such a fact should be announced with so much hilarity seems just as reasonable as the demonstration with which 'the king drinks to Hamlet'. But so it was, and gaily dressed ladies were seen hastening to a certain building at the western extremity of Melbourne. It was a very hot day, a north wind blowing, and sending a cloud of dust before it, which by no means improved the stylish bonnets and jaunty hats bought expressly for the bazaar. Sometimes the gust would rend open the flimsy covering of tissue paper that enveloped treasures destined for the fancifully decorated stalls; but the ladies were too zealous to be deterred by either dust or hot winds, and so they drove or walked up the steep hill, and mounted the sandy eminence crowned by that nondescript edifice. Several august visitors honoured the bazaar with their presence, and the National Anthem testified to the loyalty of Victorians; but these visitors causing the attendance of some officers in uniform, such a number of young ladies came pouring in, who in their turn attracted a few strangers, yes, even that most uncomfortable looking of all bipeds – the 'new chum'.

'Haw! Haw! 'Spose we take a turn into that wooden building, and patronise the, hum, what's going on?' says a swell, attired in broadcloth and 'belltopper', to a friend, who, for the first time, has donned a suit of grass-cloth.

The 'new chums' enter the building, and assuming that air of superiority so peculiar to a certain class of Englishmen till they find out that there are people in the world as good as themselves. After paying a shilling each, they are immediately presented with a letter apiece (postage, 2s. 6d.). One of these epistles contains a *mal à propos* quotation, the other gives the gentleman information respecting the state of his own heart. The strangers wander up and down between two rows of miniature toy shops, which all more or less resemble four-post bedsteads tricked out with coloured calico, strips of mosquito net, artificial flowers, and green boughs. The atmosphere is rather heavy with the strong odour of Australian shrubs, but the place is gay enough, and, who'd believe it? Our friends acknowledge that some of those women are really as good looking as any you would meet out of London, and much better dressed; so, perhaps, there may be something decent in Australia after all! We will leave them to the care of the ladies, who soon let them know that the Christian precept relative to the taking in the stranger had not been forgotten in Australian practice.

And now, having no money to spend ourselves, we will just inquire if the pockets of that old Scotch shepherd are better lined than our own, or, if not, what could possibly have induced him to visit a bazaar.

'Good morning to you, Andrew Ross – you don't look as if you had forgotten your old master, Angus McAlpin, though he was such a tyrant.'

'Na, na,' replies friend Andrew, 'I dinna forget the laird. I forget naething that minds me o' auld Scotland; and it's just that air that brings me here the day.'

'"Bonnie Prince Charlie!" Ah, my friend, that air and that Prince have laid ancestors of yours in their graves.'

We do venerate old associations, so we will sit down with you on the steps of the platform, and ask a few more questions. 'The ship in which your daughter has come out is in quarantine at the Heads, is she? Well, never mind, she'll be released very soon. How now! What ails the man? What does he see in that very old-fashioned snuffbox, which Miss Bessie has put in a waxflower case, and suspended from the centre of her stall, adding the quotation, "Bonnie braw John Highland man!"'

We'll take a glass of lemonade at the refreshment stall whilst Andrew Ross pays his devoirs[8] to Miss Bessie Garlick.

The young lady smiles very charmingly, and producing a green velvet smoking-cap with a gold tassel, asks if the gentleman would like to buy it, adding, 'Everyone who smokes must have such an article.'

Not quite true that, Miss Bessie, or there'd be a rise on velvet and goldthread. But, says old Andy, 'Na, I dinna smoke – I snuff; and I hae a liking to that box.'

'That box! Well, you shall have it for two pound.'

'Twa pund's a deal o' money for a puir mon; but it war the Laird's, and the last day he left his hame.' A tear glistens in the dark grey eye of the old shepherd, and,

---

[8] Compliments or respects.

drawing forth a small leathern bag, he takes out two one-pound notes.

Bessie Garlick, who is a good-hearted girl, notwithstanding a few peculiarities, does not like to take the old man's savings; so, reaching down the box, says, 'You shall have it for ten shillings if you can prove it to have belonged to Mr McAlpin.'

'I never tell a lie, Miss,' replies the shepherd.

'I don't mean to hint at such a thing, but Mr Silverton told me it belonged to him, and was given to him by a man who went to England lately. I can't understand why he should care about such an ugly box; and as for that man – he was decidedly the most odious wretch I ever saw.'

'The box was the Laird's, far a' that Miss – and here's his name.' Andrew Ross is showing Bessie a little silver plate under the lid, which, being near the hinge, had escaped her notice, but now she distinctly reads, 'Angus McAlpin' and says, 'Here take it – I only wanted to plague Mr Silverton.' She gives old Andrew the disputed article, but cannot stay talking to him any longer, as some more aristocratic purchasers are at hand.

The snuffbox is of little intrinsic value, but it is dear to Andrew Ross. It was in the possession of his master up to the day of his death; and many, many years ago, when the Laird and his shepherd were both young, one evening, whilst wandering over their native hills, Mr McAlpin picked up a pebble, known as the Cairngorm, and fancying it to be of more than usual brilliancy, he had it set in the lid of a snuffbox. Perhaps the conversation that took place on that day might have been particularly interesting to both parties, as there always seemed to be an association connected with the box; so much indeed, that McAlpin promised to leave it as a legacy to his faithful shepherd. And now, those days – the days when Angus McAlpin wooed his Lucy, Andrew Ross, his Jessie – seemed to return, and half sorrowful, half pleased, the shepherd leaves the gay scene, but good news awaits him without. The emigrant ship is released from quarantine, and the father hastens to welcome his child – may joy attend them both.

Scarcely had Andrew Ross made his exit by one door ere Pierce Silverton entered by another, and, after strolling carelessly along, he came up to the stall of the Misses Garlick. He had, of course, been assailed *en voyage* by a shoal of saucy little girls, who are in the habit of going up and down, thrusting their shoulders out of their frocks, and hawking flowers or tawdry cushions, or something equally useless. At length, having got rid of this small fry, so troublesome to the quidnuncs[9] of bazaars, Mr Silverton was at liberty to compliment his fair friends on the exquisite taste of their arrangements; and then, after propitiating them by making several purchases, he said to Miss Bessie, 'And now my snuffbox, if you please.'

'Yours! I've found you out, Mr Silverton. It wasn't yours at all. It belonged to Mr McAlpin, and I've just sold it to an old Scotchman, who got very sentimental on the occasion.'

'Sold it, the d—!'

'Mr Silverton!'

Well might the fair Bessie exclaim, for it was the first time she had heard anything like an oath from his lips.

'I beg your pardon,' apologised the gentleman, 'but it is enough to put anyone out of temper to come broiling here on a day like this.'

---

[9] From the Latin *quid nunc?* or what now? Gossips or busybodies.

'I dare say you wouldn't have grumbled if Miss McAlpin had come with you.'

'Don't know – I didn't ask her; but Bessie, my dear girl, where is the snuffbox?'

'Sold it, I tell you. How troublesome you can become when you like. If you wanted the box, you should have come earlier.'

'I was coming, but a friend kept me in conversation; and I wish he had been at Hong Kong.'

'Because he prevented that very elegant purchase. There's some mystery about this old box, and I'll find it out, see if I don't.'

Mr Silverton turned pale, and taking a flacon of eau de Cologne from the stall, he applied it to his nose, and sprinkled his fingers, abusing the weather all the time; Miss Bessie, however, took care to make him pay five shillings for the loss her property had sustained – a piece of extortion to which the gentleman submitted without murmuring – and, having apparently forgotten all about the snuffbox, he invited the young lady to partake of ices at the refreshment stall.

Very agreeable did Pierce Silverton make himself, for he likewise treated the other two sisters to ices; bought a pineapple, a quantity of peaches, plum cake, and about a pound weight of the most delicious French bonbons; he then paraded through the room with the fair Bessie, which ceremony being concluded, they ascended the staircase, walked along the gallery, went on the balcony, and made themselves rather conspicuous. No one would imagine that Mr Silverton cared anything about Flora McAlpin; in fact, he almost denied the soft impeachment to Bessie Garlick, who, poor girl, felt happy once more, and deeply penitent for her theft of the snuffbox.

When they had sufficiently enjoyed the hot wind from the top of the building, had almost succeeded in blistering their feet by treading on half molten lead, had contemplated the rising columns of dust, and experienced a few other delights peculiar to the city of Melbourne, the thermometer being at 90° in the shade, and no one knows where in the sun, they again descended, and then went in search of a cool place, which was only to be found relatively speaking. Mr Silverton immediately suggested lemonade and sandwiches, and Miss Bessie gratefully accepted the offer – that of his hand would have been more welcome still, but who knows what may follow?

'Oh, you are too generous! I really cannot allow you to spend so much money,' exclaimed Bessie, on seeing him invest a £5 note in a few trifles for herself and her sisters.

'Nonsense; I don't go to bazaars every day, and I am determined you shall not forget this.'

And Bessie never did.

But Mr Silverton was subjected to other penalties, as a deputation of ladies from all quarters waited on him, to request he would put in to some half score raffles; and then he was compelled to make another tour of the bazaar (always accompanied by Bessie Garlick), for a great many things still remained to be done. He had not yet tried his fate at the wheel of fortune, or drawn from the lucky-bag; the little paste-board witch had not yet pointed with her wand to the magic circle on which his destiny was written; and, owing to some unspeakable cause, the fair post-mistress had not forwarded his letters; a neglect speedily amended, as a dozen epistles now came showering in. At length, all duties being complied with, Mr Silverton took his departure, with his purse considerably lighter, however his heart might be.

CHAPTER XVII

Mrs Roberts's Rubbish Drawer

WHILST FLORA MCALPIN was exerting herself in the metropolis to save her lover, the friends she had left were no less active. Too much zeal, however, is sometimes as injurious to a cause as too much apathy, and in this way, the position of Herbert Lindsey was rendered still more precarious by the extreme anxiety of one of his warmest adherents.

We have already remarked that Mrs Roberts had become very feverish from the injury her ankle had sustained, as well as from the excitement produced by other causes; and scarcely did the coach in which Miss McAlpin travelled towards Melbourne leave the courtyard of the hotel, ere Mr Garlick was summoned to exercise his professional skill. The young surgeon being unwilling to undertake the responsibility of the case alone, requested that Dr McDare might be called in. This was done, and happily by the joint efforts of the two practitioners, Mrs Roberts was soon pronounced convalescent. A refreshingly cool breeze had sprung up, which, after several days of excessive heat, was doubly grateful, and produced a most salutary effect; so (excepting a little lameness) it was hoped that the sufferer would be as well as ever. Meantime her attendants, having been greatly alarmed, had bustled about in a nervous manner; sometimes raising the invalid in her bed, sometimes shaking up her pillow, but generally doing quite as much harm as good – a great deal more in one instance, for they contrived to drag the little silk necktie from its hiding place; and (no one knew how) in course of time, it found its way to the quarters of the police.

The next morning a couple of these gentlemen waited on Mr Roberts, to inform him that it was their painful duty to arrest his wife as an accessory with Herbert Lindsey in the murder of the late Angus McAlpin.

Mr Roberts started with surprise, swore with anger, and told the officers to go to a warmer place than the Southern Cross; which they did not, at least, just then; but, on the contrary, declared they would not stir until Mrs Roberts obeyed the summons. At length, and with some difficulty, bail was admitted, as, according to the doctor's certificate, a removal would certainly endanger the life of the invalid. The good lady was therefore allowed to recover a little, and was then informed of the whole affair. Being still unable to attend on the justices, a magistrate (not O'Twig) vouchsafed to attend on her. She could not deny that she had herself found the handkerchief near the spot where McAlpin's body had been discovered. 'But,' she added, with the ready repartee of her nation, 'if he had been killed then, I should have seen him too; so I don't know why you have come here bothering me.'

She was reminded that there was a dense mass of scrub on that part of the plain, on one side of which the dead man might have been lying, whilst she was tripping along on the other; and then she was asked 'What might be her motive in taking up the handkerchief?'

'Just to get it cleaned for the poor gentleman,' she replied; adding that she was going to send it to Melbourne, to the dyers, along with a silk dress of her own.

Here Mrs Roberts burst into tears, and the doctor, asserting his authority, induced the magistrate to withdraw.

Many persons who had hitherto maintained the innocence of Herbert Lindsey, now felt their belief staggered. Mr Roberts himself looked grave, but, although annoyed at the idea of his wife being dragged forward, said, 'Perhaps Lindsey can account for this handkerchief, as he did for the other one and the bowie knife.'

'He has not accounted for them yet. Nobody believes that yarn about the bushman and his dog,' said a bystander.

And thus, events seemed to be veering from bad to worse. The gay temperament of Mrs Roberts, however, was not entirely overcome, as she had still faith in the prisoner's innocence; and faith, even in man, gives us strength, at least till proved to be vain. But the character of our hostess was not extremely equable, and she became very irritable on the subject of the article discovered in her possession; the more so when some official thought fit to appropriate the drawer itself, and after formally demanding the key, ransacked its contents in her presence. A strange medley he found. 'Odds and ends', as she expressed it herself; 'things just thrown in to be out of the way.'

There were sundry ornaments, more or less out of repair. Here, a bracelet, composed of pieces of jet, strung together on an elastic cord, which having given way, the bracelet was for the present useless. There, was a brooch, minus a pin, and, farther on, a pin, minus a brooch; a smelling bottle without a stopper; a Chinese fan in tatters; a piece of red flannel, which had evidently been tied around a swollen face; a small bottle of laudanum, and a few scraps of cotton wool; two broken locks, and six or seven keys; a pack of cards, at least that portion of a pack employed by Mrs Roberts in the cabalistic art of fortune telling; a pot of pomatum; some hairpins; and a package of tin tacks; several remnants of faded ribbon; a knot of white tape; a bunch of curtain rings; a hank of grey thread; in short, a large assortment of such articles as are usually deposited in a Rubbish Drawer.

'Bad cess to ye for rummaging my things in that way. If I'd known, I'd have put a good branch of prickly pear amongst them, and spoilt those fingers of yours, my boy,' cried the indignant lady to the zealous official.

Had she conjured up a portion of the delectable shrub which caused the policeman to wring his hand in apparent agony? No, it was merely a large carpet needle run through the skein of thread.

'Can't compliment you on the neatness of your drawer, madam,' said the wounded man.

'Take that, and see if it will improve the neatness of your hair, my beauty,' cried the amazon, flinging one of the pillows of her easy chair at the head of the spy; and adding, as he retired with the confiscated repository. 'Neatness, indeed! Who overheard of neatness in a Rubbish Drawer?'

CHAPTER XVIII

A Myth

IT WAS TRUE that a great many people doubted the existence of the bushman whom Herbert Lindsey asserted he had met, as though it is no unusual occurrence for a traveller to cross these vast plains without encountering a single human being, yet it was asked, by way of argument, 'If, on that day, other persons had been met, why should not the bushman have been met too? Or, if so, only by Mr Lindsey himself?' And thus, from not having been seen, the bushman's very existence became dubious, and he was beginning to be regarded as a myth, his dog being equally unsubstantial.

'This bushman would prove a most important witness in our case,' said Miss McAlpin's solicitor one day to her when she was giving him some additional evidence. Flora said she would offer any reward that might lead to the discovery of the man.

'We will advertise in all the leading country papers, as well as in those of South Australia and New South Wales; and, to facilitate the matter, the notices shall be printed both in English and in Gaelic,' replied the lawyer.

That evening, the advertisements were sent to all the Melbourne newspapers, and, the next day, to the up-country papers, and likewise to those of the adjacent colonies.

After this step, Flora felt a new hope dawn within her, but her solicitor kept his opinion to himself; a reserve not maintained by Mr Lindsey's country friends, who nevertheless eagerly read the advertisements. Very welcome they were at that moment, for there was nothing particular going on in the district, neither land sale nor county court, no, not even a ploughing match, nor was any matter of public interest anticipated till the assizes, and then—

'Then we shall see whether that bushman will turn up,' cried one, 'who, to believe, we must first see.'

'Bushman or no bushman, I think it will be very hard if poor Lindsey is to suffer because a man cannot or will not come forward to give him a help,' said a truer friend of the prisoner.

'I don't say Lindsey ought to suffer, but I like to see a thing sifted to the bottom,' replied the first speaker.

The scene where this discussion took place was an apartment in the Southern Cross we have not yet visited. Don't object to the locale, good reader, because nearly everything done or talked of in that township, was done or talked of in the hotel conducted by Jonathan Roberts and his wife Judith. So, if you please, I will introduce you to the public room, which we shall have no difficulty in finding, for we have only to follow our noses – and it is to be presumed that a few years residence in Victoria has sufficiently familiarised us with the odour of the plant which added to the fame of Sir Walter Raleigh.

A very good specimen of its kind is the public room of the Southern Cross, of ample dimensions in length, breadth, and height, well ventilated, and lighted by two large windows, furnished with strong venetian shutters, and curtains of dark green stuff. At the extreme end is a capacious hearth filled with huge logs, which, even in summer, owing to the size of the room and its shady aspect, are either lighted or merely require the aid of a match. Above the high mantelpiece is a glass whose frame is covered with a yellow mosquito net. On the mantelpiece itself stands a clock and a few vases, the latter being chiefly used as depositories for matches or pieces of twisted paper; around these a considerable space is reserved as a temporary resting place for pipes and cigars.

At the farther end of the room is a large horsehair sofa, and, in different directions, are clusters of round-backed chairs, some seated with cane, others with wood; a few small tables are interspersed with these, and down the centre of the apartment is one longer and more substantial; this is covered with oilcloth, and on it are placed during the day, and till an advanced period of the night, sundry trays and glasses, to replenish which affords constant occupation for one waiter. An oilcloth is on the floor, and in various places are objects of either brass or painted tin, not very elegant, but essential to a public room, and moreover demonstrating a certain amount of logic, inasmuch as if pipes are the cause, these said objects are the result.

Don't be cross, good reader, with this description, which I admit is not very refined, and be pleased to remember that it does not refer to either Parisian salon or English flower garden, but to a public room in a country hotel, which, take it 'for all in all', is quite as good as anything of its kind in Great Britain or Ireland.

On the present occasion, this apartment was rather more crowded than usual – the advertisements before alluded to having replenished a source of conversation that was becoming exhausted 'for lack of argument'.

But the public room being filled with speakers, the atmosphere soon became filled with smoke, the glasses with ale or spirits, and, as a natural consequence, the heads with nonsense.

'They'd better print their advertisements in Chinese whilst they are about it,' exclaimed one of Lindsey's doubtful friends.

'Chinese! The bushman couldn't be a Chinaman. He must be a Scotchman, from the Western Highlands or some such place. Didn't Lindsey say he couldn't understand him because he only spoke Gaelic?'

'You may as well say that he was from the moon. It's all gammon about the bushman,' answered Mr Thomas Turnside, a gentleman who, since the discovery of the handkerchief, had abandoned the prisoner's cause.

'Sorry for Roberts,' said another. 'Can't think why his wife should connive at the murder.'

'I don't believe she did that; she has only let a good-looking fellow talk her over – as women always do,' said a third speaker.

'Bother the women!' exclaimed a henpecked husband, now that he was out of his wife's hearing. 'They get gossiping together and neglect their own business. Haven't had a decent dinner since this affair was started.'

'What do you think some of them say?' asked a timid looking little man, who was making his debut in a public room.

'Who's they?' demanded Turnside.

'The women,' replied the little man.

'Pooh!' returned the voice (or pipe) of Turnside.

'Well, but it's something queer,' whispered the other.

'Out with it, then – anything for a change.'

'They say,' answered the little man, blushing, and unable to proceed; for he had never addressed a meeting before, excepting one connected with a road board, when he broke down as completely as the ruined fence he was endeavouring to get into repair.

'Well, what do they say? Nonsense, of course,' said a gentleman, who had heard nonsense talked by two wives, and was soon about to listen to that of a third.

'More than nonsense – something awful!' answered the small individual, turning pale; and sipping at his brandy and water, he continued, 'Mrs Yarnley spent the day before yesterday with my wife, and told her that soon after she came to the colony, about twenty years ago, a shepherd was murdered near the forest and his dog killed too; and that for a great many years such sights used to be seen.'

'Lord help us!' exclaimed another neophyte of public rooms.

'Gammon! If a shepherd gets murdered a score of years ago, his ghost doesn't go about murdering other men now,' said Turnside.

'Shut you up there, Smalltalk – eh!' said Turnside's friend.

Whether the little man was shut up or not, it was time to exercise that proceeding on the hotel, a hint that Mr Roberts announced by commencing to blow out the lights, which caused the public room to be cleared of its frequenters, and (after the windows had been open a short time) the atmosphere of its smoke.

It so happened that whilst Mr Smalltalk was relating his story, the waiter entered with a fresh supply of liquids from the bar, and, as it will readily be supposed, repeated the legend in the kitchen, where the cook and her assistant, Mary and the laundress, were assembled round the fire.

'Them were awful times in the bush, when the people were lost and murdered, and couldn't get Christian burial till there was nothing left of them to bury, and sorra a priest to lay them,' exclaimed the cook.

'A man that's murdered has a right to send his ghost till they get's him laid; but a dog – the Lord save us! Whenever we hear tell of one of them craythers that walks after it's been killed, you may depind upon it there's been something done that shouldn't be,' said Mary, who, turning to the kitchenmaid, added, 'Don't you renumber the story we were reading in *Reynold's Miscellaneous*, last night, Hannah?'

'Don't scare us, Mary,' cried Hannah, a great rosy Yorkshire girl, whose naturally plump arms had acquired extra development by the constant lifting of immense cooking utensils. 'A man's fetch is nothing more than nat'ral, but t' dog's bargheist* is the awfullest sight that ever I heerd tell of.'

'Weel, lasses! It's the ghaist of the laird that'll come to them that did this fearfu' deed, and may be, to them that puts the wrang where the right should be,' ejaculated the old Scotch laundress in a prophetic tone.

'How Wallace does be barking! May be it's the thunder that's bothering him. It's an awful night!' cried our friend Bridget in her turn.

---

* Ghost or spirit (author's note).

Thunder had been heard during the evening, and flashes of lightning, which had gradually become more vivid, now indicated that the storm was about to break.

'I'll engage,' continued Bridget, after a pause, 'that ye know a power o' tales, Jeannie. They say that in the ould times Scotland used to be as bad as Ireland for murders and the like.'

'Aye, aye, lassie! Many's the deed that's told, and many's the deed that's been done in puir Scotland, and there's ain I ken of.'

'And ye'll tell us, won't ye, Jeannie, whilst the water's boiling for the punch?' said Bridget in a pleading tone; then turning to her subordinate, she added in a more authoritative manner, 'Blow up the fire can't ye, Hannah? There's nothing settles the sorrows like a drap o' punch.'

Hannah took up the bellows, and seating herself on the ground immediately in front of the hearth, began to blow the fire with all her might. The women drew closer together; then, whilst the rain beat and the thunder rattled without, they prepared to make themselves pretty comfortable within, and old Jeannie introduced her long story by saying,

'This murder just minds me o' the maist awfu' tale, lassies – ain o' a murder too – and na' sae lang syne, for they say his ghaist is aft seen wi' a plaid aboot him a drippin' wi' weet, for it war sic a storm as this just noo, and in the dead o' night.'

At this moment a blinding flash of lightning filled the kitchen; it was accompanied by a loud crash of thunder, and a gust of wind so violent as to blow the door wide open. The women shrieked, and threw themselves into each other's arms, for within the threshold stood a tall pale figure, shrouded in a grey plaid, from which great drops of heavy rain fell to the ground.

CHAPTER XIX

Pro and Con

'HOOT AWA, LASSIE, is it daft ye are?' exclaimed old Andrew Ross, as he approached the terrified females.

'And is it yersel, Andy?' asked Jeannie, who was the first to recover the use of speech.

'Mysel! And who should it be, woman?' replied the midnight guest.

'And sure he is'nt 'kelt at all,' added Bridget, half dubious whether she might be addressing a creature of earth, or of some other planet.

'Ye 'll soon see that, lassie,' said Andrew; and if the hearty tones of his voice were not sufficient to convince them of his natural existence, the proof was borne out by his still heartier appetite; as, taking his seat at the table, he drew a dish of cold beef towards him, and began to demolish one slice after another.

'And what brings ye here, the night, Andy?' asked Jeannie of her countryman.

'The storm, woman, though it is not mickle I care for the like; but ye ken I gaed to the town to fetch my bairn.'

'I mind it weel – an' whar's the lassie?'

'I' the dray – but it war sae lang a' coming through the weet, that I walked the last twa mile. I ken Mistress Roberts winna refuse a shelter to the puir bairn for the night, but gang an' ask her, Jeannie.'

As it was Mary's office to attend on the lady of the Southern Cross, she volunteered to be the bearer of old Andrew's request; but her nerves not having sufficiently recovered their wonted tone to enable her to traverse the verandah and ascend the staircase alone, she engaged Hannah as companion in arms, and thus attended, went forth on her mission.

Since the murder of McAlpin, and more especially since the mystery respecting the bushman, these damsels had gone 'coupled', and (as far as their several duties would admit) 'inseparable'; magnifying all the actual dangers of the bush, and calling up others of a more idle nature, in a way that proved them to be highly gifted with imagination.

The duty of committing a disciple of Bacchus to the care of a guardian (not an angel), had detained Mr Roberts till a late hour; and, as he now approached his wife's apartment, he beheld two maidens timidly tapping at the door. It would seem that they were determined upon seeing a ghost – and the old shepherd having proved too substantial for that purpose, they now invested their employer with unearthly attributes. His costume – a suit of linen – did well enough, insomuch that it was white; neither was the light that he carried de trop, for spectres have been known to carry tapers, though it is nowhere stated that they use kerosene. As for the pipe that spirit had in his mouth, and the wide-awake, on his head – they were decidedly out of keeping. But, notwithstanding the inaccuracies of the make up, the girls squalled, fell on their knees, and begged for mercy.

'What the devil do you want here?' roared Jonathan Roberts – and in this place I must remark that a certain potentate cannot be 'so black as he is painted', or his name could not have allayed the fears of two timid maidens, who, being well read in legendary lore, knew that ghosts are too polite to invoke the name of his Satanic Majesty; and thus, Mr Roberts having established his identity, proceeded to ask, 'What that 'tarnation row was about?'

The cause was explained, and permission accorded, the damsels dismissed, and then Mr Roberts thought he might as well go and fraternise with the other imaginary spirit; not that he troubled himself at all about beings from another sphere, nor indeed very much respecting those of his own, though he deemed it prudent, considering the excited condition of his household, to look after the doors; so, after briefly informing his wife of the state of the case, he descended to the kitchen.

There he found the Highland Mary listening to the welcome of the Irish one, and directing old Jeannie to take care of her country-woman, besides giving a general admonition to the other females not to make such 'tarnation fools of themselves'. He offered a night's shelter to the old shepherd. This was gladly accepted; and the old women having retired, Mr Roberts pushed the whisky bottle within reach of his guest; he then asked a few questions relative to the state of the weather, the rise of the river, the fall of the funds, and other matters that might either send customers to the Southern Cross or keep them away.

Andrew Ross, not being a man of many words, was accustomed, when at a loss, to inspire himself with a pinch of snuff; and, all at once, Mr Roberts saw the light of his lamp reflected on the cairngorm of poor McAlpin's snuffbox; a circumstance which caused him to remark, 'So he gave you this, did he?'

'Na, it wun na the Laird; it war a young lady at a fancy kind o' a sale,' replied Andrew.

What a young lady should be doing with an ugly Scotch snuffbox was sufficient to cause surprise, even to a Yankee; and Mr Roberts having exhibited symptoms of that weakness, Andrew related the occurrence. The shrewd American at once detected some discrepancy between Silverton's statement, namely, that the box had been owned by a stranger; and the fact, for which he himself could vouch, that it did once belong to Mr McAlpin.

'I reckon there's something at the bottom of all this,' said the landlord.

'An' mair, it may be, than some folk would like the warld to ken; but a' will come right if we bide a wee,' replied the visitor.

The cunning American and the cautious Scotchman alike agreed that the matter should be kept quiet; Andrew consenting to hide his treasure from the public gaze, and Mr Roberts making a note of the circumstance; which note he determined should be forwarded, the next morning, to the prisoner's attorney. Suddenly, however, he changed his mind, not in consequence of diminished zeal, but because he thought it would be as well to see the lawyer himself. This project he only confided to the old shepherd, doubting not that he would keep the secret, which was rather more than he could expect from his wife. But that good lady being in a comfortable sleep at the moment he entered the chamber to bid her farewell, she did not thoroughly awake till her lord was some miles distant; then, remembering something about his departure, she remarked, 'He ought to know his own business, and it was a good thing to get rid of men sometimes, because they do so interfere when there's a thorough cleaning.' We will therefore leave Mrs Roberts to indulge in that domestic pastime, and accompany her husband to the metropolis.

Arrived there, his first business was to communicate with Mr Lindsey's attorney respecting the incident of the snuffbox. Perhaps the shrewd lawyer did not think the evidence would be of much importance, for he made no remark, although, as Mr Roberts observed, he noted down something in his pocketbook.

A great deal often comes out of a trifle, was the reflection of our American; and, as the bazaar was to remain open another day, he sauntered to the building we have already visited. Somewhat of its gay appearance had disappeared, as the stalls were beginning to look bare, the fair shopkeepers weary, and the green boughs faded, the flowering shrubs smelt more sickly, and the currant cakes less attractive except to the flies and mosquitoes; but none of these circumstances disturbed the tranquillity of Mr Roberts, who, after buying a little ordinary looking snuffbox at the most ordinary looking stall, went away. Nevertheless, he lingered outside the building, probably because he saw an old acquaintance; who, on approaching him, exclaimed, 'Bless me, Roberts, what has brought you to Melbourne?'

'A little matter of business; but I should like to see Miss McAlpin before I return,' answered the American.

'All right; she is staying at my mother's. Come and take tea with us in the evening. Mother will be at home, and so will the girls.'

'Thanks – I will drop in.'

'You're a brick; but how goes it with Mrs R?'

'Getting quite hearty again. I left her in a comfortable snooze. But if you're going in there, I'll take leave of you till evening.'

Mr Roberts went to visit a countryman of his own, and Mr Philip, whom we suppose our readers have already recognised, to inform mother of the arrangement he had made for the evening.

Mrs Garlick did not, as a rule, approve of her son's acquaintances, and the Yankee hotel keeper formed no exception; but Mr Philip drew the argument to a close by saying he wouldn't stand any humbug, as the Roberts were always very hospitable to him; and so the lady put the best face she could on the matter – rather a sour face at all times was that of Mrs Garlick – but no one seemed to pay much attention to it that evening, as she sat over an interminable piece of knitting.

Miss Susannah poured out the tea, and talked *sotto voce* to her intended. The other sisters were at the bazaar; therefore, Miss McAlpin, Mr Silverton, Mr John Speedy, Mr Roberts, and Philip Garlick made up the party.

As Miss McAlpin and Mr Roberts had already discussed matters relative to the prisoner, the conversation was general. The American, unlike the old shepherd, did not require the aid of snuff to supply him with speech, although he flourished a snuffbox before the eyes of the company; rather ostentatiously too, for it attracted the observation of Mr Phil, who exclaimed, 'What, taking to snuff, Roberts?'

'Don't know, just to give this fancy article an airing, bought it at the bazaar.' As Mr Roberts said this he observed Pierce Silverton turn quickly round; but Mr Speedy suddenly exclaimed, 'I say, Silverton, you were sold about your snuffbox; Miss Bessie has made it over to a rum looking old Highlander, and so you must look out for another souvenir of your friend Smith; but, I say, what did you see in that great brute?'

Mr Silverton here stooped to pick up something, and on again raising his head appeared unusually flushed, as he said, 'Ah! poor Smith, a sad thing when a decent man cannot get anything to do in a colony like this.'

'There are plenty of stones to break; and if I am not mistaken, Mr Smith has tried his hand at that sort of work before now, and very likely will again if he should ever come back,' replied Speedy.

'Nonsense,' said Silverton. 'He hasn't been accustomed to manual labour, and wouldn't have strength to—'

Here Mr Speedy indulged in an outburst of laughter; and, on recovering his gravity, exclaimed, 'Strength! By jingo, I shouldn't like a blow from that fist of his.'

The conversation was now interrupted by the entrance of Miss McAlpin, who during the last quarter of an hour had been concluding a letter to her lover. This she confided to Mr Roberts, asking him to forward it. He promised to do so, and soon after took his leave. He did not, however, return to his home till he had paid another visit to the solicitor; then, as that gentleman made a fresh entry in his notebook, Mr Roberts thought something might yet turn up to save the prisoner. But in spite of this comforting reflection, his mind would revert to the long chain of evidence to be brought forward for the Prosecution.

CHAPTER XX

THE LOVING AND THE LOVED

MR. SILVERTON ALSO reminded Miss McAlpin of this painful fact. 'It was his duty to do so,' he said, 'lest the stroke might ultimately prove more than she could bear.'

'Yes, yes; I dare say you mean well,' she replied, 'but I cannot bear to hear a doubt cast on him. I know he is innocent, and all the lawyers in the world would not convince me of the contrary.'

'But, my dear Miss McAlpin, although we may assert his innocence, our opinion will be of no avail if the jury should find him guilty.'

'They dare not. A wooden headed set of idiots presume to asperse his character.'

Very unbecoming, no doubt, was it in Miss McAlpin thus to designate that glorious institution – a British jury – and also nonsensical. But with regard to talking nonsense, a little latitude must be allowed to all women, and especially to one who felt herself aggrieved on so tender a point as did Flora at that moment. Perhaps too, she had, like a friend of our own, once inquired what sort of people were generally chosen to act as jurymen, and been answered, 'Oh! fellows with heads that will stand a deal of punching' (morally it is to be presumed); or perhaps, like ourselves, was in the habit of encountering one who had formerly sat on a jury – a remarkable jury – in fact, who may be considered as a sort of historical juryman, but whose head is decidedly of the most wooden of all wooden heads. All this, however, cannot excuse Miss McAlpin's informant, as he seems not to have regarded that part of the British constitution – trial by jury – as a real blessing, one that ought to be eulogised like roast beef, strong ale and, perhaps, November fogs.

But the life of Flora's lover is in the balance, and she does not pause to venerate Messieurs Les Têtes de Bois.

Well there must be something in a name after all. 'Têtes de Bois' does not look so very bad; not quite so well perhaps as 'Cœur de Lion', but not greatly inferior to 'Front de Bœuf'.[10] Pardon this digression, gentle reader, we are trying to convince ourselves that there is no such thing as a 'legal injury'; and that we should always be meek and bow the neck to insult and oppression.

We do not try to convince that proud girl who feels the indignity to which he is submitted; we do not try to convince the fond heart that must break if … if … But she cannot contemplate what the catastrophe may be – death! – the death of a dog! – and eternal infamy to rest on the name that was to have been hers! Pierce Silverton tells her to reflect on these things. It is very well that she regards Pierce as a friend – as one who is doing all in his power to save Herbert; but if anyone else had even dropt that hint, Flora McAlpin would have told him to 'begone'. Even as

---

[10]   Reginald Front de Boeuf is a Norman villain in Sir Walter Scott's *Ivanhoe* (1820). His name means 'ox-faced'. *Têtes de Bois* means 'wooden heads'.

it is, her eyes flash, and she looks so like her father that Pierce turns pale and trembles.

'I know him to be innocent,' she exclaims, 'and his innocence shall be proved if I spend the last shilling I have in the world.'

'I will assist you,' says Pierce, after a pause, 'but – nay – listen a moment, Flora, if the verdict should be unfavourable, and the sentence pronounced by the law be—'

'I defy the law! That sentence passed on Herbert! Oh God! Oh God! Do you wish to drive me mad that you stand talking there, Pierce Silverton?'

Flora withdrew the hand he had taken within his own, and motioned him away with a haughty gesture, but presently continued more calmly, 'I will watch his case to the end; but if his life should be sacrificed, I shall not survive – I will not.'

She left the room, and Pierce Silverton began to fear that such a heart might break, but would never yield to oppression.

And that was the young girl who, three months earlier, had been seen skipping over the plains – singing to her birds – blushing, smiling, and often hesitating about some trifling project? Just so. But then she had not been called on to act; her life at that period was a tranquil dream, now she was awakened to a dreadful reality. Pierce Silverton did not know what her purpose might be; perhaps she had formed none – perhaps she was waiting the result of the trial – but he knew whatever she might determine that would she execute. He had not previously arrived at this estimate of her character; and though he found it to be more violent than he anticipated, he loved her the better. He admired her courage, her resolution – the sort of antique grandeur which made her stand apart from tamer and less vigorous women. If he had loved her when surrounded by the graceful attributes of domestic life, he adored her in her present strange and almost isolated position. Why it should be isolated may appear strange, for she was young, handsome, and supposed to be an heiress; but everything in her temporary home was so ungenial – she was so much an object of wonder and affected sympathy – so absorbed by one only thought, that she might almost have been regarded as a creature of another sphere. Weak characters, when they do not envy, generally admire strong ones; and, perhaps, it is not so unusual as it may at first sight appear for the character of a woman to be stronger than that of a man. But if this apparent reversal of the order of Nature should be always unbecoming, some poets are very much at fault in their delineations. In this instance the lady had the advantage; and thus Pierce Silverton, who, for three years, had thought Flora McAlpin a sweet girl, now looked up to her as a being to be worshipped, and considered the object of her passionate love as one to be envied; aye, even though he was en-compassed by the terrors of the law, and perhaps destined to undergo the most dreadful of all deaths.

The role of Mr. Silverton was, or ought to have been, one of considerable dignity, for he had assigned to himself the character of a disinterested friend – the guide and supporter of a young girl under very trying circumstances; and if suspected of loving that fair girl (so long as he kept his passion under control), his conduct was only the more praiseworthy.

Mr. Argueville, who was a man of the world, probably thought Pierce Silverton to be quite as much actuated by love as by friendship.

Mr. John Speedy thought – and said, too – that Pierce had a sneaking sort of a fancy for Miss Flora; and Miss Bessie – but she might be jealous – couldn't see why Mr. Silverton didn't get rid of the whole concern.

It is very strange what ideas people form of each other, and of each other's business; but the strangest part of this affair was, that Mr. Silverton should think it worth while to give himself any trouble whatever about Miss Bessie Garlick. Was he a double-dealer? A male coquette? Or did he (just the least in the world) love the poor girl who, though not romantic, nor likely to make a fuss about devoted attachment, would prove a good, sensible, managing wife? Nobody understood the state of the case; and Silverton's real, his absorbing love of Flora – the love that for three years had turned astray all his thoughts and acts from their natural aim – was unrevealed to his most intimate friends; all was mere surmise, but it was evident that, from some cause or other, Mr. Silverton was very attentive to Bessie Garlick. 'It is true,' she reflected. 'He has not yet made me an offer, but he has just stopped short of that; and perhaps he may speak out as soon as this horrible affair is settled some way or other.'

Meantime Mr. Pierce Silverton has plenty of business on his hands – too much indeed – and Bessie tells him that he does not look so well as when he came down from the country, and she thinks he is very ridiculous to make himself so anxious.

'Ah, poor Lindsey!' sighs the disinterested friend.

'Poor Flora! I suppose you mean,' says the jealous maiden.

Mr. Silverton admitted that he was deeply distressed on account of the young lady, and Miss Bessie recommended that he should take a good rousing pinch of snuff. Not a very sentimental remark, it must be confessed, but one that probably suggested itself to Miss Bessie from the conviction that it would call forth a little attention to herself. Why, she neither knew nor cared, but, as the result proved, she was right in her conjecture; and Mr. Silverton forthwith proposed a visit to the Museum, and another to the Royal Park – dividing a whole afternoon between ugly fossils and uglier monkeys.

Mr. Silverton had no special object in proposing a visit to a couple of institutions which would not seem to present any very great attractions for a pair of lovers; perhaps he imagined that Bessie had a taste for science, and perhaps he knew Philip and young Speedy to be elsewhere. However it might be, he engaged a car, and bravely confronting a dust storm, drove away with the young lady.

Bessie was in a sportive mood on that afternoon. She was so proud of her imagined conquest that, after boasting as she had done to her mother and sisters, she was now intent on exhibiting her captive to the astonished passersby. She chatted and giggled along the road; and Pierce, lost in his own thoughts, with difficulty contrived to answer her in monosyllables. But, when arrived at the Museum, notwithstanding his preoccupation, he performed the part of cicerone pretty well, explaining the manners and customs of certain birds and beasts; very interesting no doubt, though infinitely less so to the fair Bessie than an offer would have been. All at once she determined to provoke him by a little agacerie,[11] and as they were then standing before a receptacle or mineral specimens, she pointed to one, in that alarming manner peculiar to some ladies who make use of a parasol to indicate any

---

[11] Allurement or enticement.

object placed within a pane of glass, and then tapping her companion on the arm, exclaimed, 'Look! look! Mr. Silverton. Well, I do declare! That yellow stone is just like the one in your old snuffbox.'

Violently lively young ladies are sometimes too fatiguing for the nerves of delicately organised young gentlemen; therefore, it is no wonder that Pierce did start a little, but the next moment he recovered sufficiently to take the damsel's hand in his own, and to say, 'My dear Bessie.' She thought the offer was coming at last, and therefore bent down her head in the most becoming manner. But in vain did her eyes seek the dusty floor – the offer did not yet come, although 'My dear Bessie' was repeated. Thinking this a prelude, she remained silent; and at length Pierce said in a faltering tone, 'I have something to ask of you, my dear girl.'

If silence means consent, consent should imply something definite, and Bessie Garlick, being a practical young lady, at last thought the gentleman, having forgotten his own part, was acting hers, namely, silence; so to give him his cue, she said 'Well?'

To which he replied, 'Bessie, you and I have been friends for a long time.'

'Yes – yes,' murmured Bessie.

'I have a favour to ask of you – a great favour.'

'Well – what is it?'

'That – that you will not talk about that snuff box.'

'Hang your trumpery snuffbox.'

So saying, Bessie flung herself away from Pierce Silverton and the collection of minerals, and sought the region of stuffed cockatoos. Thither Pierce followed, and was perhaps somewhat surprised at seeing a big scalding tear on her high coloured and rather high boned cheek. Oh! What would he have given to perceive such a sign of weakness in Flora? So he thought even at that moment, and he sighed. The thought could not be read, but the sigh was, though not correctly, but it served his cause and Bessie looked appeased, as, again taking her hand and drawing it through his arm, he once more prefaced his speech with 'My dear Bessie'. This time she did preserve silence, and Pierce continued, 'That snuffbox belonged to poor McAlpin, and on the very morning he was murdered he gave it to me. Now, as the most trifling incident connected with that fatal day will be discussed, it is probable I may be asked how the article fell into my possession.'

'Then why did you say that the man Smith had given it to you?' Bessie very naturally asked.

'I was thinking of a pocketbook that somehow or other had found its way amongst your pretty little knick-knacks – and poor Smith having just gone, and left it with me, and – one thing or other – in short, I scarcely knew what I was saying; but, though it is very well known that I was elsewhere, and could not by any chance have had a hand in the murder, yet there are some people whose imaginations being evil, will suspect anything. And if there should be an inquiry about this d— I beg your pardon – this old Scotch article – in fact, lawyers are the devil, and when they begin to talk, no one knows where they will stop.'

Bessie looked rather aghast at this speech, either because it contained a profane word or two, or because she did not understand what it meant, and no wonder. But Pierce Silverton was squeezing her hand so tenderly, and looking so pleadingly into her eyes, that she whispered, 'I'll deny everything about the box – I'll say whatever you like – indeed I will.' In short, she offered to tell as many fibs as could reasonably be expected from a young lady who had been subjected to a severe course of training.

'Nay, I do not want you to tell anything that is not true. Thank heaven, I have nothing to fear; but the fact simply is that McAlpin did give me the box, and I don't want to be bothered with any stupid questions; though if I had cared about the affair being known, I should scarcely have left it in your way to play tricks with, you little gipsy.'

Mr. Silverton looked as if he would challenge the scrutiny of the world, and at that moment his arm found its way round Bessie's waist; look and gesture together gained his cause, for she answered, 'I will never joke about that box again,' and she never did.

'You are a good girl, Bessie, and you may command me for life,' he replied with emphasis. Flattering and vague language; but Bessie sipped the honey of flattery without heeding the thorns of doubt, she was in such a delightful turmoil – Pierce holding her hand all the way back to Melbourne; but the only actual promise he breathed in her ear was, that as she seemed to admire the stuffed cockatoos so much, he would bring her a live one the next time he came down from the country.

Mr. Silverton ought to be considered a fortunate man, on that day at least, being all in all to Bessie Garlick, and, notwithstanding a thousand anxieties, he very much occupied the thoughts of Flora McAlpin, as no sooner was she alone, than her conscience smote her for the harshness with which she had treated her true and dis-interested friend. Poor Flora! She was not very wise in the world's ways; nor would we have any girl of twenty-one to be so. But we will not destroy her illusions; and though her faith both in Lindsey and in Silverton may prove vain, we will leave her to enjoy yet longer the sweet but treacherous dream of youthful confidence.

'I was unkind to Pierce when he wished to prepare me for … for— But if he knew half my wretchedness, he would forgive me – he is so generous. He has not spoken of…,' Flora paused in her soliloquy and blushed, for she knew that Pierce loved her, and her alone. 'Yes, generous in many ways – he has not yet touched my father's legacy. He will leave me in undisputed possession of my father's house – I wish I had a sister – I should so like dear Pierce for a brother!'

But Flora's meditations were interrupted by the car driving up to the door; Pierce Silverton and Bessie Garlick alighted – both still covered with dust, though very different were the separate expressions seen through that unbecoming cloud. The lady looked red and radiant – the gentleman, pale and perplexed. They entered the house – the one with a bounding (not to say a bouncing) step; the other with an air of listlessness and languor.

How ill he looks, thought Flora; and, with the generous impulse of her nature, she went to meet the object of her solicitude, saying, 'I am afraid you will think I was very rude and unkind this morning, but do not be angry – I was so wretched that I scarcely knew what I was saying.'

She held out her hand, and the look of candour that was her principal charm – (it is always a charm in woman, for it cannot exist with rigidity) – went right to the heart of the unhappy lover.

'Angry with you!' he exclaimed. 'Oh! I could not be so. You may say what you like, Flora, and you know it.' His hand, that had lain passively in that of Bessie Garlick, now trembled within the soft fingers of Flora McAlpin.

The conscience of the tender hearted girl was appeased, and she sat down to talk of business with her friend. Her mission was accomplished – she had done all she could for Herbert; both attorney and counsel were in possession of all the bearings of the case, and now she was anxious to return to the country. She could not be with him, it is true, but she could be nearer. She would see him once, after which she would seclude herself in her own house until the trial, and then wait somewhere close to that dreadful courthouse; that is, if they did not compel her to be present at the hearing.

Silverton did not think this would be required; it was well known that she did not meet Herbert till the day after the murder; and he was sure that all parties would spare her feelings as much as possible. He was glad she had made up her mind to go home; and though he could not now reside in the house with her, as he had done in her father's life time, he would take lodgings as near as possible, and endeavour to give her all the consolation in her power.

She thanked him with one of her sweet smiles; and saying she should not see him anymore that evening, as there was to be a party in honour of Mr. Philip's visit, again retired, leaving him all unmindful of the dust in his beautiful hair and whiskers, although some young ladies were coming to tea.

This fact, however, was soon announced by Bessie Garlick, who entered attired for the festivity, in a shining gauzy dress, her fat neck and arms unshaded, and her hair most elaborately dressed. 'Lor! You're not going to sit down to tea all dust, you great guy, are you?' exclaimed the young lady, who had been rather annoyed at Mr. Silverton's lengthened interview with Miss McAlpin.

'No, to be sure not; but I'll be with you directly,' he replied; and, without waiting for any farther argument, left the room.

The party assembled, and Philip, the hero of the feast, immediately inquired for Miss McAlpin.

'She isn't coming, and we shall do a great deal better without her – she's so mopish,' said her rival.

Whether Mr. Philip was of the same opinion or not, he made no remark, but did his best to amuse the young ladies by recounting some of his practical jokes; and so the evening passed amidst the delights of turn trencher, riddles, and other pastimes, that rather inconsistently hold their places in extremely rigid households.

When the guests had departed, Mr. Silverton informed his hostess and daughters that, in consequence of a letter just received, he should be under the necessity of returning to the country by the first train in the morning.

'Indeed!' exclaimed the matron. 'So soon?' cried Bessie.

Mr. Silverton put the 'amount for board and residence' in the hand of the elder lady, and bestowed a loving glance on the younger, adding, 'But I hope soon to be back again.'

As the train was to leave very early, he took leave over night; and Bessie, though sorrowful, consoled herself with the reflection that Miss McAlpin was not going the same day.

Wait a little, Bessie, perhaps Mr. Silverton may arrange the journey more to his satisfaction than to yours. Leaving so early, he would have had time to proceed by the coach; but at the town where he should have changed one conveyance for another, he happened to fall in with some young men of his acquaintance – gay fellows they were, rather of the stamp of Philip Garlick than that of Pierce Silverton – and as these gentlemen were also friends of Mr. Phil, they naturally inquired about his welfare.

'All right, and coming up tomorrow,' replied Pierce.

'Then, by Jove, we'll have a night of it – better join us, Silverton,' said the foremost of the group.

The traveller agreed to do so; and a very joyful party was arranged forthwith. Pierce did not state that the young surgeon was to accompany Miss McAlpin, although such was the state of the case, and with the sanction of his mother and sisters, who were so attentive as to conduct Flora to the railway terminus, and see her safely deposited in a comfortable carriage, charging Phil to take the greatest possible care of her; and, perhaps, thinking that if anything should happen to break off the match between her and Mr. Lindsey, the accomplished Philip might stand a chance of 'catching an heiress'.

The young gentleman, without any *arrière-pensée*[12] was attentive; and the young lady as well pleased with him as she could be with anyone. But as our travellers did not leave at so early an hour as Mr. Silverton had done, they were not in time for the coach, as they expected to be. Miss McAlpin waited for that of the next day, and Mr. Philip for that of the day after, as the party was so jovial, and was kept up to so late an hour as to render him perfectly oblivious of all sublunary things. Therefore, when Flora seated herself in one of Cobb's Royal Mail and Telegraph Line of Coaches, she was speedily followed by Mr. Pierce Silverton.

[12] Ulterior motive.

'Is that you?' she asked in pleased surprise.

'Certainly – and why not?' he replied, with an air of unusual gallantry.

'Oh, because I thought you were at Mount Alpin by this time. But where is Mr. Garlick? The coach will start in a minute or two.'

Mr. Silverton briefly explained that Mr. Garlick would probably swallow a considerable amount of soda water before he could travel. But in a few minutes they were en route, unaccompanied by any other inside passenger. The fates had favoured Mr. Silverton's scheme; there being at that season some extraordinary excitement in Melbourne, which caused every lady to go there, and none to come away.

But why he should submit himself to the torture of hearing the woman he loved talk of another man, is a thing that can only be surmised by one whose passion is as desperate as that of Pierce Silverton.

The route was not the same that Flora had previously taken, as she intended stopping at the town where the sessions were about to be held. Pierce Silverton knew of her determination, and was most sympathising. And now they were approaching that town. Flora was aware of this, as the road, which in winter must be diabolical, and even now was anything but pleasant, suddenly became tolerable; but the comparatively easy motion of the conveyance did not appear a source of gratification to her, for she violently shuddered; and, perhaps, if she had not removed her hat and laid aside her gloves, she would have fainted.

Pierce, observing her extreme paleness, took a bottle of essence out of her reticule, and poured it on the damp cold palms of her trembling hands. 'Miss McAlpin! Flora! Are you ill?' he asked.

'No – no,' she faltered, 'tell me when we come in sight of the courthouse and of— .' Her eyes closed, and she lay back in the coach.

'Yes – but why did you come this way? It will be too much for you.'

'No, it will not. I am better now.' And she roused herself with an effort.

'Then, it is there.'

A turn of the road brought them in sight of a dark stone building, with a strong iron gateway. Flora gazed with straining eyes, for she beheld the gaol in which Herbert Lindsey was awaiting his trial!

CHAPTER XXI

THE GAOL

I T WAS THE opinion of Napoleon that courteousness of demeanour is not suited to the vanquished and oppressed, who, on the contrary, should maintain a certain amount of haughtiness and reserve; and for this reason the great conqueror admired one amongst his foes, who, when imprisoned, and being asked what he desired, replied, 'To be let alone, and not indebted to any one for pity.' People will always differ as to what is most becoming in others, and it might be more Christian like, under any circumstances, to be resigned than haughty; yet, although Napoleon may not be set up for a saint, we will let him pass for a hero, and also as no bad observer of men and women. Judging, therefore, from the standard he had formed of propriety, he might have admired Herbert Lindsey, who (the first impulse of indignation having passed away) was haughty and reserved enough for Napoleon the Great, and for all the eagles in his Imperial army into the bargain.

Not a 'model prisoner', according to the views of those who think incarceration a likely process to induce penitence – a very mistaken idea, and one rejected even by the refractory urchin who is locked up till he promises amendment. It is true that when sleepy or sick of his prison, he may promise all sorts of things to get free, but away he goes with a pouting lip and a lowering brow.

But poor Herbert had not the inducement of liberty held out to him, for nobody said, 'If you will promise not to slaughter another highlander, you shall go free to study the art you love – the nature you adore.' It certainly is not reasonable to suppose that anyone would say this to a man committed to stand his trial for murder. Neither is it much more reasonable to imagine that he, conscious of his own innocence, would be extremely meek whilst unjustly imprisoned.

Until the gentlemen whom Flora disrespectfully termed 'wooden headed' have decided the question, we do not know whether he is innocent or guilty; so, for the present, we must take his word – his honour as a gentleman – his oath as a Christian – and suppose that he did not commit the deed. Having made that assertion, he asked why he was to be imprisoned like a felon.

'Oh, we do not regard you in the light of a felon at present, Mr. Lindsey,' replied the governor of the gaol, a very bland sort of person. 'But you must be aware that having been committed for trial, you cannot be set at liberty till that is over. I am very sorry for all this, and sincerely hope that you may be able to establish your innocence.'

Herbert knew how strong was the circumstantial evidence against him, and thought his fate was sealed, but he remained silent.

The governor grew sympathising, and asked if the prisoner had any request to make.

'Only to be let alone, and not troubled with condolence,' replied Lindsey, in almost the same words as those used by the Irish officer who thus won the admiration of Napoleon. As Herbert spoke, his gesture was haughty, and even tinctured with a little military stiffness, perhaps.

And then the governor retired with a bow, far less proud than that of his captive.

There were several opinions abroad respecting the conduct of Herbert Lindsey. Some persons arguing that his attitude of reserve was becoming an injured man – others, who probably thought the 'prison made the crime', said he ought to be more humble; but in his case, as in that of many others, the oppressors were more eager to reform the conduct of the oppressed than their own. There were some too, who, remembering how Herbert had treated his midnight guests, expected that his sojourn in the gaol would be a career of knocking down gaolers; and they were greatly surprised when told that Mr. Lindsey was as gentle as a child – that he never so much as found fault with his food, or showed the slightest disposition to any kind of mutiny.

But Mr. Lindsey was otherwise troublesome, inasmuch that he had become a 'popular prisoner'. His reserve had first won him respect; and when he did unbend, his gentleness gained him admiration. Nevertheless, his conduct was not altogether conventional, as, in spite of his dangerous position, his natural character would sometimes appear, and a relish for humour break through the more tragic surroundings of the scene.

His paintbox had been confiscated, perhaps as being too great an indulgence for a prisoner – perhaps lest he should be tempted to break his fast on vermilion and gamboge.[13] Pen and ink, however, were permitted, and pen and ink sketches executed without any permission at all, but simply for his own amusement, as if seen, pens, ink and paper would speedily have been confiscated.

Amongst these specimens of art was an alarming caricature of O'Twig, and the touching up of this gem had solaced many a lonely hour. But Herbert was beginning to weary of this amusement, and even the haughty reserve he thought essential to an injured man was growing irksome, for his character was eminently social. Nevertheless, his dignity must be maintained, and all complaints avoided, as only fit for a set of fellows who cry out for porter, and an extra allowance of food.

And now the time appointed for his trial was drawing near, and the danger of his situation increasing, not merely because the approach of the catastrophe painted each circumstance in more vivid colours, but the danger was really greater, for though link after link was added to the chain of evidence against him, there seemed to be no witness on the other hand who could break these links asunder. It is true that numerous friends were ready to vouch for his honour – his humanity – his Christian principles – but what would they avail if the jury should pronounce him guilty?

And there he lay – stretched outside his narrow bed – gazing upon the rays of the setting sun that shone upon the plastered walls, and thinking of the brilliant landscape that sun lighted without. His cell was not so very dreary for a cell, but it was a prison still.

He had been dreaming of some gorgeous palace, enriched with gems of art, that he had once visited; and, on awaking, his eye fell on the scanty furniture of a gaol.

---

[13] A mustard yellow pigment.

He had been dreaming of some vast forests and trackless plains, that he loved on account of their freedom and immensity – for Herbert Lindsey, like many another artist whose educated eye had been pleased with the rich park like beauty of English scenery, having grown familiar with the grander types of nature, admired – nay, almost worshipped them for their majesty. But now freedom was exchanged for imprisonment – boundless space for the narrow confines of a cell.

And so he lay, dreaming of liberty and of love – 'of love in vain' – of Flora dying of grief, and of himself, sacrificed to appease the spirit of McAlpin.

The gaol chaplain entered – a benign, kind-hearted man. He and Herbert Lindsey had not very well understood each other at first, because the manner of the reverend gentleman slightly implied that the prisoner was a culprit, and Mr. Lindsey told Mr. Stewart that it would be quite time enough to exhort him to penitence when he was pronounced guilty. But the clergyman was merely discharging the duties of his office in tendering advice and consolation.

Herbert, in consideration of his visitor's spiritual calling, gradually became less haughty. The first visit was short, and the chaplain, depositing some books on the table, withdrew. The next day he called again, and sighed, as he perceived that the books had not been touched.

'Do not think I am without religion, Mr. Stewart; if I were, I could not endure my present misery, but it is hard to be regarded as a criminal,' said Herbert, for he interpreted the sigh of his visitor.

Mr. Stewart was a man of tact as well as of feeling, and therefore led the conversation to other subjects; speaking (or he had travelled) of scenes endeared to the prisoner's memory, of the profession he had chosen, and of all its elevating tendencies; and, by degrees, developing these finer shades of character, often seen both in the lover of art and in the admirer of nature. Lindsey's heart warmed to the subject, and Mr. Stewart, on again taking leave, thought that delicately minded young man could never have committed murder. Meditating on all the contradictions of frail humanity, he retired to his study. His conversation with the artist had led him into a poetical train of thought, and by chance, the first book he selected, was a volume of poems by Thomas Hood. It opened upon the subject of Eugene Aram,[14] and then Mr. Stewart reflected that all murderers had not been branded ruffians.

Since that evening he had had several interviews with Herbert Lindsey, and many and conflicting were the impressions they caused and now he found the prisoner more overcome by the sense of his position than he had hitherto been.

Herbert arose to receive his visitor, and for the first time complained of his destiny.

'It is hard,' he said, 'very hard for one who loves liberty as I do, to be immured in this wretched cell – and to think that I shall only be freed by death – and such a death – and for the crime of another.'

'Ah! my friend,' said the clergyman, 'there is One who died for the crimes of all!'

'That is true! But to think of the stain that will rest on my name – the name of my father.'

---

[14] Eugene Aram (1704-1759) was an English schoolteacher and philologist convicted of murder. Thomas Hood's illustrated ballad, *The Dream of Eugene Aram, The Murderer,* was published in 1831.

The good clergyman made some passing remark, to the effect that sin should be avoided for its own enormity, rather than for the disgrace it may entail on a proud family; and again he mused on human inconsistency, as he thought that pride – pride of race – had more than once preserved men from evil.

But Herbert Lindsey had other visitors – some of his more jovial friends. They did not come very frequently, as the prison authorities were rather severe on this point, but they came quite often enough to inform the captive of what was going on without, and of the efforts Flora was making to discover the bushman.

'And it is Flora's money that is spent for all these advertisements,' said her unfortunate lover one day when Mr. Roberts called to see him.

'Never mind whose money it may be. The first thing is to save you – legally, if possible.'

'What do you mean, Roberts? If I am saved, it must be legally – and if murdered – legally too, I suppose.'

'Well, keep up your spirits – all may yet be well, for every honest fellow is in your favour – and I can tell you that some people may find themselves in a fix yet.'

After this somewhat vague speech, Mr. Roberts said he'd better 'slope', and did so accordingly. It was time, for notwithstanding his usual caution, he was nearly betraying a secret – namely, that there was a plot to rescue the prisoner. But if Mr. Roberts found it difficult to preserve silence on the subject, some of Mr. Garlick's friends – with whom the scheme had originated – found it impossible; and the consequence was that a request was despatched to Melbourne from the governor of the gaol for a reinforcement of mounted police.

It has been stated that the prisoner had few visitors – partly because knowing there was a difficulty made about granting leave, he was too proud to solicit a favour; besides he was, comparatively speaking, a stranger in that locality. Had he been allowed to remain in the little township, amongst the habitués of the Southern Cross, the number of visitors would have been greatly increased, but only petty sessions being held there, his removal to the chief town of the district had been rendered necessary.

A fortnight – one little fortnight – was now all that remained ere the trial, and still no additional evidence in his favour seemed to be forthcoming. Sad and almost helpless he lay, as was his custom, watching the last rays of the setting sun – the only cheering visitant to his dreary abode – when he heard the low soft tones of a woman's voice, welcome anywhere to him; but ten times more welcome within those walls! He started up, and in another moment Flora was in his arms.

The sight of her lover chased away the feeling of oppression that had overpowered her during the journey, and, with a glow of enthusiasm on her cheek, she exclaimed, almost joyfully, 'Herbert, dear Herbert, you will be saved.'

'Dearest Flora – my angel – for such you have been, and such I shall regard you, even if—'

He was unable to conclude. The long confinement and the sudden visit of Flora acted on his overwrought mind, and throwing himself in a chair, he buried his face between his hands.

She withdrew them gently, saying, 'Will you not look at me, Herbert?'

Another thought then seemed to cross the mind of the unhappy man, for, rising and withdrawing to a little distance, he asked, 'Flora McAlpin, do you believe me innocent?'

'I do – I do. Oh! Herbert, how can you ask such a question?'

And again she threw herself into his arms.

'May that belief console you, dearest,' he said as he kissed her cheek, 'but you cannot save me. I know how strong the circumstantial evidence is against me, and I have only my word to offer in defence. Flora, I am already condemned.'

She used every argument she could think of to soothe him, but her presence – her constancy did more than words. Hope again returned to his heart, and vows of love were renewed almost beneath the shadow of the scaffold.

Presently a rude tramping of feet was heard without; and Lindsey, who, even amidst his sorrows, feared lest the conduct of his beloved should be exposed to misinterpretation, asked,

'How did you come?'

'With Pierce Silverton. He procured an order from the sheriff, and took all the trouble upon himself. You cannot think how kind he has been, Herbert,' was her reply.

'God bless him. But where is he now, dearest?'

'Waiting in the corridor to take me back.'

Herbert gave a signal that was understood by a turnkey, who immediately entered, and the prisoner asked if the gentleman outside could be admitted.

The turnkey replied, 'There would be no objection.' He was a good-hearted man, that turnkey, and if he had had his way, the prisoner would soon have been free without waiting for the permission of judge or jury.

Pierce Silverton entered, and clasped the hand of Herbert Lindsey within his own.

'Pierce, my dear friend, how can I thank you for your care of Flora?' exclaimed the prisoner.

'Command me in any way. Would to heaven that you were at liberty again,' replied Silverton. His voice trembled, and his countenance denoted extreme anxiety. This was remarked by Herbert, who asked if he was ill.

'Not ill, but very uneasy. We are all uneasy about you, Lindsey; and there is nothing so trying as suspense. I don't know how you bear it as you do.'

'Conscious innocence sustains me, or I could not bear it.'

A look of lofty endurance lighted up the countenance of Lindsey as he spoke. Pride and trust in her lover shone in the eyes of Flora; but intense agony was written on the brow of Pierce Siverton, and, as if to render the group more remarkable, a tear stood on the cheek of the turnkey. Thus it may chance that human sympathy and heavenly compassion are to be found even in that sad abode of crime and misery – a gaol.

But the moment of parting has arrived. Flora is again confided to the care of Pierce Silverton, and Herbert Lindsey is once more alone.

CHAPTER XXII

The Courthouse

THE BUILDING WHICH served as the court, in the town where the trial of Herbert Lindsey was to take place, had been crowded from an early hour; and the reserve in which the building stood was likewise thronged with persons of all conditions, anxious to know the fate of the prisoner. Summer was drawing to a close, but the day was nevertheless extremely hot – thick dust in some places – a quartz soil in others, scorching and blistering the feet of the bystanders long before the hour when the sun had attained his full power. Most oppressive would be the heat in that courthouse during the long afternoon, but dread of this seemed not to deter the eager crowd. On they came, through the burning streets – along the ill-made road – over the vast plains; in carriages, coaches, buggies, dogcarts, gigs, drays, and all sorts of conveyances, light and heavy. On they came, mounted on thoroughbred horses, on horses half-broken, and on horses of every description; slowly pacing along, or furiously galloping, according to the distance of the journey, or their own previous delay.

The assizes naturally bring a number of persons to any town where they are held, but these persons are, generally speaking, either officially connected with the business on hand, or attend 'on compulsion' as witnesses. On this occasion, however, interest in the prisoner more than trebled the number of those who sought temporary accommodation in the various 'hostelries'.

A thriving trade the proprietors of these establishments would drive, for a few days at least. Beds had been bespoke beforehand, extra cooks engaged, and an extra quantity of provisions laid in; stables were overcrowded, and grooms everywhere in request. Breakfasts were prepared soon after dawn, and they seemed likely to succeed each other till after dinner.

But as we have lost sight of Mrs. Roberts since the confiscation of her Rubbish Drawer, we will briefly state that after having been examined, she was allowed to go free, as not suspected of being accessory to the murder, although she was ordered to attend as a witness.

'And if I don't give them the benefit of my tongue, may I bite it out,' she exclaimed to her friend Mrs. Busselman – a lady who exercised the same métier as herself, and in whose hotel she took up her quarters during the trial.

Harry Saunders, who had likewise been subpoenaed, was abiding in another hotel, but, unlike Mrs. Roberts, he determined to say as little as possible. These two witnesses had long since known that their attendance would be required; neither was Mr. Philip Garlick greatly surprised when informed that he would be called upon to give evidence.

His sister Bessie, however, and Mr. Speedy, were (to use the language of the latter) taken aback. The young gentleman, who was rather glad of an excuse to 'cut the lectures at the university for a week', bought a very swell looking suit, and did his best to train his moustache for the occasion. The young lady thought it would be good fun to be a witness, and said she would treat the barristers to plenty of sauce; but, as the time approached, her courage seemed to be 'oozing out of the palms of her hands', at least her hands were very hot, and her new gloves very soon split; but that might have been caused by her tight-fitting dress, and the violent efforts of two housemaids to squeeze in her waist.

Pierce Silverton, Mr. Roberts, and old Andrew Ross were also in court, but not the Highland bushman.

And where was Flora?

She had no friends with whom she could reside during these anxious days, so there she sat, in a small upper room of the Royal Victorian, that commanded a view of the courthouse. Her landlady – Mrs. Busselman, already mentioned – was very attentive, and Mrs. Roberts extremely sympathising. Every dainty was forced upon her, but she could neither eat nor drink – neither sleep nor talk, nor do anything but think of Herbert; yes, she could do one thing more – she could pray for him!

The courthouse was approached by a deep porch, entered by two side doors. Within this porch some shade was to be found, and also under the verandah at the back of the building, every other part of which was exposed to the scorching sun.

A great many policemen were in attendance, many of whom consisted of that part of the force denominated the mounted police. No attempt at rescue had yet been made, and this was chiefly attributed to rumour;

nevertheless, it was considered prudent to have these gentlemen at hand, as a crowd of stalwart young fellows had sworn, even if Lindsey were found guilty, that the extreme penalty of the law should not be carried into effect. As the compulsory attendants on authority and the voluntary attendants of the prisoner were pretty nearly matched in strength, a thought suggested itself to one or two observers that a riot would be a formidable thing, if determined men were united in purpose, and knew what they wanted; which, it is perhaps fortunate, they seldom do.

Very crowded was the courthouse, many persons being refused an admittance, and others advised not to press in such numbers into the gallery, for, though it looked so strong, yet nobody knew if the pillars could bear such a weight, as they had never been tried to that extent before. But even personal danger seemed to be little regarded, so great was the excitement about the trial. A half-suppressed murmur of 'There he is!' escaped the crowd as the prisoner entered the dock. Paler than usual was Herbert Lindsey, but perfectly calm, carefully dressed in black, and of a most gentlemanly appearance. He surveyed the judge, the jury, the crowd – and smiled, but rather with the eyes than the lips, as he recognised his friends.

The first formalities were concluded, and in a clear voice he pleaded, 'Not guilty!' After which commenced the hearing of the evidence for the prosecution; in fact, it seemed like a repetition of the examination, although several other links were added to the chain, slight in themselves, but adding strength, as they served to connect what otherwise would have fallen apart. The bowie knife, the strips of linen, the stains on his own garments, the dark brown hair found on the scrub so closely resembling that of the prisoner, all these were enumerated.

Harry Saunders was examined; and, in a low tone, with evident reluctance but without prevarication, he testified to having seen blood on the wrist of the artist, as well as dripping from the sponge; neither could he deny that the prisoner seemed agitated on perceiving the state of the sponge; but, when asked if he had previously looked like a man troubled in mind, he replied more emphatically than he had hitherto spoken, 'No – not a bit of it!'

The motive was urged – the animosity of Mr. McAlpin to his daughter's suitor; and then an angry flush suffused the brow of Herbert Lindsey as the name of her he loved was uttered in that court. His own exclamation, 'Blood – blood on my hands, and on my soul for ever,' which it will be remembered had been heard by the policemen, next formed a subject of comment. Then the handkerchief was produced, which Mrs. Roberts was compelled to identify, crumpled and soiled as it was, as if a blood-stained hand had clutched it from the throat of the murderer; evidently the fingers of the victim had been dyed in his own gore. Many persons turned away sickened at the sight, and, as it was observed, the prisoner more than all.

The question of the handkerchief having brought forward Mrs. Roberts, it was not very easy to keep her to the point, for she persisted in saying, 'Though I did find the handkerchief, that does not make him out to be the murderer – he might have taken it to tie up the bushman's leg; he might have—'

And when told that her suggestions were not required, she added, 'Faith, then, it's easier to set a woman a talking than to get her to stop; and I'll engage that some o' ye that's got wives knows that!'

A little interruption was caused by this sally of Mrs. Roberts, but, after order was again restored, attention was directed to a small camel hair pencil, and to a saucer of porcelain in which a tint of ultramarine had been mixed. These articles had been discovered near the place where the body was found – what more likely than that the artist's paintbox should have been upset in the struggle? The various objects that had undoubtedly belonged to the prisoner – the suspicious motive – the absence of anyone else on the spot – all combined to fix the guilt on Herbert; and when the evidence for the prosecution was concluded, many persons – who had previously supposed him to be innocent – now changed their minds; and more still hesitated. The defence was not to be entered into till the morrow, and the court rose at a late hour.

Still more intense was the anxiety on the following day, when the defence was opened, though it was expected to be very feeble; for what was there in the prisoner's favour, save the testimony of good character and honourable principles, as sworn to by certain individuals? These, however, were numerous, many having come a great distance for no other purpose. Some surprise was, however, manifested when the prisoner's counsel seemed to make a point of the mystery connected with the snuffbox, which article, according to the evidence of Saunders, was in the possession of McAlpin the morning he rode forth for the last time, and which was afterwards found in the dressing table of Mr. Silverton, who said it had been given to him (according to the oath of Mr. John Speedy) as a keepsake from a man named Smith, on his departure for England, but (according to the statement of Mr. Silverton himself) by McAlpin.

'Mr. Silverton did not take snuff – then why give the box to him?'

'To get the cairngorm in the lid fastened, it having become loose?'

'What jeweller had done this?'

'Mr. Silverton had done it himself?'

'Then he must be very expert, as no trace of the stone having been loosened was apparent.' But as there was no reason why Mr. Silverton should not be an amateur jeweller, the incident of the snuffbox was considered frivolous, at least until it obtained a little more importance in the first place from the statement of old Andrew Ross, which statement, though rather tedious, was certainly clear; in the second, by the explanation of Miss Bessie Garlick (if the term 'explanation' could apply to that young lady's confused and contradictory answers).

Poor Bessie! The tables were turned; and she herself received a rebuff instead of bestowing one on the counsel, as she had intended.

Some questions were then asked respecting the man Smith, who, according to the version of Mr. Speedy, had left the snuffbox with Mr. Silverton, and who had slept in that gentleman's room the night before his departure.

'Very condescending on the part of Silverton! What induced him to take so deep an interest in this person?'

Mr. Silverton explained that 'Smith, having a large sum of money about him, would otherwise probably have gone to a low public-house, have got drunk, and in the morning have found himself penniless. Surely that was no unusual occurrence in the colony?'

'Unfortunately not. Then, it was to presumed that Mr. Silverton had taken care of the man from a motive of Christian charity. Was he in the habit of exercising his benevolence in that disinterested manner?'

'No – but he felt for this person, as having been an old servant of his late friend.'

'Did anyone remember a man named John Smith who had been in the employ of the late Angus McAlpin?'

Several persons remembered two individuals known by these two names, but as no one could tell where either of them resided, as they had both been discharged some time ago, all that resulted was that Mr. Silverton's protégé was called 'John Smith,' that he had 'gone to London,' and had a mother living 'somewhere.'

A few people thought that this catechising would give a favourable turn to the prisoner's case; but, if so, Mr. Pierce Silverton might be open to suspicion, and this could not be, as Mr. Dixon (the gentleman who had come forward at the examination) stated that he had seen McAlpin after Mr. Silverton had parted with him, and that he himself and the said Mr. Silverton had ridden on together, and been in each other's company for several hours. In short, the prisoner, and the prisoner only, could be traced to the spot, at the time when the murder had been committed.

It was presumed by a few persons in court that Mrs. Roberts's suggestion, respecting the silk handkerchief having been used as a bandage, might have been taken up by the counsel for the defence; but the prisoner had denied this, saying that early in the morning, in fact, just after starting on his journey, he had bathed in the river, and on afterwards looking for his necktie, could not find it, and at last, supposing it had blown away, gave up the search. But, as the distance between the river and the place where the body had been found, was fully nine miles, it could scarcely have blown so far. This statement told greatly against the prisoner, nor would the suggestion of the bandage have served him much, as the very existence of the bushman was doubted.

His counsel made the best of a bad cause, and expressed the greatest indignation at the idea of fixing such a crime on such a man. Whilst in the midst of the defence, Mr. Roberts was called out of court; old Andrew Ross, tired perhaps of the proceedings, had also gone away; his absence had not been observed, and probably that of Roberts might not have been, if he had not knocked someone over in his impatience to get out, and thus created a disturbance; but this was soon forgotten in the feverish excitement of the hour, the conviction that, although the learned barrister was talking most eloquently, he was talking 'in vain.' Presently a piece of twisted paper, stuck on a pole, was handed to him over the heads of the crowd; he read it; whispered to the judge; and at that moment a great clamour was heard without. There was a rush towards the building – a shout. Mr. Roberts re-entered, accompanied by Andrew Ross, and followed by a stranger holding a large dog by the collar. The animal seemed more accustomed to the lonely forest than to a crowded court, for he barked rather savagely, looked round him, and then, with one bound, leapt into the dock, and licked the hands of the prisoner. Two or three people were upset, and so was a considerable amount of legal etiquette, as the stranger addressed the judge, jury, counsel, and crowd promiscuously, and to little purpose it was supposed, for he spoke in a tongue unknown to any of those learned gentlemen, versed as they might be in the classics; but Andrew Ross, interpreting his native Gaelic, exclaimed, 'It's Evan Gillispie, the bushman, an' he'll take his Bible oath that he crossed the bit o' plain wi' the puir lad, an hour or mair afore the laird had left Mount Alpin!'

Several persons in court, on being asked if they understood Gaelic, answered in the affirmative, and it was evident that there could have been no previously arranged plot between the stranger and the old shepherd. The bushman was therefore placed in the witness box, duly sworn, and then allowed to give his evidence; and, in his own language, he admitted the statement of Herbert as to the assistance he had given him, and the employment of the linen to bind his wound, showing at the same time another piece that exactly corresponded, and saying that the sponge had been used to wipe away the first stream of blood, and the knife to cut through the hem of the handkerchief. On being cross-examined, he said that, having parted with the prisoner, he himself struck into another track and soon left the district, crossing the boundaries of the colony – that he had not heard of the murder for a considerable time after it occurred. In fact, not until the advertisement in Gaelic was shown to him. Then, although engaged to accompany an exploring party towards the interior, he had hastened to give his evidence in favour of the prisoner. All this while the dog, which the police in vain had tried to remove, was giving his testimony of gratitude to the man whose timely aid had perhaps saved the life of his master; and half the women in the court were crying their eyes out.

The late arrival of the last witness interfered with the usual routine and formality of the proceedings; but, after a little delay, order was once more restored, the judge summed up, and the jury retired. It was supposed they would almost instantly return; for, notwithstanding the incident of the handkerchief – which still remained unaccounted for – opinion had veered round, and Herbert Lindsey was considered to be innocent.

Great impatience was manifested as the jury lingered so long, but amongst them was a gentleman, whose head 'did require punching' – a certain Mr. Oakenhed, who insisted on going through a repetition of the evidence, maintaining that as one man had been murdered, another ought to be hanged; indeed, he seemed more anxious to appease the spirit of the dead than to do justice to the living.

At length, however, he did acquiesce in the opinion of the other gentlemen, and the jury re-entered. There was a moment of breathless suspense, but it was succeeded by the most heartfelt joy, as the foreman pronounced the verdict of 'Not guilty!' Still greater was the satisfaction when the judge, addressing Lindsey, told him that he would leave the court without a stain on his character.

As his friends crowded around him to offer their congratulations, he expressed his gratitude for their exertions – 'Thank you, thank you all,' he exclaimed, and then, turning to Pierce Silverton, he added, 'And Flora! Oh! Where is Flora?'

CHAPTER XXIII

Many Passions

'**G**O AHEAD, AND I'll show you where she is,' said Mr. Roberts, answering the question that Lindsey had addressed to Silverton; and, leaving the courthouse together, they hastened to the Royal Victorian.

Flora had heard the shout that echoed the verdict, and knew he was safe, but her long-sustained spirit now gave way, and she fell weeping into his arms. Some joys, like some sorrows, are too sacred for the public gaze; therefore, we will not intrude our presence on the lovers; but, if we visit their friends, we shall find that the satisfaction was general. And now it transpired that, for many miles around, persons had been on the lookout, hoping (though almost against hope) that the bushman might make his appearance, and when at last he did so; almost on the spot where Herbert had formerly met him, he was accosted by the brother-in-law of Mrs. Roberts, and driven by him towards the scene of the trial, in the most tearing American fashion ever before witnessed. Arrived at the outskirts of the town, the rattling dusty vehicle excited attention, and the cause of so much speed explained by the announcement 'Another witness – the bushman!'

And now the honest fellow is consigned to the care of old Andrew and Harry Saunders, and very joyful they all are together. Mrs. Roberts is laughing, crying, chattering, and threatening what she will do to that 'varmint O'Twig, though he does be a peahen!' The good-hearted American is rejoicing that such a fine young fellow has got out of that 'tarnation fix'; and Mr. Philip Garlick is running about engaging all his acquaintance to get up a dinner in honour of the prisoner's release (but that is to be held at the Southern Cross).

And where is Pierce Silverton? For Herbert, when asked about Flora, did not await the reply – Pierce heard him not, as he fell down in a dead swoon on the floor! Such might have been expected from Flora, or indeed, from any woman in the court far less deeply interested in the result of the trial; but a man has no right to faint unless from physical exhaustion; doubtless, this was the case, as the court had been oppressively hot, and poor Silverton was so extremely delicate! They brought him water, smelling salts, and eau de Cologne, and called him 'a great muff'; but he soon recovered, and then fervently exclaimed, 'Thank God! Thank God! He is saved!'

'What a sympathising friend!' 'What a tender heart!' 'What deep feeling!' ejaculated the bystanders, as Pierce Silverton, leaning on the arm of a great powerful fellow, left the courthouse. He retired to his own room (it was in the Royal Victorian) and there Herbert, on hearing of his friend's indisposition, immediately hastened, saying, 'My dear Pierce! What is all this? You are too kind! Too sensitive!'

And again Pierce Silverton thanked God who had ordered the events of the day.

'Never saw such a nervous fellow in all my life!' said Phil, who was called in to administer his aid; he suggested a stimulant – in fact two or three; but, as Mr. Silverton decidedly objected to that sort of treatment, he went on the other tack and composed a sedative; this Mr. Silverton drank, and said he thought he could sleep, upon which his friends retired; but, whether Mr. Garlick had not been very careful in the preparation of his drugs, or whether the patient repeated the dose too frequently, was not known, for though the phial was found empty, it had apparently been upset, but when Mr. Speedy (who, in consequence of the crowded state of the hotel, shared the same room with Mr. Silverton) entered, he was alarmed by a strange gurgling sound, emanating from the throat of the sleeper. 'Halloo! Come here, Garlick! What the deuce is the matter with this fellow?' he roared out – and just in time – for had not Silverton been immediately aroused, he would never have woke again.

It now and then happens that people become extremely sympathising – that human nature seems to shake off the selfishness and apathy that have clogged its better part, and really to feel for the serious affections of others! And so it happened on this occasion, public interest having been excited for Herbert Lindsey, now that he was safe, perhaps required another object, and therefore turned to the kind-hearted, interesting young man, who felt so deeply for the welfare of his friend. It is very certain that Mr. Silverton ran no risk of dying for want of either sympathy or attention. Flora, who owed him so deep a debt of gratitude, sent Herbert from her side to give his assistance; Bessie Garlick, who hoped to take care of him for life, ran screaming about, as if to convince people how unfit she was for such a duty; and Mr. Roberts, who actually took him in hand, saved his life by the means which, under some circumstances, might have been extremely injurious – keeping him awake with talking. At the end of two days he was almost well again, and Mr. Philip Garlick was relieved of the terrible apprehension that his heedlessness might have cost the life of a friend.

And now, those whom the excitement of the trial had drawn to that town, dispersed and returned to their different homes. Herbert Lindsey was informed of McAlpin's will, which clearly stated that if Flora became his wife, she would forfeit all claim to her father's wealth; whereas, if, on the contrary, she espoused Silverton, she might enjoy all the rights and privileges of an heiress; likewise of the middle course – allotting her a portion if she married either some indifferent person or nobody at all. Herbert then said, 'Flora, you are free; I will not urge you to fulfil the contract existing between us.' But the use Flora made of her liberty was to resign it again – a proceeding which caused her lover to look so proudly triumphant, that she, probably thinking it would not quite do to let him understand the extent of his power, said 'she did not intend to marry him directly.' And then, Herbert, who, a minute before, had offered to give her up altogether, looked disappointed, and asked, in that low murmuring tone, half of doubt, half of sorrow – 'What! No?'

'No,' said Flora, 'it would not look well after the very decided part I have taken. It would seem as if – as if I was quite as anxious to be married as to save your life.'

'If you don't intend to marry me, Flora, it would have been quite as well not to have saved my life.'

Upon which Flora coquetted as if to illustrate the truth of the Poet's verse:

> O woman, in our hours of ease—
> Uncertain, coy, and hard to please.[15]

At length, it was arranged that the marriage should not take place till a year after her father's death – and it now became necessary to form some plan for the future, as the property Flora inherited from her mother had been greatly diminished by law costs, and as it will readily be understood, Lindsey's funds were not increased by three months' idleness.

Where then was compensation for an impoverished exchequer – for unworthy suspicions – for the insult of a committal – for tedious imprisonment? Where? But awaiting that reward with which Heavenly justice requites earthly wrong.

But the lovers are content to wait for better times – they are both young, hopeful, and confident of each other's truth; there is no one to forbid their marriage, and so, willing to accept the penalty of narrow means they quietly and simply discuss their plans for the future. Herbert will only be too happy to abandon his wandering habits, and Flora, after having played the heroine with some success, to retire into the more natural position of domestic life. The likeness to her stern father now seems to have faded away, and her countenance again resumes the expression of her mother's gentle face.

Pierce Silverton, 'the mutual friend,' is admitted to their conferences, – nay, he is invited, and how can he resist the request of Herbert, or the pleading eyes of Flora? She

---

[15] From Canto VI, Stanza XXX of Sir Walter Scott's 1808 poem *Marmion*.

seems to ignore his love for her; it would be indelicate to allude to it – it might render Herbert uneasy, as well as embarrass the position of all parties, and then (she tries to think) there may be nothing in it after all.

Herbert Lindsey is not a man of great observation. Artists and poets live so much in a world of their own that common events which attract the attention of inferior intelligences are apt to escape their notice altogether; but Silverton, being on his guard in the presence of his friend, the fleeting changes of colour and expression which pass over his face are naturally attributed to delicate health; moreover, the character of Lindsey is so unsuspecting! He has such reliance on mankind in general, and the deep interest so lately manifested in his welfare (an instance of nature acting under a generous impulse) has also aided to paint poor humanity in glowing colours. But if he is thus favourably disposed towards society at large, how much more must he be so towards his own tried and trusted friend? The friend of Flora – the man who endangered his own health by such constant exertions – the man who submitted to censure for having espoused the cause of a suspected murderer.

Herbert Lindsey could not therefore imagine that Pierce Silverton would indulge in the vain hope of winning the affections of Flora, and if a passing thought that the frequent presence of a lovely girl might inspire him with a passion for her, honour would undoubtedly soon overcome the temptation, and Pierce Silverton prove himself to be a sincere and disinterested friend.

If, when under the influence of sorrow and disappointment, we are led to regard everything en noir, we are not the less induced by happiness and content to view surrounding objects en rose; and it was thus that pleasure, hope, and gratitude aided the sanguine disposition of Herbert Lindsey in picturing the scene where Flora dwelt as a paradise, and her friends as almost divine. His newly recovered liberty also lent another charm to existence, and led him to discover new beauties in inanimate nature. With what pleasure he again resumed his professional labours, adding one sketch to another; and when not disposed for landscape drawing, he would turn to portraiture – and sometimes, by way of amusement, to caricature – a fertile imagination and a good memory helping to fill out scenes that had fleeted away; thus, the courthouse, although at the time of the trial invested with so much terror, now furnished several groups – humorous, as well as severe – gay, as well as grave; here were barristers, in their gowns and wigs; there, bushmen, in shooting jackets and Napoleon boots, and all relieved by a background of eager faces.

One day, whilst occupied with sketches of this description, he perceived Harry Saunders lurking about, and, knowing that his portfolio possessed a wonderful charm for the honest countryman, he beckoned him to approach. Harry eyed the sketches with the curiosity of a child, and, like a child, turned eagerly to look for his own portrait, saying, in a tone of disappointment, 'You haven't put me in the picture of the courthouse, Mr Lindsey.'

'No,' replied Herbert, 'there is old Andrew Ross doing duty as witness. Does he not look well with his long white hair and beard?'

'Yes, it's as like him as two peas are like each other – and there's Mr Silverton, and Mr Roberts and the Missus, and lots of folks, but—'

'But you are not there – and I suppose you thought I had quarrelled with you. Eh, Harry?'

'And if you had. Mr Lindsey, you'd a right to, because I haven't behaved as a man should.'

'Ah! How's that?'

'I've often been going to speak to you about it, Mr Lindsey, but you see when a man's ashamed of himself, he doesn't like to talk.'

'I should think you about the last man in the world to do anything to be ashamed of, Harry.'

'Oh! Mr Lindsey, it quite cuts me up to hear you talk in that way – for – for—'

'Well, out with it – what have you done?'

'I'm dashed if I didn't think it was you that murdered the master!'

'You did – did you? Hum!'

'I never was so bothered in all my life, because you don't look like a chap to do a thing of that sort, but you see there was the blood on the sponge, and you turning so terrible white – I'd rather have been shot than have had to speak, but when a man's put on his oath, on one side, and them lawyers a' dinning at him o' t' other, he's forced to speak, though 't were agin his own father.'

'Appearances were against me, I must confess; pray don't think anything more about the part you were forced to play. But I see now what made you stand first on one leg, and then on the other, and seem so little like yourself; so you need not wonder that I left your portrait out of the courthouse scene. You looked a great deal better when I set you to root up the gumtree.'

'I'd rather root up a whole forest of gumtrees, and eat them afterwards than have to say what would put an honest man's life in danger.'

Herbert laughed at the idea of that substantial sort of food, and Harry added, 'Well, I thought all along it would be queer if a man who laughs in that hearty sort of way could kill anyone.' But he had now made his peace with Lindsey, and the frank manner in which the young artist held out his hand – just as he had done at their first meeting, convinced the penitent countryman that he was forgiven.

Herbert afterwards related the incident to Flora, remarking that the honest countenance of Saunders would never serve to depict remorse.

'That must be rather a difficult passion to portray, I should imagine, but of course, the natural countenance can have nothing to do with our feelings,' was her reply.

'Sometimes I fancy not, and sometimes I think that if we make mistakes, nature does not; but these ideas are dangerous, for, although the clear open brow of our friend Saunders would not illustrate that of a conscience-stricken villain some of the best fellows in the world would make capital models for all sorts of assassins and schemers; there's Pierce Silverton, for instance, in spite of his beautiful features—'

'Goodness Herbert! How can you talk so? There cannot be a more amiable man than poor dear Pierce.'

'I know that, Flory; and he cannot have any cause for remorse, but we were speaking of types of character, and I explained that a somewhat contracted brow and compressed lips, even if handsome, are – but that sort of thing is only conventional, and we artists are a set of humbugs.'

Flora was quite satisfied with that somewhat illogical explanation, and Herbert knew very well that the moody expression on the brow of his friend was merely caused by failing health, and he sighed to think that this was the prevailing opinion – for such it was, as many people when they saw Pierce Silverton, would exclaim, 'Poor fellow, he's not long for this world!'

Mr. Silverton consulted Philip Garlick, who advised change of air; recommending a trip to Queensland before the winter set in; but there seemed to be no immediate cause for apprehension; and the thoughts of most people in the neighbourhood were then directed towards the dinner to be given in honour of Herbert Lindsey. The Southern Cross, though always brilliant on such occasions, never shone with such lustre as on this festival; all the previous dinners, whether of Freemasons, Odd Fellows, or Volunteers, being completely eclipsed. The choicest wines were supplied – the choicest delicacies served; Bridget and her assistants working with hearty good will – and the most respectable people for miles around honouring the feast with their presence. Not Mr. O'Twig, however, as very important business called him to Melbourne, which was quite as well, as it is probable the stewards would not have allowed him to purchase a ticket at any price. Mr. Lovelaw was, however, admitted, and Mr. Lovelaw said in his speech that 'He had formerly venerated Herbert Lindsey as a martyr to the laws of his country, but he now looked on him as their hero.' The speaker then likened his young friend to Quintus Curtius,[16] but no one seemed to understand the simile, nor, as it is probable, the speaker any more than his hearers.

The address of Mr. Garlick was very much more jocular – that of Pierce Silverton, more sentimental, and,

---

[16] A Roman scholar and author of a history of Alexander the Great.

when he wound up with his own gratitude to Heaven for the safety of his friend, he became truly sublime. Mr. John Speedy having been entrusted with the tribute to the ladies was about to prefix Mrs. Lindsey, but suddenly remembering that there was no such person, and being aware that it would not be correct to introduce the name of Flora McAlpin, he made a touching allusion to the Goddess of Flowers, perhaps being inspired by a great bouquet on which he kept his eyes during his very remarkable speech, until recollecting that Miss McAlpin had not enacted the part of a Niobe[17] during her stay in Melbourne, a circumstance which had then called forth his gratitude, 'because', to use his own words, 'it shuts a fellow up to see a woman cry', therefore getting a little hazy about the Maid of Saragossa,[18] he exclaimed with considerable emphasis, 'She sheds no ill timed tear.' After which he sat down to the great relief of the company in general, and of Herbert Lindsey in particular.

Various songs and speeches followed, all more or less appropriate, and, to quote the language of a brilliant reporter, 'The festivities of that joyous evening terminated at an advanced hour in the morning.' That morning, however, was not particularly joyous, as headaches prevailed throughout the township but perhaps apprehending the effects of sudden reaction, most of the party thought it advisable to let their hilarity subside very gradually, and accordingly got up an impromptu feast, although with diminished splendour, and then in the course of a week the inhabitants got over the effects of the 'recovery'.

---

[17] A tragic figure from Homer's *Iliad*, whose fourteen children were killed by the gods.

[18] A heroic Spanish woman from the early 19th century, mentioned in Byron's *Childe Harold's Pilgrimage* (1812-18).

But if it will impoverish a man to give a succession of feasts, it will not enrich him to depend on the feasts of other men, so it is just as well to awake to the consciousness of this before people grow tired of giving the said feasts. Herbert fortunately aroused himself ere there was any danger of learning this unpleasant truth from that most convincing of all teachers – experience, and he then learnt another circumstance – that the public mind occasionally reverted to the fact that the real murderer had not been discovered. There were some very material individuals who reminded each other that 'Someone must have done it.' A few, with still more obtuse intellects, would add 'What if this Lindsey did it after all!' And then they proceeded to argue that, although the bushman saw him cross that part of the plain, he might afterwards have turned back on purpose to murder McAlpin. In short, Herbert Lindsey had been so fêted and applauded that people were beginning to grow jealous of the hero, whose praises they had lately sung. Some of these people, on various pretexts, broke through their engagements, and postponed, sine die,[19] the portrait taking projects into which they, had, once eagerly entered. And thus, when Herbert Lindsey was on the eve of starting for South Australia, he received a couple of letters to this effect; the one being dictated by fear – an absurd woman having taken it into her silly head that if Mr. Lindsey was admitted to her house, he might be tempted to murder her harmless old husband, and (what would be equally improbable) to fall in love with her very unattractive daughter. The other epistle was the suggestion of envy, the writer being one of those

---

[19] From the Latin, without day; to postpone without setting a future date.

pests of society – a man somewhat important in his own neighbourhood, and very much so in his own opinion, and, therefore, unwilling to be eclipsed by the hero of the hour.

And then, notwithstanding his own single-mindedness, Herbert perceived that he stood in the shadow of suspicion; that the jury's verdict of 'Not guilty' – the judge's assertion that 'he left the court without a stain on his name' – were neither sufficient to stifle the whinings of folly, nor the murmurings of jealousy. He felt disheartened, for his illusions were beginning to disperse, and even to stand out in all the hideousness of their evil passions.

'I must go, Flora,' he said. 'I will cross every foot of ground I trod on that unfortunate day. I will challenge my accusers, and if anyone dares insinuate in my hearing that I raised a hand against your father, I'll horsewhip him to death!'

And so, being anxious to prove that he was not a murderer, he asserted his intention of becoming one.

'I don't see why you should excite yourself in that way, Lindsey,' said Pierce Silverton, who was present. 'You are acquitted, and if these talking fools give you any annoyance, bring an action for libel against them at once.'

'I have had enough of law. I will take it into my own hands next time.'

'But why not travel by the coach to your destination? Why trouble yourself to go over that ground again? You may be sure that it has been searched more than once.'

'My presence on that spot may perhaps convince some of the ignorantly superstitious that I should not be likely to cross a tract of country where I had committed such a deed.'

But it was the hard-minded – the wilfully blind, not the timid nor the superstitious, whose opinions Herbert Lindsey had to combat. He went, and in a few weeks the envy and the admiration he had excited were alike forgotten.

Flora naturally felt lonely after the departure of her lover, but she did not give way to low spirits; she had no right to do so, as if she had chosen, she might have joined her lot with his and accompanied him on his journey. One motive for not doing so has been already explained – but though she spoke of waiting a year out of respect to her father's memory, she had a vague presentiment that the mystery connected with his death might yet be cleared up. She was not much more solitary than she had been at Mount Alpin, as her father when at home had generally surrounded himself with persons towards whom she felt no sympathy, and with whom she seldom associated. So she now amused herself, as she had formerly done, with music, books, needlework, and in writing to Herbert.

Pierce Silverton, who no longer resided at Mount Alpin, had taken up his quarters at the Southern Cross, although scarcely a day passed that he did not visit Flora. Once he alluded to the will. It was a delicate subject, to which Herbert did not like to refer, indeed it required all Flora's tact to prevent a jealousy of Silverton from being excited in her lover's breast. 'Did your father ever say he should like you to marry Pierce?' Herbert had then asked of Flora, who replied, 'No, but he once told me he had made up his mind who should be my husband, and he would let me know when he thought fit. But I fancy he made the will from some impulse or other, and very likely he would have destroyed it if he had lived, particularly if he quarrelled with Pierce – and this very often happened.'

But now Pierce himself spoke of this will, and as he was so deeply interested in the matter, it is almost a wonder he had not done so earlier. Very timidly did he hazard its introduction. First of all by extolling the virtue of filial duty. Flora looked very sad, for she was by nature gentle; and her rebellion against her father had caused her much sorrow. 'It will always render me unhappy to reflect that I cannot obey his wish,' she exclaimed.

'That you cannot! But it is not likely you should have been much attached to your father – you saw so little of him during your childhood.'

'Oh! Do not say that I did not love him, for in spite of his occasional violence, I venerated the very ground he walked upon.'

'I did not think that your affection for him was so strong.'

'I do not make a parade of my sentiments, but no daughter could love a father better than I did, and I am miserable whenever I think of my disobedience.'

'And if that reflection should hereafter arise?'

'It will. Oh! do not speak of it. Do you wish to make me wretched, Pierce?'

'I? Oh! Flora, I would save you from the torments of self-reproach.'

Flora buried her head on the sofa, and wept bitterly. Pierce took her hand; he had held it within his during their journey together, it then lay passively in his own, but now it trembled, and Pierce hoped.

'Flora,' he exclaimed almost solemnly, 'your father beholds you from his grave!'

Flora started in alarm. Some Highland superstition perhaps crossing her mind, and she exclaimed, 'Where, oh! Where?'

'Forgive me, I did not mean to frighten you; but Flora, obey your father's will and marry me.' So saying, Pierce knelt at her feet, and pressed her hand to his lips. She gazed at him with surprise, and making an effort to withdraw her hand, said 'What do you mean? Are you mad?'

'I shall be if you refuse – Flora, I love you.' He then threw his arms around her waist; but, at length releasing herself from his grasp, she said, 'Pierce Silverton, how dare you address such language to me – to the betrothed of your friend?'

'Because it is your father's will – because if you marry Herbert Lindsey, your own conscience will whisper to you that you have given yourself to his murderer – and because I love you to distraction.'

'Now you have spoken the truth – but I despise your perjured love. You know Herbert to be innocent, and such conduct is unworthy of yourself and insulting to me.'

Flora was about to leave the room, but he still held her hand – yet he did not dare to rouse her anger, for he knew that if once banished from her presence, he might never see her again; therefore, after a moment's pause, he said, 'Forgive me, Flora, you do not know what I have suffered in preserving silence so long; you cannot guess one half my misery.'

She gazed on him, and saw on his countenance that anxious expression which Herbert had termed remorseful; and then her anger changed to pity, and she said 'I do forgive you; but never speak on that subject again.'

'Say that we are friends, at least.'

'Yes, but—' She turned away confused by his ardent glance. He dared not trust himself to speak, and, after passionately kissing her hand, he left the house, mounted his horse, and galloped furiously away. When Flora was once more alone, she burst into tears, overcome by contending emotions, for she scarcely knew whether to blame or to pity her unfortunate lover; but the latter feeling got the mastery: how, indeed, could she be severe to him whose sorrow she had caused?

Silverton did not call at Mount Alpin on the next day, nor yet on the second, and Flora, notwithstanding her love for another, thought of him a great deal; she felt embarrassed also because there was now a subject on which she could not speak to Herbert. Whilst absorbed by these meditations, Philip Garlick rode up to the house; she heard him ask to see her immediately, and thought, as he entered, that he had never looked so grave before.

'I am sorry to be the bearer of ill news,' he said, adding, as he observed her look of alarm, 'Nay, do not be frightened, it is nothing about Lindsey; but poor Silverton is very ill – in a very bad way indeed.'

'Good heavens,' she exclaimed, 'you don't say so! What is the matter?'

'A sudden attack: he came riding up to the hotel like a madman, the other evening; and, as I was told, caught a sudden chill, but his nervous system has been out of order this long time, and if he doesn't take care it will be a case with him. I knew you would be very sorry, and yet thought it better to tell you; but don't fret, we will do all we can for the poor fellow.'

'Mrs. Roberts will take care of him! Won't she?'

'I believe you – all the women at the Southern Cross are fighting who's to be head nurse. But I must be off. Shall I give him your love?'

'Say I hope he will soon be well again, and advise him to keep quiet.'

Philip rode off, muttering to himself, 'well' and 'quiet! Hum! I never heard of any good arising from these sentimental friendships.'

But Mr. Garlick was not the only person to divine the cause of Silverton's illness, which was at once attributed to a 'love fit' by Mrs. Roberts, as well as by her maids, all of whom took the deepest interest in the case, Mary and Harriet, having abandoned their ghost stories for equally fabulous legends of broken-hearts, and Bridget exerting all her skill in the manufacture of broths and jellies. Their efforts, united to those of Mr. Garlick, saved the life of the patient, but a thorough change of air and scene was insisted upon, and at the expiration of a few weeks, Pierce Silverton left the district, though without seeing Flora. But before his departure, he despatched a note to her, containing merely the following words:

'Forgive – and pray for –
'Yours till death,
'Pierce Silverton.'

He could only pay a flying visit to Mrs. Garlick and her daughters, as the Sydney steamer was to sail the day after his arrival in Melbourne. In vain the ladies urged him to wait for the next, but having torn himself from the spot where Flora resided, he was anxious to leave the colony as fast as possible. Poor Bessie began to suspect the cause of the false one's complaint, and when he took leave of her, said peevishly, 'Get along, if you won't stay with those who can take care of you – you deserve to be ill.'

But whilst conflicting passions were agitating the breasts of these – our leading characters, there was a more humble individual who was absorbed in 'one only thought' – deep, deadly, and resistless – that of Revenge – not exhibited in stormy demonstration, but in persevering activity, and he who thus dedicated a portion of his remaining existence to that motive was no other than old Andrew Ross – his object being the pursuit of his master's murderer, demanding the consequent penalty (on whomsoever it might fall) – 'a life for a life!'

He haunted the plain where the death-stroke had been given; he searched the grass – the sand – the scrub – and the creek; in the latter, though not recently dropped there, he found a broken bridle and a stockwhip; these had apparently been lost on the verge of the creek farther up the country, and since washed down by the winter rain. Old Andrew exhibited his treasures to Mr. Roberts, who, after turning them about for some time, said they were ordinary things that might have belonged to any stockman in the district. 'Weel! Weel!' replied Andrew, 'wait a wee!' And he did wait, but not inactively.

Meantime winter was passing away, and the public mind becoming diverted from the murdered man, and also from the survivors, by events of local interest, private quarrels, and public meetings, peculiar to a Little Pedlington[20] in any part of the world.

Herbert Lindsey had not yet returned from his professional trip, which (as he wrote to Flora) had proved far more remunerative than he had at first anticipated,

[20] A reference to John Poole's *Little Pedlington and the Pedlingtonians,* published in 1839, an amusing account of the 'habits and manners' of small town English life.

indeed, he had sufficient occupation to engage him several months longer. It was said that Mr. Lindsey having vanquished the prejudice once conceived against him, had become almost as great an idol in his present neighbourhood as he had formerly been in that of the Southern Cross; a rumour had also got afloat that he had engaged the affections of the daughter of a wealthy settler, whose corn fields and vineyards had long rendered the young lady a great object of attraction. This report reached Pierce Silverton in Queensland, and contributed far more than a tropical climate had done towards his recovery; therefore, with as little delay as possible, he embarked for Sydney, and from thence, for Victoria.

It was not generally supposed that Miss McAlpin had heard anything respecting Herbert's fickleness, as they continued to correspond pretty regularly, and she seemed to be in her usual spirits, but it was observed that as soon as she was told of Mr. Silverton's expected return, she invited Miss Bessie Garlick to keep her company – whether with the intention of making a match for that young lady, or as a blind towards promoting her own, no one could say.

When Pierce Silverton, who, a few months earlier, had been almost lifted into the coach, now alighted from the same conveyance with a light step, and walked quietly into Mrs. Roberts's parlour, the good landlady scarcely recognised him again; at length, after a look of pleased surprise, she exclaimed, 'I am glad to see you looking so well, Mr. Silverton. Oh, how delighted Roberts will be, and Miss McAlpin, and everybody else!'

Mr. Roberts soon entered, and confirmed his wife's promise as far as he was concerned, and the next day Miss McAlpin spoke for herself. Pierce lost no time in paying his visit to her, and she advanced towards him with her usual frankness, holding out both hands as she said, 'Oh! How happy I am to see you restored to health!'

'Thank you, dear Miss McAlpin,' he replied, kissing the hand he held within his own. He answered all her questions respecting Queensland, its climate, and its cotton, but presently added, 'I could think of nothing the whole time I was away but of returning to you, Flora.'

Again he called her by her Christian name; but, having done so for the last two years, the circumstance might have passed unnoticed now, if he had not looked so lovingly into her eyes, and then she blushed – and then Pierce hoped once more.

Whilst in Melbourne Mr. Silverton had shown himself extremely ungallant, having actually shirked the duty of accompanying Miss Bessie Garlick on her visit to the country. It has been seen that, on the occasion of Miss McAlpin's journey, he contrived to finesse a little, and now he was equally successful – first of all saying he could not leave so soon, and then (the young lady having agreed to wait a couple of days) starting off by rail, and writing a hasty apology on the pretext urged by all gentlemen – 'unexpected business'. But Miss Bessie, in her turn, arrived at Mount Alpin, where she was most cordially welcomed by her young hostess, and towards whom she felt so grateful that she could not neglect her, especially when Mr. Silverton called; but Miss McAlpin did not seem to adopt the prejudice about the number three spoiling company. Sometimes when Mr. Silverton did not call, Miss Bessie would propose riding over to the township to 'look him up' at his hotel, and if Miss McAlpin hinted at the impropriety of this step, she had always Berlin wool to match, or some other purchase to make, though she had left the metropolis so lately. Upon the whole, however, they all seemed to spend their time agreeably enough during that pleasant spring – the sweet Australian spring! – which, after those terrific gales have subsided, is so balmy and genial, not visiting you with hail, sleet, or snow, as if winter had come back to pay a debt not demanded of him.

And so, for the present, all was calm and tranquil in nature – but, in the heart of man! – oh! who can fathom its mysteries?

CHAPTER XXIV

DESOLATION ISLAND

ROM THOSE RICH Australian plains, smiling in peace and plenty, we must now turn to 'the wild waste of ocean', and there we shall perceive a majestic ship drifting through a narrow channel. This is not her course; and we might imagine that she had sea room enough without getting amongst those rocks, but she has outrun her log; and though her captain was positive that he should not sight Kerguëlen's Land[21] till noon on the next day, a little before midnight, the man on the lookout suddenly calls aloud, 'Land ahead!' The ship is sailing thirteen knots, and though by taking in sail her speed can be checked, it is too late to alter her course. In a few minutes another cry is heard, 'Land on the larboard bow!' On she goes, her tall masts gently bending and her sails swelling before the breeze. It behoves her commander to be on his guard, as the curvature of that rocky outline indicates an inner barrier in two directions.

---

[21] Now known as the Kerguelen Islands (Captain Cook had called them the Desolation Islands), located in the southern Indian Ocean roughly midway between Australia and Africa.

'Why do they shave the land so closely – surely there is plenty of space here, almost in mid-ocean?' asks a landlubber, who, from his cabin, surveys the threatening rocks.

'Hard-a-port!' shouts the captain.

'Land to the starboard,' calls the man on the lookout.

There is a rush on deck, and screaming, praying, and cursing, as all became aware of their perilous situation – for the ship is running down a channel between Kerguëlen's Land and a reef of rocks, in dangerous proximity to the mainland. The entrance to this channel is about nine miles in breadth, and though this at present may afford room for a ship of burden, yet the channel soon narrows, for the reef does not run parallel with the mainland, and in a very little time the distance between them is lessened to five miles. Fortunately, the night is fine, and the moon shines brightly on the perilous track, so clearly indicating each projection of rock, as to add to the terror of the passengers, by rendering their danger more apparent. Even the hardiest of the crew is not without apprehension, as, though many amongst them have sighted Kerguëlen's Land before, none have been in that channel – if channel it be, for some persons say it is a mere inlet to a cluster of rocks, which, on the farther side, will form a promontory, a sport for the ocean, but affording no safety for man; others there are who suppose that a passage may exist between the rocks, but one of no avail for a ship of considerable tonnage. In either case death seems to stare them in the face, as on the larboard side appears a mass of dark solid rock crowned with snow; on the starboard, a jagged and crenulated reef, stretching nearer and nearer towards the mainland. Straw and twigs are now seen on the surface of the water, which indicate its shallowness. Every moment they expect to strike; and some, who preserve their presence of mind, resolve calmly to await the catastrophe, knowing that their small remaining chance of preservation would only be the more imperilled by a frantic rush to the boats. A still more dreary fate arises to their imagination, as 'Desolation Island' offers no means of subsistence save that afforded by a few coarse vegetables. But they prepare for the result, taking every precaution that human foresight can suggest, and then praying to that God who can restrain the fury of the waves, and compel the rocks to yield a shelter. This rational portion of the passengers are, however, extremely limited, terror and dismay having overcome the majority. Nevertheless, the vessel sails gallantly on, answering her helm to perfection, and it may be that she will yet bear them safely through the channel. The moment is one of extreme anxiety, and the captain, though a very jovial sort of man, now looks grave; the sailors are earnest and obedient, and a manly spirit prevails, which suggests that the first objects of care should be the most helpless. But it is impossible to preserve order; most of the women will degrade themselves by screaming in a most insane manner, and a great many of the men continue to curse and to clamour, even when threatened by a terrible death. Some of these rush to a boat, the tackle of which had been loosened, though not cut adrift, as the captain explains that is not at present necessary, and he begs the passengers to keep quiet, but very few heed his advice. Suddenly a grating sound is heard – it is echoed by a shriek of 'She has struck!' There is another rush on deck; women and children are trodden under foot by big burly men, who think of nothing but their own preservation – one amongst these, more brutal and more animal in his instincts than the rest, cuts the tackling of the boat; she is hastily lowered by powerful fellows, who leap into her, but a few minutes afterwards she is swamped, and the greater number of those she contained either sucked under the vessel, or dashed upon the rocks.

Had they awaited, they would have found their alarm useless – the vessel had not struck, but her escape was most providential, for her keel did actually grate on a sunken rock; so lightly, however, that she received no injury. And now the summit of the reef appears lower, presently it slants downwards till it can scarcely be seen close to the water's edge – rocks still remain, but soundings are taken, the water is deeper and deeper, and the ship can now ride clear of the rocks that threatened her with destruction: she stands off from the land, and a hearty cheer announces that the *Robespierre* is again on her course in the open sea.

CHAPTER XXV

THE RETURN OF THE *ROBESPIERRE*

'I SAY, CAPTAIN, THERE'S a boat with some poor fellows rowing for their lives,' said Mr. Manners, one of the cabin passengers of the *Robespierre*, as he perceived in the moonlight a boat following the track of the vessel; it was the one that had been so rudely lowered, and which, having drifted on a flat part of the island, had afterwards been regained by the survivors.

The captain swore at the insolence and insubordination of the men, but eventually he ordered a rope to be thrown to them, and had the boat proved seaworthy, she would have been safely towed to the ship; but a plank in her side having been stove in, she leaked to such an extent that the greatest exertions were required to bale out the water. This was not immediately perceived on board the *Robespierre*, and although within hail, the men were too much exhausted to make themselves heard, but, guessing how matters stood, the captain, after venting a few oaths upon them, put about, as much as the close vicinity of the island would permit. Another boat was also lowered, as that containing the men was observed to be sinking; but this second boat was greatly endangered by the eagerness of the occupants of the foundering one to regain the ship, which quite equalled their former impatience to leave her. Brute force and selfishness seemed alone to sway the minds of the greater number, but there was one amongst them in whom these qualities predominated to a greater degree than in his companions, for as a couple of poor fellows were endeavouring to climb the ship's side, he stepped on their shoulders and caught at the rope which they were unable to reach, finally regaining the deck, whilst his frail supporters were plunged into the sea, and one of them (a mere stripling) was never recovered.

'You confounded ruffian,' said the captain, in greeting to his unruly passenger, 'it's you that cut the boat adrift, and now you've drowned a better man than yourself.'

'That's as it may be, captain; one man's life is as good as another's, and my maxim is, first come first served, either afloat or ashore,' replied the fellow, in a tone of indifference.

The captain called him a 'selfish scoundrel', and a great deal more swearing followed, in which it must be confessed the captain played the principal part – his antagonist being either too apathetic, or too much exhausted, to speak with much fluency; he pleaded the latter cause, but apparently as an excuse to get that sovereign remedy – brandy; and, after his submersion, his efforts in rowing, and in baling out water, brandy would naturally be administered by most ship surgeons. After draining the bottle, he rolled into his berth, saying, 'drowning was a death only fit for a rat or a blind puppy.'

'Never trouble thee-self about it, lad, drowning won't be thy lot,' exclaimed one of his acquaintance; but the fellow was already in a swinish sleep, unmindful of the lives his selfishness had sacrificed, and ungrateful for his own preservation.

There was mourning on board the *Robespierre*, as several of the unfortunate beings who had been drowned by the swamping of the boat had relatives behind them; amongst these were a father and a brother of the youth on whose shoulders that strong man had mounted when he regained the vessel.

'Where is that brute, Jarvis?' asked the brother of the poor boy as he entered the cabin where the ruffian lay sleeping off the effects of the brandy; but a man, occupying an adjacent berth, begged him to 'Go away or there'd be more mischief.'

'No, I won't, till I've had my revenge on that scoundrel,' replied the youth, who was immediately followed by the aged father exclaiming, 'Nobody shall screen that scoundrel from me; it is he who pushed my poor boy into the sea, and he shall answer for his death.'

The conversation at length roused the sleeper, who, with a great oath, told them to be off, and that he wanted to sleep.

'Sleep! And after sending him to his cold grave,' exclaimed the father, approaching the ruffian with a menacing gesture.

'Come none of your gammon, or I'll send you both after him,' said Jarvis, springing out of his bunk.

High words followed, and to these succeeded blows – the hand of the ruffian grasped the white locks of the aged man, and the youth lay bleeding at his feet.

The disturbance increased, till all classes of passengers came rushing towards the steerage, where the scene of strife was enacted; but at length the captain interposed, and quelled the disturbance by putting Jarvis in irons, in which manner he passed the remainder of the voyage.

A fortnight later the *Robespierre* cast anchor in Hobson's Bay, and as the sun shone on her white sails, and the deep blue waters of the Australian main reflected her tall masts and graceful outline, she seemed too bright and fairy-like to be the abode of violence or of evil passions.

CHAPTER XXVI

ASHORE

NOWHERE IS HUMAN nature exhibited with more truth than amongst the mixed community of a crowded ship – amongst people who embarked for the most part in amity towards each other, but who are now aroused from their better feelings by petty animosities – by the inconvenience attendant upon limited space or by want of occupation, and who jostle one another, and strive for pre-eminence as in the wider world, where every trade and calling illustrates the jealousy between man and man. But when they part at length, probably to meet no more, a kind of forgiveness of the past – a desire to obliterate all remembrance of injury – generally takes the place of ill-will; just as if they were making their peace with the dying, and (to continue the simile) after our fellow passengers of a voyage have been gone a few weeks, they become as entirely forgotten as fellow passengers through life who have gone to their graves.

The passengers of the *Robespierre* formed no exception to this prevailing rule; for when they parted, those who bid each other farewell at all, did so for the most part, without any ill-feeling; indeed, they had very little feeling excepting for themselves, which, it will readily be imagined, was not an ill one.

Landing in Melbourne, there is another resemblance to human nature at large; for how varied are the interests of the motley groups which, liberated from the confinement of the ship, are now turned loose upon the shore. First of all comes the old colonist: he naturally feels himself at home, though he may express some surprise at the additional improvements, the handsome buildings, and the tall trees that meet his eye; but this surprise will be proportionate to the length of his absence, as well as to the expansiveness of his temperament; and it may be that there are certain old colonists who think that the place did quite as well when there were no buildings, excepting some inconvenient wooden constructions, and very little verdure to be seen; for their memory reverts to a time between the periods of felling the trees planted by the hand of nature and of replacing them by that of art. Some of these very old colonists have been absent long enough to be as much surprised at the sight of a railway carriage near Hobson's Bay as any of the aborigines could possibly be; and, perhaps, they almost fancy they can't be in Melbourne at all, since it is possible to land without sticking fast in the mud, and especially as an Albert car now waits to bear them to a handsome hotel, instead of a bullock dray, to cart them to a wretched shanty. And thus the ancient colonist goes on his way, half proud of the improvements, and half resentful that more recent comers are better lodged than he was in former days.

The man of progress comes next, and being about the most rational amongst the throng, he will probably rejoice at the aspect of the gay city; that is, unless he should be greeted with some unpleasant intelligence respecting insolvencies, absconding debtors, failures in mining speculations, bushfires, or any other ill of colonial life.

After him the new chum is seen tripping jauntily along, quite proud of his superiority, and looking with such condescension on the benighted beings he has come to civilize; but he nevertheless wears that uncomfortable aspect which, no matter in what part of the world, is peculiar to the Englishman *dépaysé*.[22]

They are not all Englishmen though, for there is a friend from the Emerald Isle, who is more at his ease because he is confident of some big man's patronage; and, on the strength of this security, he makes acquaintance with half a score of government officers, waiting about their doors, as his forefathers have done times out of mind in the 'Old Country'.

And the North Briton too! But he, having calculated his chances beforehand, though he may be lost sight of for a while, is still thought to be getting on; and, if it is not known where he is gone, the general conclusion is that it will not be 'bock again'.

Then we have the honest artisans – poor men! How you will be disappointed, for you won't get half the wages (or in accordance with Colonial usage, the salary) you so fondly anticipated! Very likely indeed you won't get any at all, as a number of works have been stopped, and the 'old hands' turned adrift.

'But how are we to live?' ask the disappointed mechanics. 'Things are twice as dear in this colony as at home!'

---

[22] Displaced from one's home country, or disoriented.

'You should have thought of that sooner, my friends; but as you are here, you must live on your wits – if you possess any – or on those of your friends – always supposing that you have friends, and that they will let you exist in such a manner – but lest I should embarrass myself with these suppositions, I must leave you to take your chance, with the sincerest regret for your plight.' (I can afford pity).

Well, the passengers of the *Robespierre* have landed – half of them never to see the other half again, and the other half not caring whether they do or not. But they are not all selfish; there is Charles Manners, Esq., for instance, who, though he has resided twenty years in the colony, is as fine a specimen of an English gentleman as anybody in the world, even as his own brother who inherits the paternal mansion of Castle Manners. But Mr. Manners having been absent from the colony for nearly a year, is now warmly welcomed by his friends, who have come to meet him on the wharf.

As he was leaving the vessel, the man Jarvis (now released from his irons) came to ask if the gentleman could help him to any light employment, as his money was out.

'Go and break stones at once, or, faith! You'll be forced to do so one of these days. If ever I catch you in my district, and you don't mind your behaviour, I'll send you to the lock-up – you confounded ruffian!'

Now Mr. Manners being a very gentlemanly sort of person, this phraseology appeared rather strange to his friend, who had gone to meet him; but as Mr. Manners was also a man of determination and a P.M. (though very different to O'Twig), it was quite evident, if the occasion should offer, that he would put his threats into execution. The conduct of Jarvis having been explained, Mr. Manners' friend naturally turned to take another look at the unprepossessing countenance of the individual who had provoked such language, and the scrutiny was concluded by the remark, 'I've seen that fellow somewhere before.'

But the 'light employment' demanded by Jarvis was given, together with a moderate salary to the father of the poor lad, who had been so roughly pushed into the sea, and a letter of recommendation to the brother. Mr. Manners then went to pass his first evening on shore, in the society of his friends.

Amongst the guests was Mr. Argueville, the barrister who had so ably defended Herbert Lindsey, and as he was slightly acquainted with Mr. Manners, the conversation eventually turned towards the recent trial.

'In my opinion, young Lindsey is an honest honourable man, his very countenance would go far towards acquitting him,' said the barrister; 'but as for Miss McAlpin, she is the most spirited girl I have seen this long time.'

'It would appear that she is sincerely attached to him,' interrogated Mr. Manners.

'I should think so – she admitted the engagement in the first interview I had with her, though I was afterwards informed that she regarded it rather as a point of honour – as a contract entered into at the suggestion of her mother, and one that she felt called upon to regard as sacred; the more so, since her betrothed had fallen into trouble.'

'Hum! She is not an unlikely sort of girl to take these ideas into her head; at least, if I may judge from a certain exaltation of sentiment which she appears to inherit from her mother. I knew Mrs. McAlpin well many years ago, and therefore feel a strong interest in her daughter. She is my ward, you know.'

'I am aware of the circumstance, and if you had been in the colony, the poor girl need not have taken so prominent a part; but it is highly creditable to her, whether she be sincerely attached to Lindsey or not.'

'Who told you that she was not attached to him?'

'Why, I was told so in strict confidence, and should not have spoken to you on the subject were you not her guardian; besides, there is a good deal of stupid business about the will, and, after all it is quite natural that the young lady should endeavour so to shape her course as not to forfeit a just inheritance.'

'Yes, but she is totally free in that respect, as far as I can see.'

'I don't agree with you there, for if she should marry Lindsey—'

At this moment a lady began to sing in so very high a key that the gentlemen, not being able to hear each other speak, broke off the conversation, Mr. Manners saying that he should like to discuss the subject with Mr. Argueville at his convenience.

CHAPTER XXVII

Day Dreams

MR. SILVERTON WAS sitting one afternoon in a small room that he usually occupied at the Southern Cross. He was giving audience to the superintendent of the Mount Alpin station, to a stockrider he had lately engaged, and to three or four other people of higher or lower degree, for Mr. Silverton was now a man of some consequence, although his exact position was not very clearly defined. During the lifetime of Mr. McAlpin, he had been his agent, but now the station itself being debateable property, he could not be said to be the agent of its late owner's daughter – neither was he the real possessor of those broad acres, though it was beginning to be hinted that he would be hereafter, and the husband of the young lady into the bargain. He had been spending a great part of the morning in her society, and, although Bessie was decidedly in the way, he did contrive to be alone with Flora for five minutes, during which he talked of devotedness, of unalterable attachment, and of everything just stopping short of 'Love'. This word he did not dare to utter, as Flora turned away, looking (as he thought) a little angry at first, and then very sympathising. Another moment and he would have risked a second avowal, but Miss Garlick entered, and Pierce Silverton fell from the seventh heaven to the lower earth.

But now he was haranguing his employees with the authority of a master, though every now and then he referred to their common interest in Miss McAlpin's affairs with so much patter that he seemed to be less their lord than her slave. At length his satellites vanished, and he stretched himself on his sofa to dream of love.

Very much at his ease was Mr. Silverton in his inn. Mrs. Roberts liked everyone to be at his ease as well as herself, and certainly no one ever studied the comfort of lodgers as she did.

The public room – before alluded to – was not her province; but there was another apartment devoted to boarders, and there she would occasionally sit when certain friends were present, or when the coach brought any passengers she delighted to honour. In this room, breakfast, dinner, and a substantial repast, inviting the advantages of tea and supper, were duly served; and there Mr. Silverton partook of his meals with the other boarders, but he had the entrée to another room, very neatly furnished, and possessing very little of the ordinary hotel character, with the exception of an elaborate display of plate and pickles, glass and gewgaws on a substantial sideboard. The window of this apartment, opening like a door, was dressed with curtains of washed muslin, inside others of green damask. The verandah, which shaded three sides of the house, being barred off in front of this room by a light wooden railing, approached by a small gate.

To inhabit this privileged spot it was necessary either to pay a very high price, or to be a very great favourite with Mrs. Roberts. In this latter respect Pierce Silverton stood only second to Herbert Lindsey; but, notwithstanding the good landlady's hospitality, she had an eye to the main chance, and therefore it is to be inferred that Mr. Silverton did pay for the good things he enjoyed. At all events he was surrounded with a great many luxuries. Plenty of wood to burn if he was cold – a cheerful aspect; added to which, every appurtenance for making his room as dark as he chose, and (in consideration of his health) heaps of pillows and cushions strewed about the sofa, as well as permission to kick away the antimacassars if he thought fit; and, every day, jellies and blancmange served in such profusion that the sight of them would have made young O'Twig's mouth water for a week. But a pet invalid is always a privileged person – very much to be envied when not particularly ill and possessing a good income, moreover one who imagines his love suit will be successful at last.

Such, at that moment, was Pierce Silverton; and, if he had no other anxiety, he might truly be pronounced a happy man – so he was for the time, as he lay fast asleep dreaming of Love and Flora.

CHAPTER XXVIII

Awaking

Pierce Silverton dreamt that he had heard the bells ringing for his marriage, but his dream and his sleep were suddenly ended by a ringing of another sort – the thirsty frequenters of the public room summoning the waiter to replenish their glasses. Pierce started up, and the airy vision of a bridal procession faded away.

Considering the happy nature of his dreams, his awakening thoughts were strangely painful; perhaps reality had too quickly succeeded to imagination, and the objects of this harsh exterior world too rudely crowded on the sweeter creations of the 'Ideal'; but, after a little white, he thoroughly roused himself, and went into the dining room to discuss common-place events with common-place people.

The mail had arrived, bringing him two or three letters, although of little importance, as it would seem, for they were soon read and thrown aside for the daily papers.

He glanced at the leading article – shrugged his shoulders at the politics – skimmed over the general news – just saw that there was a list of births, deaths, and marriages, and then looked over the shipping intelligence. This was an important item to Mr. Silverton, as the wool season had commenced, and he would soon have to busy himself about exports, etc. So, having conned the 'Projected Departures', he naturally turned to the 'Arrivals'. Amongst these he saw the name of the *Robespierre*. All this time he had been sitting on the edge of a table in the dining-room, but now he took the journal into his own apartment, where he again threw himself on the sofa.

Why did he sigh so heavily? What ill-news met his eye? What news of any kind, excepting the arrival of Mr. Manners, and he was an old acquaintance – a friend – and all the other passengers were strangers. But there might perhaps be some melancholy association connected with that ship, or he might be deeply shocked by the intelligence, briefly stated, respecting the swamping of the boat. But it sometimes happens, notwithstanding the general urbanity of Mr. Silverton, that his manner was rather peculiar. This, however, might proceed from delicate health – an admitted excuse for shortcomings of all sorts. Be it as it may, the journal was cast on the floor, and when Mary summoned Mr. Silverton to tea, she found him resting his head on the table in the most disconsolate of attitudes. After calling to him several times in vain, she shook him gently by the shoulder, and then he looked up; but such gloom was on his countenance that the tender-hearted girl returned to the kitchen with tears in her eyes, bewailing the destiny of those who are crossed in love.

'Serve him right!' exclaimed Harry, who was present. 'What business has he to be hankering after another man's sweetheart?'

'Oh! But love can't be helped Harry.'

'Eh! What's that?'

'Love comes and goes without our bidding, Harry.'

'The devil it does! And so if that Yankee driver makes love to you, you mean to say that – but hang me, if I stand this gammon!'

And so poor Mary, who sought to excuse the weakness of one man, roused the jealousy of another.

But, contrary to the expectation of Mrs. Roberts (who had been informed by her faithful domestic of Mr. Silverton's apparent illness), that gentleman seemed quite himself on the following morning; and, at his accustomed hour, rode to Mount Alpin.

On arriving there, he found Bessie Garlick alone, and to her great delight, he began jesting with her as he had formerly done, pelting her with cotton-balls and every other article that came in his way. The poor girl's hopes were awakened, and she fancied that her empire was about to be restored; but, thinking it was now her turn to play the tyrant, she said:

'Get away, you disagreeable creature! Do you think I am going to take any notice of you, after your ingratitude?'

'Oh! Bessie, why have you not more pride than to betray your secret to one who loves you not?' But, notwithstanding the ingratitude, and perhaps the treachery of Pierce, he was too generous to exhibit any signs of triumph; on the contrary, he took her hand very kindly, saying, 'Wait a little, Bessie, and you'll find that I can appreciate your goodness?'

At that moment Flora entered, very much to the annoyance of her rival, and, for the first time, not to the satisfaction of Pierce; but as she did not seem to be displeased at his evident familiarity with Bessie, he soon recovered his self-possession – or rather, he forced himself to be gay, and, as a natural consequence, overacted his part. At length, when his excitement subsided a little, he told Miss McAlpin that he had news for her.

'What is it? Anything about Herbert?' she asked.

'No, although I have heard that he is getting on famously – quite taken up with a pretty hem! A landscape he is painting. But it is of Mr. Manners I have to speak; he has returned, and here is a newspaper, where you will find an account of his voyage.'

Miss McAlpin expressed her satisfaction at the idea of so soon seeing her father's friend again, but scarcely had she done speaking, ere the gentleman in question was announced.

He was warmly welcomed by those whom he immediately supposed to be lovers; and when, at a later hour he accompanied Mr. Silverton to a part of the station which, in the lifetime of McAlpin had been little better than waste ground, but which was now in a state of high cultivation, he thought it would be the best thing that could happen if these young people were to make a match of it, as Mr. Silverton was a clever managing fellow, and that wandering artist not fit to marry a girl like Miss McAlpin.

Mr. Manners then complimented his companion on his improvements, and the conversation turning on the Will, he added, 'I should inform you that I am in possession of a letter addressed to me by Mr. McAlpin shortly before his death, in which he stated that– but I am not at liberty to reveal all at present, so I shall merely say that the writer wished to put Lindsey to the proof, and the time has not yet arrived for the ordeal to cease.'

'God grant he may be worthy of her, and that these rumours may be false! But I should not have spoken of this,' said Mr. Silverton.

Then, as both gentlemen seemed anxious to preserve a degree of reticence, and neither to be very well able to do so, they, by tacit consent, changed the subject to more indifferent topics.

'Oh, by the way,' said Mr. Manners, 'I have a favour to ask of you.'

'Command me in any way,' replied Mr. Silverton.

'It is only a trifle. Can you find employment for a poor fellow who came out in the *Robespierre*?'

After a moment's. hesitation, Mr. Silverton made inquiries into the man's character.

To which Mr. Manners answered that his protégé seemed a decent lad, a stranger in the colony, that his brother had been drowned at sea, and, added the gentleman, 'I feel a strong interest in the youth, as well as in his rather, and would take him into my service, but that he wishes to be near the old man, whom I have consigned to our friend, Roberts.'

Mr. Silverton now spoke with more certainty, and said he would employ the young man at once, and do anything else to oblige Mr. Manners.

The gentlemen soon after rode together to the township, where Mr. Manners heard several rumours relative to the fickleness of Herbert Lindsey; and though he highly recommended the reserve of Pierce Silverton with regard to his friend, he thought he would observe what was going on with his own eyes, and his residence being near the spot where the young artist was then sojourning, he would have an excellent opportunity of so doing.

A day or two later, Mr. Manners left for South Australia, and things seemed to be going on in their usual way – Mr. Silverton paying his daily visits to Mount Alpin, yielding himself more and more to his passion for Flora, but at the same time endeavouring to amuse Bessie with his occasional attentions; yet whenever a letter was received from Lindsey, he could scarcely suppress his agitation, although he flattered himself that these letters were becoming less frequent.

At the same time, the conduct of Flora did not altogether escape comment; but, if in explicable to the public in general, it had evidently satisfied her guardian; as, according to a dialogue which had been overheard, when that gentleman expressed some surprise that she should remain in that secluded spot, instead of living in the metropolis, she had replied, 'I suffered so much whilst I was there, from being forced into notice, that I have resolved to remain quietly here till the expiration of the year; it will then be time enough for me to act.'

This speech certainly admitted of more than one interpretation, but that of Pierce Silverton was, that she intended to watch the conduct of Herbert, and if by any means convinced of his infidelity, then – he might hope.

And thus, forming vain schemes for future bliss, he spent many a solitary hour. Some people called him a lazy fellow, but others took his part, saying it was needful for him to rest in the day, as he did not rest at night. But he was again aroused from these sweet visions, and this time by a man who entered the apartment through the little gate on the verandah.

Seeing a dark shadow, Pierce started from his couch – a shadow of coming evil it seemed to be, or why did the cold drops of perspiration stand on his pale forehead, as he exclaimed, 'You here? What brings you to me?'

'Want of money, Mr. Silverton; and that often makes a man do many a queer thing, as I think you ought to know by this time,' answered the stranger.

'What do you mean? I do none of those things you call queer for money,' replied Silverton angrily.

'No,' said the man, with an insolent grin, 'you are too much of a gentleman for that, and too much of a Christian not to help a poor fellow – so you'll just have to help me.'

'Again, so soon – I shall be ruined at this rate.'

'You'll be ruined if you don't, Mr. Silverton.' And the man, rapping his nose with his broad forefinger, looked the impersonation of vulgar defiance.

'Well, wait here, and I'll see what is to be done. There's some brandy, and now keep yourself quiet till I come back.' So saying, Mr. Silverton, after securing both entrances to the room, went away; his absence lasted some considerable time, and the twilight was far advanced when he returned. 'Come along,' he then said to the stranger; the man nodded in reply, and immediately followed his patron.

At a late hour in the night, Pierce Silverton re-entered by the window, and, throwing himself on the sofa, exclaimed, 'My God! Is this persecution to last for ever?'

CHAPTER XXIX

A Wedding

'CROFTS, MY MAN, this won't do at all – a horse, valued at a hundred guineas, gone out of the stable whilst you were spinning your 'tarnation yarns to those girls in the kitchen. Do you think I shall stand that?' exclaimed Mr. Roberts, in an angry tone, to an old man who had recently entered his service.

'I do not know how it happened, sir,' replied the man, 'but I'll take my oath that I locked the stable door last night.'

'After the horse was stolen, I suppose.'

'No, Mr. Roberts, before, and that I'll swear to,' said Harry. 'For I was with Crofts; indeed, it was I that did lock the door, because he had his hands full of candles and things.'

'You did, did you, Saunders? Well, I can't doubt your word,' said the landlord.

'And it's the first time mine was ever doubted, sir,' added the stranger sorrowfully.

'Why, you see my man it won't do to trust strangers in a colony like this, though you do look like an honest fellow, and I don't want to be hard upon you, especially as you were recommended by Mr. Manners; but there's no time to be lost. Eh, there – police!'

And, on being joined by the official, Mr. Roberts walked away with him to take steps for the recovery of the animal and the apprehension of the thief.

This little incident, as it may he supposed, collected a crowd in the courtyard of the hotel; for, in the first place, a number of people were anxious to clear themselves of all suspicion, and, in the second, those who could not be suspected were equally ready to give their suggestions and advice. The boarders left the breakfast table, the servants their work, and a number of people from all parts of the township thronged about the doors. Some of the late risers came hurrying down stairs one by one, and amongst these was Mr. Silverton, looking unusually pale and ill; but he, like all those who kept a horse in the stables of the Southern Cross, went to see if it had been stolen; indeed, from the general solicitude, anyone would imagine that a whole army of plunderers had invaded the premises, instead of a solitary individual. But the gentlemen having satisfied themselves as to the safety of their own particular steeds, returned to the breakfast table, where they found neither the coffee, the rashers, nor any of the other delicacies, the better for the accident, although the cat might be, as she was helping herself to a dish of garfish.

Puss being driven out, and the waiter called in, the gentlemen, generally speaking, gave proof that the misfortune of Mr. Roberts was borne with considerable philosophy – by them. Perhaps Mr. Silverton took it more to heart as he did not eat, though he recovered sufficiently to ride off at the usual hour to Mount Alpin;

and on his return from thence to undertake a journey to Melbourne.

It is true that he had a great deal of business there, which we will leave him to transact, as we have to accompany Mr. Manners to his home – a pleasant one in every respect, and pleasantly situated amongst cornfields and vineyards, being likewise the home of a charming wife and four lovely children.

Charles Manners was a happy man, which he deserved to be, but he was also a man of importance – the great man of the neighbourhood – and this he likewise deserved a great deal better than most people who have honours showered upon them; but, perhaps, at that time, Mr. Manners would rather have been without these honours, as they called him away from his domestic circle too soon after his return; though, having undertaken the onerous duties of a public man, he was not a person to neglect them, and, therefore, he may be excused if he was somewhat strict with those who were less scrupulous. Amongst the individuals whom he intended to keep up to a fulfilment of duty was Mr. Lindsey, and very properly, too, for it would be a shame, after all the sacrifices Flora had made for him, if he should act unworthily towards her. So it fell out that when Mr. Manners had been a few days at home, and had discussed family matters and English news with his wife, that he asked her if she had heard anything of a young fellow named Lindsey?

'There was a great deal of interest felt about him at one time,' replied Mrs. Manners, 'and I think he might visit in the best society if he chose, but they say he is so taken up with Annie Lowe, that he does not care to go anywhere.'

'And who is Annie Lowe?'

'Mrs. Lowe's daughter, to be sure.'

'You don't mean Mrs. Lowe – poor Tom's widow?'

'Yes, I do.'

'Why, her daughter must be a mere child – about twelve years of age, I suppose.'

'Nonsense, Charles! She is turned sixteen – a year older than our Clara. But you men are so stupid about ages; I dare say you have forgotten how old your own children are?'

Mr. Manners proved his stupidity by guessing at least a couple of years younger than they were.

'There, didn't I say so?' exclaimed his wife triumphantly.

But he seemed to submit very passively to her raillery, for he did not reply; and, as a great deal of business had accumulated during his absence, he probably soon forgot all about Annie Lowe's age and Herbert Lindsey's infidelities; both circumstances, however, were forcibly recalled to his memory the next day when he visited the neighbouring town.

It has already been stated that Mr. Manners was a magistrate, and a good one, but as we shall not be called upon to see him in his official character, we will merely refer to the circumstances that took him to town, lest it should be supposed that he went there as a mere idler, which many people did on that morning; but the motive for idleness being to see a wedding, we must make an excuse for once. It was not a gay wedding, although the youth and beauty of the bride deserved one – a pretty little thing she was, looking so happy, as she leant on the arm of that handsome young man, that even our grave magistrate asked the names of the parties, pointing to each individual as he did so.

'That's Annie Lowe – she's to be married today, and I am glad of it, for the poor girl was dreadfully afraid lest her sweetheart should give her the slip. It was said he had got entangled in another engagement, and—'

Mr. Manners, not having time to listen to gossip of this nature, remarked, 'Poor girl! She is very young to be married; but,' he added, pointing to the gentleman who was leading the bride into the church, 'who is that good-looking fellow?'

'That? Oh, that is Mr. Lindsey. I thought you knew him,' answered the magistrate's informant.

'The scoundrel!'

'Ah! I see the view you take of the late trial, and, between ourselves, I am of the same opinion, for who else could have murdered McAlpin?'

'Poor McAlpin!' said Mr. Manners with a sigh, the remembrance of his old acquaintance effacing from his mind the fickleness of Herbert Lindsey. But the conversation being here interrupted by the approach of a brother magistrate, the two dignitaries went to take their seats on the bench. No sooner, however, was the business of the day concluded, than Mr. Manners wrote to Pierce Silverton, requesting him to prepare Miss McAlpin for the distressing intelligence, or at least to prevent her from becoming first acquainted with it through the columns of a newspaper.

'At all events, there is an excellent fellow ready to take the place of this Lindsey, so I hope the poor girl will not break her heart about the good-for-nothing rascal,' was the concluding remark of the worthy magistrate, as he related the circumstances to his wife.

'The deceitful man! I am so glad that I never invited him here; for you know, Charles, that Clara might have taken a fancy to him, and then—'

And then, Mrs. Manners congratulated herself on her own prudence, which, like that of many other people, had been the result of accident as she had been prevented, by the illness of her children, by repairs going on in the house, and by other domestic causes, from receiving company since Herbert's visit in the neighbourhood; though she had quite forgotten how much these circumstances had annoyed her at the time.

'I am glad you did not invite him, Lizzie; I'll have no vagabond fellows running off with any of our girls. But, after all, I am as well pleased that Master Lindsey has left the coast clear, for it will greatly simplify matters.'

Mrs. Manners then became very anxious to know how a dilemma could be simplified by being doubled, but her husband only replied that 'Time would show.'

CHAPTER XXX

A Coup d'État

THE LETTER OF Mr. Manners was forwarded to Pierce Silverton in Melbourne, and, upon receiving it, he immediately hastened back to the country, deliberating all the while as to what steps should be next taken. Not wishing to be the bearer of ill-tidings, although extremely anxious that these tidings should be communicated, he resolved to go immediately to Mount Alpin, thinking that some unforeseen accident might have occurred which would guide his future movements. On arriving there he found a clue to direct him through the tangled path he had to tread – for a tangled path all must tread who deviate from the straightforward way. And it was the absence of a 'straightforward man' that aided the 'double dealer' – we allude to Harry Saunders, who had gone some distance up the country to visit a sick mother; and as it was the duty of Harry to meet the mail and take any letters it might bring Mount Alpin Station to their destination, Pierce Silverton at once saw what advantage he might reap from this accidental occurrence. But when Flora asked him which of the men in his employ could be best entrusted with the charge, he hesitated, saying one always forgot everything – another patronised public-houses too much – in short, Mr. Silverton found some objection to all the servants.

'It is very tiresome!' said Flora, rather pettishly. 'I hate the idea of having my letters delayed or lost.'

'I will bring them up for you, if you desire,' replied Mr. Silverton in the most natural tone in the world.

'I don't like to give you so much trouble.'

'What nonsense! Don't I come here every day? But will you excuse me for a moment? I have a message for Miss Garlick.'

This anxiety respecting Miss Garlick so completely threw Flora off her guard that all her former confidence in Pierce Silverton returned, and thus when he left Mount Alpin that afternoon, he thought the game was in his own hands, and forthwith resolved on a *coup d'état*. All *coups d'état* are of rapid execution, and therefore Pierce Silverton nerved himself for the enterprise. He had already skirmished about for a considerable time, and now, nearly a year having elapsed since the death of McAlpin, Flora would very soon either marry Herbert or reject altogether; it would not, therefore, be expedient for her to receive his letters, as he might explain something about that wedding, or perhaps Mr. Manners might do so – he having, by this time, ascertained that Mr. Lindsey was the gentleman 'who gave away the lady', not the one 'who received her'.

'How could you be so stupid?' Mrs. Manners demanded of her husband, when she was correctly informed of all details connected with the bridal procession. 'For', she added, 'if Annie had been coming out of the church with Mr. Lindsey, instead of going into it, then it would be evident that he was her husband. But, I declare, Charles, you seem as ignorant of wedding etiquette as if you had never been married yourself, nor given away half-a-dozen girls in the course of your life time.'

On receiving this lecture, Mr. Manners admitted to his wife that he was stupid, and to his conscience that he was unjust. Unjust, and a magistrate! His honourable nature could not bear that reflection, so he immediately set about doing the very thing that he had proposed to himself to do on arriving in his own district, namely, to observe the conduct of Herbert Lindsey; therefore, the next day he paid a visit to the artist's studio, where he found a large collection of sketches in different stages of progress, and the artist himself working away for his very life.

It was such an easy thing to gain the confidence of that single-minded young man, that Mr. Manners soon drew from him his motive for so much over-exertion, which was an earnest resolve to pay back the sum Miss McAlpin had advanced for his law expenses, and then to go on working until he could maintain her as she deserved.

'I am afraid you will not be able to do that in a hurry,' said Mr. Manners.

'As she deserves – No! But at least in such a way that she will never feel privation,' replied Lindsey – a remark which caused Mr. Manners to perceive that the artist was himself enduring privation. It was scarcely worthwhile clearing up the mystery about Anne Lowe, although Mr. Manners did ask a few questions respecting her, to which Herbert replied that he was the intimate friend of her lover, and acted towards him just as Pierce Silverton would act towards himself.

'Oh, Herbert! Herbert! That ideal world of yours has sadly destroyed your perception of the actual one! Sadly? No – the sadness will come when you can see clearly – when you taste of the "bitter fruit" that grows on the tree of knowledge!'

'Well,' said Mr. Manners, as he rose to take his leave, 'since Miss McAlpin has, with a delicacy I honour, refused to marry in haste, and as I am a sort of guardian of hers, I shall probably be in the neighbourhood about the time specified – it is not far distant, I think.'

'No; thank goodness.'

Mr. Manners went away, doubting very much whether Mr. Silverton would 'thank goodness'; for he did not think his friendship for Flora quite as platonic as that of Herbert for Annie Lowe.

But we must now return to Mr. Silverton, whom we left somewhat abruptly. We could not very well do otherwise, as the interview between Mr. Manners and Herbert Lindsey was taking place about the time that Flora was expressing her anxiety respecting her letters, and (it being impossible to explain the two circumstances together) we have turned to the 'denouncement' of the more truthful, as being the clearest and best. Had Pierce Silverton done so, what misery to himself and others would have been spared! But he was growing desperate, as several things had lately occurred which might – he cannot grasp what they might do, for he does not know how he may be implicated in two or three ugly transactions – quite unjustly perhaps – for instance, there is that affair of the horse-stealing, of which he was as innocent as the child unborn – a circumstance that would be evident to the most careless observer. How could he wrench the door from off its hinges? For it had been discovered that the lock was all right, the door having been opened by some other process. But if Mr. Silverton's conscience is clear about the theft of the horse, he might, nevertheless, have to answer some disagreeable questions respecting an acquaintance who is not troubled with a conscience at all, and he almost envies him on that account – for it is conscience that is undermining the health of Pierce Silverton – conscience as much as his restless love. And yet there is nothing that can extricate him but a *coup d'état*. Flora must be his, at any price; and after all, it surely will not be so very difficult to obtain her? Has he not the letter of her guardian, stating that Herbert is already married? But, with regard to other letters yet to be written? Well, they won't be received – so Mrs. Manners and Lindsey may write away to their hearts' content!

'But they may come!'

'Aye – there's the rub!'

And he may come again – that troublesome man without a conscience – that man whom no money will satisfy – he who has already received such large sums to leave his benefactor in peace – he may come, though he swore to stay away; but he does not regard an oath; he regards nothing, either human or divine – nothing but his own worthless life and the gratification of his brutal passions – that man, who would do anything if prompted by ungovernable rage. Ah! People who would – keep these men away! A horrible thought suggests itself to Pierce Silverton, but he resists the temptation. Oh! If he could have resisted others! Surely nature never intended him for a villain – he is too gentle and tender hearted! Did he not absolutely faint from excess of emotion when

Herbert Lindsey so narrowly escaped death for the crime of another? But why had nature stopped short in her handiwork, and in framing Pierce Silverton – so tender hearted, so loving – did she not make him truthful, candid – and honourable? It is a bald thing to say that honour, of which men are so proud, should be wanting in Pierce Silverton; but not so strange after all, for it is not so very general, even in that extremely respectable portion of society to which Pierce Silverton belongs.

He aroused himself at length from these painful reflections – it was time – for he knew that he must now act, and quickly – Herbert Lindsey having written to Flora, stating the day when he will come never to leave her again! There are so many tender allusions to the last meeting in the letter, that Pierce Silverton tears it into atoms. It is true that the writer did not intend these loving expressions for any eyes but hers. Well, never mind – there will only be another sin of omission laid on the broad shoulders of the public service if a few letters do go astray! And so, after calming down an excess of agitation – quite violent enough to destroy a stronger frame than that of Pierce Silverton – he canters away in a gallant fashion to see his Flora – for his she shall be, come who may into the lists!

'Here comes Mr. Silverton! How well he looks!' exclaimed Bessie Garlick to Flora, as they were sitting together on the verandah.

'I think he has been looking better of late; but he seems agitated, oh! I hope he has no bad news.'

As Flora spoke, Pierce Silverton entered the room, and Flora asked, 'Is there any letter today?'

'No; not today, but—'

'There is some news – ah tell me!'

'I cannot – I ought to have told you long ago, but had not courage.'

'Now tell me at once – directly.'

'Forgive my delay – it was caused by reluctance to give you pain; you know the interest I take in your welfare, and—'

Flora sat tapping her foot on the floor, as impatient people often do when they do not want to hear long speeches; and Bessie Garlick at length retired, half reluctant to leave these two together, but conscious that she ought not to remain. Mr. Silverton then continued, 'Here is a letter I received some time since from Mr. Manners. You know his writing – do you not, Flora?'

'Very well – yes that is his hand; give me the letter.'

Pierce obeyed silently, and Flora read: she coloured deeply, but from what emotion he could not guess, but she looked at him as if to interpret his thoughts, and after a long pause, said, 'It is false! Herbert would marry no one but me.'

'So I should have thought, had the letter been from anyone but Mr. Manners, and had not that advertisement appeared.' So saying, he handed her a newspaper, where, under the head of marriages, she read that of Herbert Lindsey with Annie Lowe, and then she sat down, speechless, breathless.

For a long time Pierce did not venture to break the silence; but at last it became too painful, and, taking her hand, he said, 'Miss McAlpin, Flora, tell me what I can do for you?'

'Wait, wait,' she said, in a hoarse whisper; 'wait till I ascertain the whole truth – till I see Mr. Manners – till—'

'Would you like to consult him? Shall I write to him to come here?'

'No – I will consult no one; but if this should be true, and—Pierce Silverton, on your honour – on your soul, tell me was that letter written by Mr. Manners?'

'So you admitted yourself; but, Miss McAlpin, allow me to remark that I do not understand your insinuation.' And Mr. Silverton walked away with an air of offended dignity.

Flora looked coldly at him, and there was another pause, after which she said, 'Speak – tell me all you know.'

'I have told you, Miss McAlpin; I have given you the letter of your guardian, and must leave him to explain why it was written.'

'He saw the marriage – or saw them afterwards – or what does he say?'

She once more referred to the statement of Mr. Manners, and then added, 'After all I have done for him! After my confidence in his truth! But I scorn him! I hate him!'

Pride now took the place of love in the heart of Flora, and sympathy, that of indignation, in the eyes of Silverton; still he stood aloof, but he must not give her time to relapse into tenderness. What should he do? If he suggested the unworthiness of Herbert, that wilful girl might even now take his part, so at length he said, mournfully, 'Oh! If he could witness your wretchedness, how he would repent his error!'

'I am not wretched, and he shall repent!' And the spirit of her father flashed from her eyes as she added, 'Thank heaven, I can revenge this injury!'

Very beautiful was Flora in these moments of excitement, and Pierce had great difficulty in restraining himself from falling on his knees, as he had done once before. If he had he would have lost everything, and even now the battle between strong passions was not decided.

But that word revenge pointed out a way – dark and tumultuous, but still the only way; so raising his voice above the soft persuasive tone he usually adopted, he said, 'Yes – you can revenge. You can spurn Herbert Lindsey when he comes to you in his poverty to demand forgiveness, and pleads as his excuse, his love for Annie Lowe.'

Well done, Pierce Silverton! You have aroused jealousy to aid the work of revenge, and Flora exclaims,

'His love! Shall I tamely wait his return? What have I to do with him? Am I not mistress of my father's wealth? And can I not use it in a way to make him repent his insult?'

'You can, and freely, if—'

'If what, Pierce Silverton?'

'If you will marry me,' and he threw himself at her feet, and clasped her in his arms as she said, 'I will.'

'Let it be soon, Flora. Do not let us wait til everybody is making merry at Christmas; you would not like that.'

The idea of Herbert Lindsey, happy and smiling in the domestic circle of his new made wife, now arose to Flora's vivid imagination, but restraining her feelings, she said:

'Yes – the sooner the better; tomorrow if you like.'

He did not dare to thank her, nor even to look his joy, for, as yet, she must consider him as the agent of her revenge, not the object of her love; but he kissed her hand in token of gratitude, and exclaimed, 'Thine forever – were it to be a slave!'

Flora sighed, and a shade of weariness was beginning to efface the flush of resentment; but Pierce, determined to make all safe, continued, 'You promise me Flora, and tomorrow? You will need very little preparation, for you are more beautiful in this morning dress than Annie Lowe in all her bridal finery,'

The lips of Flora curled with disdain, as she said, 'Pierce Silverton, before I was conscious of Herbert's unworthy conduct I wrote to summon him; but it he should so far presume on my former love as to venture into my presence, he shall find me your wife, and although I may not require much preparation, I will prove to him that I am not so distressed as to neglect appearances, for I will be dressed like a queen! Make what preparations you choose, and come tomorrow, at this hour, I shall be ready.'

Pride, jealousy and revenge had won for Pierce Silverton the promise that his long enduring love could never have done; but he little heeded how she had been won, as he poured forth his passionate vows to an ear that scarcely heard, and kissed a cheek that did not change colour beneath his touch. But he was happy – so happy that all dangers and anxieties were forgotten.

The *coup d'état* had been eminently successful.

CHAPTER XXXI

TO BE MARRIED TOMORROW

F LORA DID NOT pause to meditate upon her hasty engagement, neither did she weep for the fickleness of Herbert, nor her heart beat with the timid joy of a girl about to become a bride; but as soon as Pierce left, she went to her own room to make a few preparations; the hint that she would require none, which in the first instance had aroused her pride, now caused her to survey her graceful figure with more complacency than she had ever done before. 'More beautiful than Annie Lowe – I should think so indeed!' was the thought that crossed her mind, if her lips did not give utterance to the expression. Flora, however, was not a vain girl, although she could not be so strikingly handsome without knowing it; but it was not to gratify her vanity – too weak a passion for her nature – that induced her to take a costly dress from her wardrobe. That dress had been worn on a very different occasion; for Miss McAlpin, having been gifted with considerable dramatic powers, had once been requested to join in 'Private Theatricals' – the part allotted to her being that of Julia in the Hunchback.[23]

---

[23] James Sheridan Knowles' popular play *The Hunchback* (1832) was performed in Australian theatres in the 1840s and 1850s.

She possessed a good deal of the passionate nature of that heroine, but for the present emergency, it was sufficient that she possessed the bridal dress required for the last act. Magnificently beautiful had she looked in it on the night of those theatricals; and it was with a strange mixture of gratified pride and haughty disdain that she drew forth the gorgeous costume, and throwing it on the bed, exclaimed, 'There, it will serve as well for one piece of acting as another.'

Whilst thus employed, her maid, having knocked several times at the door without receiving an answer, now entered. The girl looked a little surprised at the display of so much finery, but Miss McAlpin said, in a tone of indifference, 'Things of this sort require airing sometimes, Margaret.' And then, if Margaret had previously suspected the destination of the dress, the manner in which her young mistress tossed it about would at once have caused her to think differently, as wedding dresses are always supposed to be treated with the greatest respect. But Margaret having come to summon Miss McAlpin to dinner, it now became necessary for her to sit down to that meal, if not for the sake of her own appetite, at least for that of Miss Garlick.

Bessie looked puzzled, as she heard Mr. Silverton say something about important news – bad news, as she understood; but Miss McAlpin, though she did not appear, was certainly not altogether herself.

At length Bessie hoped 'that there was nothing the matter with Mr. Lindsey?'

'Oh dear, no,' replied Flora, 'Mr. Silverton's news was not of half so much consequence as he supposed.'

The young hostess served her guest very plentifully, and herself also, although she left what is termed a 'wasteful plate'.

Dinner being at length concluded, Flora, saying she had letters to write, again retired to her own room. 'I will not say anything of this to her, for she will only make a scene,' she exclaimed, half aloud; and thus it would appear that the idea of casting Miss Garlick for the part of bridesmaid did not occur to Miss McAlpin – indeed, it is probable that she thought so little of the bridegroom, as not to think at all of the supernumerary characters: but, as she considered that a certain amount of attention was due to her guest, she wrote a brief note, to be given to her on the morrow; another, also, to the young lady's brother, in which she requested him to make Mount Alpin his home, as long as his sister desired to stay there.

Scarcely had she finished, when a note was brought her from Mr. Silverton: it ran thus –

> 'Dearest Flora, – A vessel is to sail for England
> in a few days. Would you like to go there?
> Ever yours,
> Pierce Silverton.'

To this she merely replied –

> 'England will do as well as any other place.
> F. McA.'

'So much the better,' soliloquised the bride-elect, 'it will give me something to do.'

And, perhaps, it was quite as well to pack boxes as to sit down and cry; for she succeeded in tiring herself almost to death, and in causing her tea not to be such a mere pretence as dinner had been.

Whether she was to go to the clergyman to be married, or the clergyman was to come to marry her, she did not know. Neither did any thoughts of bride cake or bride favours enter her head; but having told Mr. Silverton to make whatever arrangements he liked, it is to be inferred that she had a tolerable opinion of his good taste. Suddenly, however, the idea of travelling with Pierce crossed her mind: it was associated with the recollection of a former journey in his company – when she was about to visit the gaol. Then arose the memory of all she had suffered. 'And it was for this!' she indignantly exclaimed.

But what do all these reflections now avail, Flora, as you are to be married tomorrow.

Mr. Silverton set about the preparations for his marriage with a great deal of savoir faire; he bought the ring and two immense bride cakes, without either of these remarkable purchases exciting particular attention; it is true that he said the former was for a friend, and having occasionally been so condescending as to execute a commission or two for Mrs. Roberts, and the confectionery articles being ordered to be sent to the Southern Cross, it was naturally supposed that a bridal feast was to be celebrated at that hotel. Mr. Silverton then called on a clergyman respecting the license but the reverend gentleman not being at home, the visitor left his card and his compliments, and said he would call again in the evening. He would have liked to have gone back to Mount Alpin, but not knowing exactly in what mood he might find Flora, he thought it better to restrain his inclinations; therefore, to fill up the time, he walked about the township, looking in through the shopwindows and wondering what sort of a present he could make his bride. There was very little to tempt his fancy, so thinking he should have a better choice in Melbourne, and a better still in London, he contented himself with the most expensive diamond ring he could find; and as he entrusted this costly gem to one of the men usually employed about the station, Flora might have wondered (had not her thoughts been otherwise occupied) why the same man was not fit to be entrusted with letters also.

The next duty of Mr Silverton was to walk into the stable yard, where his host happened to be, and accosting him in a careless manner, he said, 'Roberts, a friend of mine will want your pair of greys tomorrow.'

'Very good! But where are they to go?'

'I will give you all particulars in the morning; it is only just now that I have been informed myself.'

'All right! Your friends are decent fellows; but I don't let out those greys to all sorts of rowdy chaps.' So saying, Mr. Roberts walked off, and Mr. Silverton, thinking that his preparations were nearly completed, wondered why people made such a fuss about weddings. He then bent his steps towards his own sitting room, and having missed his dinner at the table d'hôte, requested that some little trifle might be served in his parlour.

He had not enjoyed a dinner so much for many a day; nor had the wine been so well flavoured, nor he felt so happy; nor, when he took an accustomed siesta, slept half so sweetly, for he dreamt he was to be married tomorrow.

CHAPTER XXXII

Two Crimes

A GAIN, THE AWAKENING was terrible; again, did the eyes of Pierce Silverton fall on the dark shadow, which, on a former occasion, had put all his sweet visions to flight. It looked more ominous this time, for the room was only lighted by the moon; but in Australia, the moon, when full, and the night fine, is bright enough to render even minute objects tolerably distinct; and thus Pierce at once read the determination of his visitor written in coarse lines on a face swollen with drink, and inflamed with passion, far more so than usual, for that man had lately been dismissed by his employer, and his character was so bad, that it would be extremely difficult for him to meet with another. Desperation alone could have driven him into that neighbourhood, where he was suspected of having committed more than one crime of great enormity. It might be the desperation of hunger, if his habits of intoxication had not already destroyed his appetite; but there are natures in which all the coarser propensities combine together: not unlikely this, as they are not counterbalanced by the qualities of mind.

And thus, although he had enemies on all sides, he came there, even as a wolf will leave the forest when assailed by famine. Like the wolf also, he came for prey; and now, without giving Pierce Silverton time to collect his thoughts, he said roughly,

'Well, you see I've come again!'

'I see you have – and would rather see the devil. What brings you here? But I need not ask – the want of money, I suppose.'

'You've hit it – and now shell out!'

'No, I will not. It is scarcely a month since I gave you a hundred pounds. I have not spent so much as that myself in the time.'

'People live according to their tastes, and my fancies are rather expensive.'

'Then why don't you work like a decent man? It is a shame to see such a great strong fellow living in idleness.'

'Idleness, do you call it; but I can tell you it is no joke to spend one's life in breaking in them brutes of horses.'

'No – nor in stealing them either. And now tell me what possessed you to take a horse from these stables the last time you were here?'

'Just to carry me across the country, to be sure; and that's all along of you, 'cos you kick up a row about my being here.'

'I think I have a right. If I find you the means of existence, I shall dictate where you are to live; so, once for all I say, it shall not be in this colony.'

'Now that's what I call right down hard. This here colony is the one I affection the most of all the lot, besides, I like to be near a friend.'

'Do you know that it is quite possible to tire a friend with too much importunity?'

The expression of the man's face became more brutal than ever, and he said in a determined manner, 'I'm not a chap to stand any gammon; and you know I've a claim on you.'

Then a look of deep anguish clouded the countenance of him who a few hours earlier had thought of love alone; but, after a few moments' reflection, he said,

'That has been paid over and over again. I gave you three hundred pounds at the time, three hundred pounds more when you had spent the first in drunkenness and debauchery – this being with the understanding that you should stay in England; and, even when you returned, contrary to your oath, I gave you one hundred pounds; making in all seven hundred pounds within a year, and all this to a man who is a great deal better able to work than I am.'

'But, may be, I have a sweetheart to keep. Folks say that you're making up to the old chap's daughter; so I think you might have a fellow feeling for an old friend.'

Anger at this remark banished all other passions from the breast of Silverton, and he said,

'Do not dare to couple the name of that lady with the infamous women you frequent!'

'All a matter of taste, Mr. Silverton,' replied the man carelessly, 'though they do say she's a stunning fine girl – so here's wishing you joy!'

The man filled a tumbler from the decanter of pale sherry that stood on the table, and, after draining it, said contemptuously, 'Pugh! It's no better than water. Haven't you got any brandy, Mr. Silverton?'

'No, I do not take brandy.'

'That makes you the milksop sort of a fellow you are; but the bar's handy, so I'll trouble you to ring the bell.'

'I shall do no such thing; you have had too much already, and— but you must be mad! Do you want to be seen here?'

'Why, not exactly. You see I can do a thing in a genteel sort of a way. I came in through that snug little gate of yours, Mr. Silverton, and if you'll just fork out another hundred pounds, I'll take myself off till—'

Till you have spent it, I suppose. But I have not another hundred pounds to spare. I promised that sum to be paid regularly twice a year, and you come to me at the expiration of the first month: but I will put up with this imposition no longer.'

'Come, Mr. Silverton, no hard words; I helped you to your fortune.'

'You did nothing of the kind – I work for my money honourably.'

'Gave you a help though, for the old chap had left you a snug little sum, and you see it wouldn't do to let him change his mind – gentlemen will change their minds as well as poor folks.'

'What nonsense this is about poor folks! Seven hundred pounds within a year for a man that has been brought up to hard labour!'

'But them vy'ges I took?'

'One of them you had no right to take. Why couldn't you stay in England when you were there?'

'England be blowed! It's a… sort of a place; and a poor devil like me can't get along there.'

The patriot drank off the remainder of the wine; but it only served still more to inflame his passions, and striking the table with some violence, he said, 'Now, Mr. Silverton, money I came for, and money I'll have, or by—'

He concluded his threat with a terrible oath, and Silverton turned pale, but he quietly said, 'Don't swear in that way, Maddox, I can't bear it.'

'Oh, you're very delicate – you can't bear this, and you can't bear that; but I'll make you bear more than you bargained for, if you don't hand out the money at once.'

'Well, sit down quietly, and we'll see what can be done. Bring me that lamp off the sideboard.'

The man placed the lamp on the table, and Silverton applied a match to it, but the double light – the strong glare of the lamp contrasting with the moonbeams – added to the ghastliness of his countenance, although that of the stranger still preserved the same look of brutal indifference.

At length Pierce Silverton took out his purse, and drawing forth a note, said, 'I will give you ten pounds, and can afford no more at present.' As he spoke, some sovereigns rolled on the floor; the ringing of the metal seemed to arouse a greedy longing in the breast of that insatiable man, who exclaimed:

'You're rich – you've gold!'

'I want it – I have some expenses to meet tomorrow.'

'A gentleman like you has only to go to his banker.'

'I do not choose to overdraw my account. I have given you ten pounds, and you may take the sovereigns that have fallen down – there ought to be five or six.'

'Five or six! We'll go halves – I've had the worst part of the work, and won't be put off with the worst pay – so give us your purse.'

'I will not.'

'Oh, you won't! But we'll see about that.'

He tried to snatch the purse which Pierce Silverton put in his pocket. The man forced him back on the sofa

– Pierce struggled to release himself, but the man held him down. Yes, there they were! Force and Fraud, contending with each other! The two crimes which so often unite in the destruction of mankind now striving for the mastery.

But in that individual case it was easy to see which would conquer. Pierce Silverton was like a child in the grasp of that strong man, who, keeping one knee on his chest, and grasping at his throat, exclaimed,

'Who's the master now?'

'Stand off, Maddox – I'll give you another ten pounds.'

'I'll have all or—' And still more heavily he lent on the chest of his victim – still more tightly he grasped him by the throat.

'Maddox! – Oh! – God have mercy on me! – Flora! – Oh, Flora!'

A groan escaped from the heart of Pierce Silverton – an oath from the lips of his assailant; both were overheard, and in another instant half the inmates of the hotel came rushing into the room.

CHAPTER XXXIII

STRIFE

'WHAT IS THE meaning of this tarnation row?' exclaimed Mr. Roberts, who was the first to enter the parlour; but he immediately perceived that a fierce struggle had taken place, and that one of his lodgers lay perfectly helpless in the grasp of a powerful man. 'Stand off, you ruffian,' he continued, 'or you will kill the poor fellow.'

'I'll kill you if you don't take care what you are about, Master Jonathan,' exclaimed the stranger; and leaving the prostrate form of Pierce Silverton, he was about to rush on the landlord; but at that moment, old Crofts, who had followed his master, cried out, 'It is Jarvis, the villain who drowned my poor boy!'

'I told you I'd send you after him – so here goes!' And so saying, Maddox hurled the decanter at the head of the aged father. He fell bleeding on the ground, and was with difficulty led out of the room.

Meantime the ruffian seeing that he must ultimately be overpowered, resolved to sell his life dearly, and rushed from one of his enemies to another, but never directing a blow in vain. It was a scene of general confusion; the women having also added to the tumult.

'Go and fight somewhere else, and don't push anyone on Mr. Silverton,' cried Mrs. Roberts, 'for I'm afraid he's badly hurt already.'

They tried to raise him, but he lay still and senseless.

'He's very ill. Oh, Roberts! Roberts! What shall we do? Mr. Garlick! Mr. Garlick! Do come here.'

The young surgeon entered hastily, but the lamp having been upset, and the moon having passed from opposite the window, he could not tell the extent of the injury, serious, however, it must be, for the pulse of Silverton did not beat.

'Get out of the room and bring a light, do you hear? Are you all mad?' exclaimed Philip Garlick; and though he did not communicate his fears, it was evident that he felt extreme anxiety regarding the condition of his friend.

All this while the cause of the accident was foaming about the room like a wild beast at bay. If one man seized him by the throat, he felled him with a blow; if another endeavoured to trip him up, he disabled him with a kick; but a light was now brought, and the landlord, taking up a bridle that poor old Crofts had let fall, slung it like a lasso, and caught the ruffian by the neck.

'Why, he is Dick Thrashem!' exclaimed Harry, who had just returned to the township.

'Thrashem! That fellow is John Smith, the man who went to England by the *Robespierre*,' cried Mr. Speedy; for that young gentleman, being now articled to a solicitor in the neighborhood, was a frequent visitor at the Southern Cross.

'He is Jarvis! I'll take my oath he is Jarvis, who came back in the *Robespierre*, and who pushed my poor son off the boat,' added old Crofts, who, though wounded, could not resist the pleasure of witnessing the capture of his child's destroyer.

'I reckon he is all those blackguards, and a dozen more besides,' said the landlord, as he tightened the lasso about the neck of the prisoner.

'Take him away, for God's sake, Roberts; and here, you women, get some hot water directly. Eh! Silverton, my dear fellow! Speak, can't you?' said Philip Garlick.

He could not – he never spake again. That strong man had crushed, or strangled him; for either injury was sufficient to destroy his delicate frame, even without the mental torments he must have long endured. Every effort was made to restore him, but all were equally unavailing; and when the truth at length became apparent, a cry of sorrow broke from those tender hearted women, who had so often and so cheerfully surrounded him with their cares.

The room was at length cleared, and the scene of Pierce Silverton's happy dreams – the scene of that fearful strife – now became the Chamber of the Dead!

CHAPTER XXXIV

CONJECTURES

'WHAT COULD HAVE caused the quarrel?' 'Who could feel any enmity to that amiable man?' 'Was that ruffian mad, or only drunk?' Or – or – it was in vain to guess. The victim could not reveal the secret, his murderer would not. But the event soon became known, and the Southern Cross was more crowded than it had been even on the day of Herbert Lindsey's committal to prison. There were also more passions let loose, and a greater excuse for their display, as, at the same time, the murderer and the murdered were under one roof. It would not, however, do to let the former remain very long there, as he had burst his bonds, and still more injuries were inflicted ere they could be replaced. Several members of the police at last arrived, and, strongly manacled, the ruffian was dragged to a place of temporary confinement.

'Eh, Harry! Where are you going at this hour?' asked Mr. Roberts, as Saunders went to fetch his horse out of the stable.

'To Mount Alpin, to be sure, Mr. Roberts,' replied Harry.

'Then mind you don't say anything to Miss Flora about this affair.'

'Me tell her! I wouldn't for twenty pounds – no, nor for a hundred.'

'And don't go about the place with that sorrowful look, or she'll guess that something's gone wrong.'

'Then hang me if I go; for I'm not one of those fellows that can put my face into joy when my heart's in mourning, and I'm right down cut up about poor Mr. Silverton – dash'd if I'm not!' And the honest countryman sat down on some logs of wood, and cried like a child.

'Sad business indeed!' exclaimed the landlord. 'But don't take on that way; and, I say, just have an eye to this place, or there'll be another horse gone. That scoundrel has laid poor Croft's head open, and Garlick says he won't be fit for work these six weeks.'

'And I'll bet what you like, Mr. Roberts, that him who did that business is the same as the chap who stole the horse, 'specially as he turns out to be that Dick Thrashem. But I wonder what Mr. Lindsey'll think of him for a pictur now. In my humble opinion it's only honest men that's good for picturs. But what that scoundrel could have agin Mr. Silverton 'mazes me.'

Harry had by this time rather bewildered himself by his numerous conjectures; his allusion to the horse, however, suggested another to Mr. Roberts, who re-marked, 'Poor Silverton said someone wanted the greys in the morning, but don't let anyone have them without telling me.'

Alas, Pierce Silverton! Other horses, and a very different carriage from that your fond fancy had dreamt of will bear you on your journey.

'The grey horses, and two great bride cakes, came here that I never ordered; and this found in the poor dear boy's pocket; and to think if he should have been going to be married – how she will take on!' And Mrs. Roberts, who had now joined her husband, displayed a wedding ring that Mr. Garlick had taken out of Silverton's waistcoat pocket; but for whom that golden circlet was intended, none could conjecture.

A sad and sleepless night was that at the Southern Cross. Anxious and restless was the following day. Mrs. Roberts, nevertheless, did not neglect her duties, and when Mr. Lovelaw called on his way to the court, she went to meet him with a melancholy smile; but, as the grief of the good landlady could not under any circumstances be of a silent character, after expressing her sorrow in the most demonstrative manner, and calling on the gentleman to do the same, she said, 'Och, then, you may tell O'Twig to get that fellow hanged, without going to the bother of having him tried.'

'My dear madam,' replied Mr. Lovelaw, 'do you not know that every man has a right to be tried, and heaven forbid that the greatest criminal should be deprived of this privilege.'

A supporter of the rights of man was Mr. Lovelaw.

It was noon, and as yet no one had returned to Mount Alpin. Most people about the Southern Cross were busy enough; and those who were not, shrank from the task of bearing the ill-tidings to the friend (they did not know that she was to have been the wife) of the dead. And that very hour was to have witnessed their union. But though not aware of (what ought to have been) her deep interest in Pierce Silverton, they were all debating who should be the informant, when a buggy was seen approaching the hotel. It came on at a rapid rate, and though its occupants did not know anything respecting the tragedy of the preceding evening, they were conscious that something terrible had transpired, for they had noticed horror on the countenances of all they met. In fact, several people, on hearing the sound of a carriage, had just looked from their doors and suddenly hidden themselves again.

'Now might one not suppose that we were bringing the plague, or some evil along with us? Just look at those people! How they seem to avoid us,' said Mr. Manners to his companion.

'There is something wrong – something terrible has happened. Horror is written on every face,' replied Herbert Lindsey. For he it was, whom the kind-hearted magistrate having injured in thought, was now over-whelming with attention.

A few minutes more, and they were fully informed of the catastrophe, although the cause was as great a mystery to them as to the most ignorant of the crowd.

'Good God! How terrible,' said Lindsey to Philip Garlick, as they stood together by the lifeless remains of Pierce Silverton. And the true man shed tears of regret for the loss of the false one.

'Poor fellow! So young, and so amiable!' exclaimed Mr. Manners; but he suddenly added, 'How does Miss McAlpin bear the shock? They were such old friends.'

'Bless your life, Mr. Manners,' said Mrs. Roberts, 'nobody has dared to tell her; and all the more because we didn't know it, that is—'

Mrs. Roberts was about to express her doubts as to the precise relation in which the dead man and the young lady had stood towards each other, but the sight of Herbert Lindsey restrained her tongue, and the thought that he might as well find out for himself.

'Come along then, Lindsey; it must be our duty to communicate this sad intelligence,' said Mr. Manners; and the two gentlemen departed for Mount Alpin.

And how did they find Flora? Like a maniac, as they supposed for the moment. But she had heard nothing of the transaction, and was very calmly preparing herself for the marriage. Not yet attired in her gorgeous dress, but wearing a loose wrapper of white muslin – her long dark hair hanging over her shoulders, for she had been in the act of plaiting it when her thoughts had reverted to Herbert's letters. What right would she, the wife of another, have to such? No – every trace of that first engagement must be destroyed; so, having collected them together, she threw them into a little grate that stood within the hearth; and after lighting a tall wax candle – probably the first that came to her hand – she was about to set fire to these once prized treasures.

The gentlemen not having seen Miss McAlpin when they first entered, asked Miss Garlick where she was; but Bessie, half suspecting that something more than friendship existed between Flora and Pierce Silverton, replied sullenly that she did not know, but she thought Miss McAlpin had taken leave of her senses.

'It is the shock – she must have heard of it. Ah, look at her!' exclaimed Herbert to Mr. Manners.

It should be explained that the dwelling was a low cottage of one story, consisting of several rooms, added at different periods to the original structure. It was rather intersected with passages, and at the end of one where they were standing was the apartment of Miss McAlpin. She had been regardless of the observation of Miss Garlick and the servants, and was now unconscious that anyone else was in the house; therefore, as she stood, in her white robe – her cheeks pale from want of sleep, her eyes straining to see the remains of her once treasured letters, her hair loose, and a flaming taper in her hand – she looked like some fanatic priestess, about to celebrate a savage rite. Nor was the idea of her madness immediately dispersed, as when Herbert approached, exclaiming, 'Flora! Dearest Flora, this sad intelligence has overwhelmed you,' she replied,

'Beware! Nor dare to insult me with your presence!'

'I insult you, Flora?'

'Yes, Sir; your presence is an insult. Mr. Manners, I request you to turn that person out of my house.'

'But Miss McAlpin, I cannot consistently do that, as I brought him here.'

'Very well, Sir, as you choose; Mr. Silverton will be here directly, and he shall interpose his authority. I must now wish you good morning.' So saying, she withdrew into her own room, locking herself in.

A most uncomfortable position for all parties; but what remained to be done? Bessie Garlick ran down the garden to the spot where she had often laid in wait for Pierce Silverton, and the two gentlemen walked about the verandah; but in the course of an hour Miss McAlpin sent word that she would be glad to see Mr. Manners in the drawing room.

'You had better not come until I ascertain what all this is about,' said that gentleman to Herbert Lindsey; and leaving the disappointed lover to overcome his vexation as well as he could, Mr. Manners proceeded to the apartment specified by the imperious heiress. There he found her sitting in great state, and attired in a bridal costume. His own experience informed him that there had been several instances of females associating the idea of a marriage with that of death (supposing a strong attachment for the decease had existed), and he immediately made up his mind that Flora was crazed for love of Silverton.

'My dear Miss McAlpin, it pains me to see you so attired at such a moment.'

'It is becoming the occasion, Mr. Manners; but if you had not been my father's friend, I should not have thought it necessary to inform you of my intentions, which are to marry Mr. Silverton this day.'

'Ah! That you cannot do.'

'I should like to know who is to prevent it.'

'The God who has taken him from you.'

'What do you mean? '

'That Pierce Silverton is dead – murdered!'

'Dead! Dead! He who really loved me – whom I would have married for revenge. Ah! God, forgive.'

Flora threw herself on her knees, and at length she wept. Then Mr. Manners knew that she was not mad. This was some consolation and cautiously and tenderly be revealed the history of the murder. He drew from her an explanation of her conduct – he informed her that as soon as he ascertained the mistake respecting Annie Lowe, he had written to clear up the mistake, and more than all, he told her that Herbert was true. 'But I will send him – he shall speak for himself,' he said in conclusion.

'No; I doubted his word, and can never look him in the face again. But I should have married Pierce had he lived; I am his affianced wife and must mourn for him.'

Had he lived, she would have repulsed him with scorn; now she forgave him because 'he loved much,' and because she could not war with the dead. She secluded herself in her own room, and Mr. Manners thought it better to leave her to herself for the remainder of the day. He then explained the circumstance as well as he could to Herbert, who asked, 'How can it have happened? Could Pierce Silverton be deceitful?'

There is a degree of sanctity connected with the dead, and we cannot speak of their errors as of those who live; and Herbert Lindsey rather attributed Flora's doubts to some accident connected either with the despatch or with the delivery of the letters than to wilful perversion of the truth on the part of his friend. As for the advertisement, no one knew how it got there – Flora could not even state the name of the paper in which it appeared, and 'hushed was now the tongue that could have told.'

CHAPTER XXXV

Conclusion

P IERCE SILVERTON WAS borne with honour to the grave, and his murderer condemned with infamy to the gallows. That trial was a mere form, for the deed was known to have been committed; but when the man Maddox (for that proved to be his real name), was asked if he pleaded 'Guilty or Not Guilty', he said, 'Why, you know I did it, and I know you'll hang me, so cut all this business short; I want to turn in and have a good sleep.'

When the sentence was passed he did not show the slightest emotion; and, on being taken to the condemned cell, instantly demanded something to eat. Poor old Crofts had died from the effects of the wound inflicted by Maddox hurling the glass bottle at his head; and when the ruffian was told of the circumstance, he said brutally, 'There's two to one – that's some comfort!'

One day, old Andrew Ross, who had never abandoned the pursuit of his master's murderer, found, buried underneath the rude flooring of a hut, occupied by Maddox at the time he followed the calling of horse breaker, an old pocketbook that had once been McAlpin's. The shepherd took this to Mr. Roberts, who gave it to the governor of the gaol, and he, with very little difficulty – for Maddox had become boastful of his atrocities – drew from him the history of that murder.

'I did it, and got well paid for it too,' he said in a tone of triumph, and he then proceeded to relate how it had occurred.

'Old McAlpin,' he continued, 'rode off with Mr. Silverton, and on the way they had a quarrel; Mac struck Silverton with his riding whip.

'I met him afterwards, and he seemed a good deal hurt, but much more vexed. I never saw him so angry. He said in a great passion, "I'd give a hundred pounds to see that old fellow's head broke." "Then if you will, master, I'm your man for that job," says I. "Very good," says he, "be off." "I goes and settles Mac, and then comes back again to Mr. Silverton for the pay. He turns round and says he didn't mean it, and he hoped I hadn't done anything of the kind. "So," says I, "master Silverton, if you ain't a man of your word, I is, and if you don't fork out handsome like, I'll swear you did it, and there's lots of folks will believe that, for they knows the rows you have had together." But it was as easy to frighten him as a girl, he was such a soft sort of a chap; why, he used to sit grieving about that old Highlander who treated him worse than a nigger. But the lots of money I got out of him, and the jolly life I led; and if I hadn't had a drop too much, and got into that terrible passion, I'd have had another hundred pounds that night, as sure as two and two makes four.'

And in this unfeeling manner did the ruffian speak of the dead. But the mystery of the handkerchief not having been cleared up, Maddox was questioned respecting it, and he replied, 'I found it down by the river side, and as it seemed a bit tasty, I put it on, and when I set upon Mac he clutched at it; but as I hear you've been wondering about that old 'baccy box, I may as well tell you that I took it out of Mac's pocket, and when I was going to England, and Mr. Silverton was so frightened lest I should give him the slip, as to stow me away in his room, I left it by mistake on his table; and so, if he told lies about it, 'tisn't my look out. He had a way, when he got frightened, of telling a lie, and then another lie to hide it; but if it hadn't been for that and his love fit, he'd have been as decent a chap as there is going. That's all I have to say. But if you call it a confession, don't put in that I am sorry; I wouldn't do such a sneaking thing as to be sorry. And now I'll trouble you for a glass of ale, for this yarning makes a man dry.'

A few days later the wretched man was executed in the town where Herbert Lindsey had been acquitted. He died as he had lived – hardened, unfeeling, impenitent; his fate excited no sympathy, but it was long before those whose sorrows he had caused could arouse themselves from the painful associations connected with his name.

Very long was it also ere Flora would see Herbert Lindsey. 'I cannot marry him now,' she said; 'was I not on the eve of marrying his friend? I shall seem too fickle.'

'It is this seeming,' replied Mr. Manners, 'that causes so much trouble. Be what you are. You were about to marry Silverton because Lindsey seemed false, and many a woman, and man too, has married unhappily from slighter causes of jealousy; you would have been as much justified as anyone could possibly be under the circumstances. But permit me to ask one question.'

'What is that?'

'Could your heart have deceived you? Did you love Pierce Silverton?'

'Love him! Oh no!'

'Herbert will think so, and so will the world if you continue to seclude yourself.'

Flora did not reply, and Mr. Manners beckoned Herbert to approach.

'Flora, I know all; I know you love me, and surely you cannot doubt my love for you,' he said, as he seized her trembling hand.

'Can you forgive my doubts, my jealousy, Herbert?'

'There was so much apparent cause for doubt that I can easily forgive that; and jealousy is sometimes a proof of love. But, Flora, if you continue to refuse me, I shall be jealous.'

'Of whom?'

'Of him you would have married; and then I shall think – what I do not wish to do – that, that perhaps he would have let me die for the crime of murder if he could thus have obtained you.'

'Oh Herbert! Speak gently of the dead.'

'And now, Miss McAlpin,' said Mr. Manners, 'I must inform you of something in reference to a letter I received from your father. Other events prevented me from alluding to it earlier, but (and I suppose it was some Highland superstition) he stated that he often dreamt your mother requested he would no longer oppose the marriage with Lindsey, and therefore if, after a year's probation (of course he meant me to act in the event of his death), this said Herbert Lindsey should prove worthy of you, you should be at liberty to become his wife.'

'My poor father!' exclaimed Flora. 'But, Mr. Manners, perhaps I ought to say, that when I agreed to marry Mr.

Silverton, the thought crossed my mind that Herbert's falseness – for I believed him false – had been ordained to punish me for my disobedience to my father.'

'Thank God that you will have no reproach on your conscience. Indeed, I do not think you could endure it,' said Herbert.

'Oh no, I am sure I could not.'

Flora spoke so naturally, that her listeners were convinced the overstrained part she had so lately acted must have been extremely painful to her. But there was much of the painful still – so many associations connected with Pierce Silverton – such numerous reports in circulation – that Mr. Manners, acting in the character of Miss McAlpin's guardian, took her to reside with his own wife till time should efface the vividness of melancholy recollections.

Some arrangement was about to be entered into respecting Herbert, but whilst it was in contemplation, he received a letter requiring his speedy presence in England; and the lovers parted, with mutual confidence in each other's truth.

Another year has passed away, and many friends with it. A fluctuating population has somewhat interfered with the custom of the Southern Cross, therefore Mr. Roberts has migrated into another district; his wife is not sorry, for her favourite, Mr. Lindsey, could not enliven the place as he used to do – which will be readily supposed, as he is in another hemisphere – and the memory of poor Mr. Silverton makes her so sad, that she has not even spirits to rail at O'Twig. But another hotel is found on the border of the county, not so very far from the residence of Mr. Manners. Flora often comes hither to talk over old times; and it may be that they do cry a little together. Harry Saunders has married Mary; they have a farm of their own, and she has no time to read novels, nor yet to flirt with a Yankee acquaintance. Mr. Philip Garlick says the township is not so jolly as it used to be, and he will look out for a practice near the Roberts's new hotel; and, as Mr. Manners will recommend him to his acquaintance, it would be a very prudent step. Bessie has gone to be a governess at an outstation, and, as her brother expresses it, has hooked a widower of sixty-four. Mr. O'Twig received a rebuff the other day for entering the court with a remarkably unsteady step; and old Andrew Ross is 'biding a wee' with the bushman till Mr. Lindsey comes back; therefore, it is rumoured that Mr. Lindsey does intend to settle at last.

And now he has come, and with all the enthusiasm of his earlier years, he hastens to Flora.

'At last I can ask you to be my wife, Flora,' he says, 'without a suspicion that I seek you for your wealth. I have inherited my uncle's property – and now, when will you marry me?'

And Flora puts her hand in his, and replies, 'In a fortnight.'

The Mount Alpin property is still retained, but the house has been demolished, and another built on a different part of the station. It is a sweet, tranquil valley, and there they hope to live during many happy years; but if at times he thinks how nearly he had fallen a sacrifice for another's crime, he remembers with gratitude the efforts Flora then made in his defence, and never reproaches her for her temporary weakness when assailed by the violence of contending passions. Happily have they passed through their ordeal – the power of the man of force having been destroyed – the arts of the man of fraud rendered unavailing.

ACKNOWLEDGEMENTS

Grattan Street Press would like to thank our home department, the School of Culture and Communication, in the Faculty of Arts. We are especially grateful for the support of our Head of School, Peter Otto; our School Manager, John Boardman; and the Faculty of Arts External Relations team, in particular Fiona Abud, Tamsin Courtney, Lucy Ayers and Jason O'Leary. Without the support of the university and our colleagues, Grattan Street Press would not exist.

STAFF ACKNOWLEDGEMENTS

Grattan Street Press relies on the talent, enthusiasm and hard work of the students involved. As the subject coordinator, I would like to thank the following students: Georgia Coldebella, Samuel Davison, Brea Derlagen, Leisha Kapor, Kelsie Kruse, Taina Manninen, Harry Mclean, Helena Melton, Chloe Miller, Megan Sahli, Pamela Smithers, Emma Sweeney, Laken Walter, Wes Whitfield and Sophie Zins. I think the future of publishing is in good hands.

Aaron Mannion (Subject Coordinator)

ABOUT THE AUSTRALIAN CENTRE

The Australian Centre is based in the School of Culture and Communication at the University of Melbourne, with Professor Ken Gelder and Professor Denise Varney as its co-directors. It aims to develop innovative research projects in the Australian arts and humanities across a range of disciplines, including Art History, Theatre Studies, Literary Studies, Cultural Studies, Media and Communication, Cinema Studies, Indigenous Studies and Creative Writing.

ABOUT GRATTAN STREET PRESS

Grattan Street Press is a trade publisher based in Melbourne. A start-up press, we aim to publish a range of work, including contemporary literature, trade non-fiction, and children's books, and to re-publish culturally valuable works that are out of print. The press is an initiative of the Publishing and Communications program in the School of Culture and Communication at the University of Melbourne, and is staffed by graduate students, who receive hands-on experience of every aspect of the publication process.

The press is a not-for-profit organisation that seeks to build long-term relationships within the Australian literary and publishing community. We also partner with community organisations in Melbourne and beyond to co-publish books that contribute to public knowledge and discussion.

Organisations interested in partnering with us can contact us at coordinator@grattanstreetpress.com.